“I just finished *The Days of A*

(even this pen.) An amazing n

dropping on life.”

—Cynthia Ozick

“*The Days of Awe* is a great Awakening elegy for all our lives even as we live them.”

—Johanna Kaplan, author of *O My America*

“For me, the most spectacular 9/11 novel so far has been the hard-to-find *Days of Awe* by Hugh Nissenson. . . If . . . you believe that at their best, novels should be transformative, should rip the dusty curtains from our everyday vision and reveal the reality of our existence; if you don’t mind being terrorized by a narrative if it takes you to a greater understanding of what it means to be alive on this earth; if you’re willing to take this ride with Hugh Nissenson, then you’re not in for a treat exactly—that would be the wrong word—but you’ll be looking at a different world when you finish his pages.”

—Carolyn See, *Washington Post*

“This is a novel to cherish and to honor.”

—George Garrett, Poet Laureate of Virginia, author of *Death of the Fox*, *The Succession*, and *Entered from the Sun*

“A deep affirmation of life in all its mystery and agony and joy”

—Frederick M. Dolan, author of *Allegories of America*

"The distinguished author of *The Tree of Life* has produced a new novel that transcends its setting."
—*Philadelphia Inquirer*

"A gripping portrait of the Jewish condition in America. Deeply ironic. A masterpiece!"
—Amos Elon, author of *The Pity Of It All*

"Solid character writing and attention to the details of daily life make the September 11 material well motivated; as characters continue to worry, kibitz, philosophize, and complain, one feels that they have a real sense of the stakes."
—*Publishers Weekly*

"A moving, thought-provoking exploration of coming to grips with mortality."
—*Booklist*

"I predict that Hugh Nissenson's reputation will rise; he will be studied by future readers."
—Irving Malin, literary critic

the days of awe

Also by Hugh Nissenson

A Pile of Stones
Notes from the Frontier
In the Reign of Peace
My Own Ground
The Tree of Life
The Elephant and My Jewish Problem
The Song of the Earth

the days of awe

a novel

SOURCEBOOKS LANDMARK™
AN IMPRINT OF SOURCEBOOKS, INC.®
NAPERVILLE, ILLINOIS

Published by Sourcebooks Landmark, an imprint of Sourcebooks Inc.
P.O. Box 4410, Naperville, Illinois 60567-4410
(630) 961-3900
FAX: (630) 961-2168
www.sourcebooks.com

Originally published in hardcover by Sourcebooks, Inc.

Library of Congress Cataloging-in-Publication Data:
Nissenson, Hugh.
The days of awe / Hugh Nissenson.
p. cm.
1. September 11 Terrorist Attacks, 2001--Fiction. 2. Terrorism victims
families--Services for--Fiction. 3. Loss (Psychology)--Fiction. 4. Middl
aged men--Fiction. 5. New York (N.Y.)--Fiction. 6. Jewish men--Fiction
I. Title.

PS3564.I8D39 2005
813'.54--dc22

2005012499

Printed and bound in the United States of America
VP 10 9 8 7 6 5 4 3 2

For Marilyn, Kore, Kate, and Alan,
and to the memory of Paul Gottlieb

Talkative, anxious,
Man can picture the Absent
And non-Existent.

W. H. Auden: "Progress?"

Artie Rubin couldn't keep his mind on Odin. His thoughts buzzed around the corpses of the two Arab kids in Nablus. At eleven, he called Johanna at her office. He read her the headline on the front page of the *Times* that was eating at him: "Israeli Raid Kills 8 at Hamas Office; 2 Are Young Boys; Palestinians Call for Revenge; Violence on Both Sides Shows No Sign of Letup."

Artie said, "The boys were brothers, five and six. One was found on top of the other."

"I saw the article. Their poor parents. Leslie and Chris are having dinner with us tonight. I made a reservation at Shun Lee for 8:30."

"Any bleeding this morning?"

"Yes. I spoke to Dr. Gunning. He's convinced it's just hemorrhoids. I hope he's right. But we'll soon know for sure. I've never had a colonoscopy, so he insisted I schedule one for next Monday at ten."

"Finally! You'll be woozy from the anesthetic. I'll pick you up."

Leslie said to Johanna, "Send Daddy my love."

Johanna said good-bye to Artie. Leslie clicked on their five bellwether stocks: Citigroup 50.34, Intel 30.30, Cisco 65.79, Microsoft 66.71, Johnson & Johnson 54.25. No significant change this week; no significant change since late spring.

Leslie said, "Chris and I are going shopping after lunch. He needs a summer jacket. I'm thinking dark brown. To go with his tan pants."

Artie drank a Bass ale. It went right to his head. He squeezed out five sentences: "The god Odin appears among us as a warrior in his mid-fifties with one blue eye; his reddish-brown beard is turning gray. Instead of a helmet, he wears a blue broad-brimmed hat and carries a magic spear called Gungnir. Men hanged from trees are sacrificed to him."

Don't start with Odin. Begin at the beginning.

Artie wrote, "*In the beginning was fire and ice.*"

He sketched Odin in pencil. The bearded, one-eyed god stood in the open doorway of a broken-down log hut with a spear in his right hand. He wore a Yankees cap. The cap and the beard made Odin look like a one-eyed Jew.

Artie tore up the sketch.

Aug. 1, 2001. Wed. Noon. *This morning began* Norse Myths Retold & Illustrated—*my 20th book on mythology in 41 yrs. My main source is 13th century* Prose Edda of

Snorri Sturluson, *trans. by Jean Young, Univ. of Cal. Press 1996. Will illustrate in style of Viking carvings; source,* Viking Art *by Charles Sullivan, Harry Abrams, 1995.*

I often wondered why I put off tackling the Norse gods. Now, at 67, I know. The Norse gods die. Much thoughts of death these days.

Though we don't mention it, the blood in Johanna's stool over the last three weeks reminds us of Johnny Havistraw, my former editor at Harper's, *who died of colon cancer in July.*

At a quarter to three, Artie walked Muggs, the Rubins' four-year-old English sheepdog, up West End. He kept on the shady west side of the street. A sparrow chirped among the leaves of the big plane tree planted near the curb at the far corner of 80th Street; it chirped louder than the traffic. Artie couldn't spot it among the leaves.

Muggs, who had never learned to heel, tried crossing 81st Street against the light. Artie yanked him to a halt.

Artie and Johanna were crazy about sheepdogs. Muggs was their fourth in thirty-one years. Johanna gave him to Artie for his sixty-third birthday. He said to the four-month-old pup, "We'll grow old together."

Over spare ribs at Shun Lee, Leslie said, "I'm three months pregnant."

Artie would cherish the moment made of his daughter's

words, the big dish of ribs, and a Chinese waiter serving a crispy Peking duck to the couple at the table to his left.

He and Johanna said, "Congratulations!" and Leslie and Chris each answered, "Thank you."

Artie said, "This calls for another drink. Waiter!" Johanna gave him a look. "Never mind, waiter."

Johanna said, "Oh, darling, we're so happy. Your guest room is perfect for a nursery. Take a long maternity leave. Not to worry about the office. I'll manage things."

My God, I'm going to be a grandfather. I want a grandson. Wait a sec! What's all the excitement? I'll be almost eighty when he's ten.

Leslie: "Chris and I went for an ultrasound this afternoon. Look at these pictures. The baby's about four inches long. Its heart is beating. This graph shows the movement. The baby's face is developing. Here it is in profile. See the nose? The smudge near the mouth is a hand. The mouth's open."

Artie reached for more sweet sauce. "When will we know the sex?"

"I have an appointment for another ultrasound the second week in September. We might know then. It depends on what position the baby's in—whether we can see between the legs."

"It's a girl," said Johanna. "Mark my words."

The waiter served steaming cloths on a plate. Artie wiped his greasy hands, lost in the loud conversation at the table on his left between a guy about thirty and a pretty redhead: "Don't you dare call me cheap."

"I take it back."

"You're sore we have to split the check."

"Forget it. Let's eat."

"I won't forget it."

"You're upset about the market."

Tonight was Johanna's turn to walk Muggs. Not a breath of air. Muggs panted. Johanna walked him around the block under the yellow street lamps. He crapped on the corner of Riverside and 81st Street. Johanna thought, I've got blood in my stool like Johnny Havistraw. She picked up Muggs's shit with a plastic bag from Zabar's and dumped the load in the steel mesh garbage can on the corner. She was reminded of tossing Leslie's smelly Pampers down the incinerator. My baby's carrying a baby. Let them live and be well. She said aloud, "That's a wish, not a prayer."

She'd quit Hebrew school in New Rochelle when she was going on thirteen. All of a sudden, it hit her then that nobody was listening to her prayers and thoughts. There's no God. What a relief. He couldn't read her mind about blond Tommy Rand who sat next to her in math.

A motorcycle backfire spooked Muggs on West End; Johanna held him short. I haven't thought about Tommy Rand in fifty years. There's no God. Artie feels the same. He goes to shul only because it connects him to his dad. Dead and gone twenty-three years. That pious old Jew still has his hooks in Artie. More than ever since he turned sixty-five. He's feeling his age.

Artie had high blood pressure. Before going to bed, he took his daily dose of 5 mg. Norvasc, 4 mg. Cardura, and 10 mg. Altace that kept his pressure normal: 120/80. The drugs made him impotent.

Artie and Johanna lay under a sheet and a light cotton blanket in the chilled air.

Johanna said, "A grandchild! I'm so happy."

"Me too. I hope it's a boy."

"I couldn't care less—so long as it's healthy."

The air conditioner whirred behind her voice.

Artie said, "If it is a boy, I'm gonna ask Leslie and Chris to have a bris."

"I wonder if Chris is circumcised."

Artie would have been happier if Leslie had married a Jew. At least Chris had money. He worked for his father, who owned and managed fifteen garden apartment complexes in southern Westchester.

Muggs sighed; he was asleep on the faded blue carpet at the foot of the bed.

Artie said, "Sweetheart, let's celebrate."

"Let's."

Artie went into the bathroom and popped 50 mg. of Viagra. It would take twenty minutes or so to work. He unbuttoned his pajama top and looked down at his big pot belly covered with grey hair and mottled by three big brown moles. He looked in the mirror at his sagging hairy tits. I'm part woman. He examined the reflection of his high, bald forehead, bulbous nose, and wrinkled, wattled neck. Two parallel wattles hid his Adam's apple. Long hairs grew out of his ears. I look more and more like Dad.

Artie slipped back into bed in his pajama tops. Johanna was wearing one of his T-shirts; it reached her thighs. She dozed off. Artie shut his eyes. Think sexy thoughts! He played with his limp cock while searching his memory for images of Johanna when she was young. He came up with her naked at twenty-two sitting on a camp bed in a sublet on East 92nd Street. She was putting up her long auburn hair. She spread open a hairpin with her top front teeth.

Johanna asked Leslie, "Is Chris circumcised?"

"How do I know?"

"You don't know if your husband's circumcised?"

Johanna woke.

Artie said, "I'm second-rate. I'm getting old."

Johanna sucked Artie's limp cock. It got hard. He went into the john and washed it in the sink. Johanna, who was naked, joined him.

She said, "Hold still," and squeezed a blackhead from his right temple.

"Ow!"

"There's one more," she said. "Don't move."

Artie diddled her pussy with his left hand. She said, "Ah!" and left off squeezing.

Johanna washed her pussy in the bathtub. Their fucking never varied. Year after year they caressed each other in the same way to the same end: coming together.

Back in bed, she lay perpendicular to him, to his right, with her head on his stomach.

They closed their eyes. Artie gently massaged Johanna's clit; it swelled under the middle finger of his right hand. She tickled his balls. They went down on each other. Johanna pressed Artie's head between her thighs. She sucked, he licked. She pressed tighter. His tongue got tired. The muscles around her lips ached a little. They kept themselves on the verge of coming.

Johanna said, "Let's fuck."

Artie pumped away till they came together. They momentarily forgot who they were; each saw a flash of light. Then, back to being Artie, he said, as usual, "That was good for you. How was it for me?" And, as usual, Johanna smiled at his nonsense. Muggs, aroused by their juicy smells, tried climbing onto the bed. Johanna pushed him off.

Artie knew her inside out: her love of Auden, Willa Cather, and the last movement—the rondo—of the Waldstein, how she moaned in her sleep, plucked hairs from her chin, strove to be a supermom. He admired her talent for making money—her honesty that inspired confidence in her clients. He knew that a sound track of melodies always played in her head. He knew the smell of her skin, her sneezing fits in the morning, how tough it had been for her to grow up with a depressive mother in New Rochelle. He knew that Johanna brushed and flossed her teeth after eating—even at work—three times a day. And how she detested the sweet smell of lilies.

The next morning at ten, Artie gave creating the universe another shot. "*Burning Muspell is in the south. Surt squats among the fires, hefting the red-hot hilt of his flaming sword from hand to hand. His hair and beard are ablaze. He exhales sparks, smoke, and glowing embers. Surt waits for Ragnarok, the final battle between good and evil, when he will vanquish all the gods and set fire to the world with his sword.*"

Artie wrote about Niflheim, in the north, packed with ice and snow, heavy with hoar frost, and the abyss Ginninsgap that yawns between the fire and the ice. "*The fire from the south melted the ice from the north. It thawed and dripped. The slush congealed into Ymir, the vicious frost ogre. While he slept, the sweat running from his hairy left armpit became two more frost ogres, a male and a female. His right leg fathered another male frost ogre on his left.*"

Artie got hooked on myths when his mom gave him an English illustrated edition of *Bulfinch's Mythology* for his Bar Mitzvah. She said, "It's an antidote to Torah."

His mom, Lea Blaustein, was born and raised in Boro Park, Brooklyn. Her dad, Hymie, was a presser, active in the ILGWU; he knew David Dubinsky and exchanged letters in Yiddish with Victor Alter, one of the leaders of the Polish Bund. Hymie and his wife Rachel taught their daughter that religion was the opiate of the masses. When Lea was fourteen, her mom died of a stroke. Hymie wouldn't say kaddish at the funeral. He told the rabbi, "I will not praise God!"

Lea graduated from Erasmus Hall High School and wanted to study law. But to her surprise, she fell in love with Sam Rubin, a dress salesman on Seventh Avenue. She was surprised because he was religious. Every morning, Sam put on tefillin—phylacteries—and prayed. He had come to the States from Warsaw with his Orthodox parents when he was seven. He and Lea discussed marriage. Sam wanted her to keep a kosher home. She refused. They compromised by not eating pork or shellfish.

They got married in 1932 and rented a three-room apartment over Ebinger's bakery on King's Highway in Flatbush. The three-room apartment smelled of freshly baked bread. Sam just managed the twenty-dollar monthly rent. Artie was born December 2, 1933. Sam borrowed fifty-five dollars from his boss to settle the hospital bill.

At Artie's bris, Sam prayed, Master of the Universe, make my son a good Jew. Worthy of Your chosen people Israel.

Sam joined an Orthodox shul on Ocean Avenue. Artie remembered going there with him on Rosh Hashana a year or so after Pearl Harbor. They walked hand in hand on King's Highway to Ocean Avenue. Artie still pictured the brass plaque screwed into the back of the pew in front of him, his black velvet yarmulke, the bearded cantor. He often thought of Dad wrapping himself in his tallis and artfully tossing the fringed ends over his shoulders. On the first night of Rosh Hashana, between waking and sleeping, Artie saw God. He was a mop in the corner of a closet. Next day, without telling Mom why, Artie sketched her mop in pencil; she said, "Very good. I can see every tangle."

Artie sensed that Mom loved him more than she loved Dad. To ease his guilt, he kissed Dad on the lips every evening when he came home from work. Artie took Hebrew lessons for six months from the melamed at Dad's shul. Then the melamed was hospitalized with bladder cancer, and Artie dropped his studies.

Mom said, "Good going!"

In the spring of '42, Sam went into business with a refugee pattern maker named Herman Levin. Herman was married to a German shiksa with whom he had fled Hamburg in 1938. He was a talented pattern maker; his clothes were a perfect fit. Herman and Sam manufactured inexpensive dresses in a loft on Seventh Avenue and 35th Street. Sam sold the dresses in the showroom up front to goyishe buyers from Filene's, Marshall Field's, the Federated Stores.

He told Artie, "Deal honorably with goyim. Your behavior towards them reflects on all Jews."

Fortunes were made in the dress business during the war, but piece goods were scarce, except on the black market. Over Herman's objections, Sam refused to pay money under the table to the big textile houses for black-market goods.

He said to Artie, "Son, I could be a millionaire if I chose. I don't choose. It means breaking the law. I won't break American law. This is God's country."

Sam believed that God rewarded him with good business for resisting the temptation to line his pockets illegally. He pulled down thirty-five thousand dollars a year. In 1945, he moved Lea and Artie to a four-room apartment on the second floor of a gray stone building on 92nd Street, off Central Park West, in Manhattan.

Sam still put on tefillin and prayed every morning. Then he read a page or two from *The Ethics of the Fathers,* but for Artie's sake, he joined a fancy Reform synagogue called Temple Rodeph Sholom on 83rd Street between Central Park West and Columbus, where the service was mostly in English and there was a concealed choir singing from a loft. Lea didn't kick up a fuss because she felt guilty for loving Artie more than she loved Sam. Sam and Artie went to Rodeph Sholom on

Friday evenings and the High Holidays. Yarmulkas were out; only silver-haired Rabbi Friedman wore one.

One time, Artie said to Johanna, "'Silver hair and a silver tongue'—that's how Dad described Friedman. He spoke in a deep, theatrical voice, rolling his r's, like an old-fashioned actor. Soon after the war ended, his sermons introduced me to sealed trains, gas chambers, and crematoriums. He taught me the word 'Auschwitz.' He said Jewish corpses were boiled down into soap in a factory near Berlin. It was discovered by Russian soldiers. Friedman gave details I never forgot. The corpses, hung on hooks, were boiled in vats. Friedman said we Jews are alone in the world. Every hand is against us. Trust only ourselves and God. If we lose faith in God, then Hitler has triumphed over us.

"I hardly remember anything about studying for my Bar Mitzvah. Dad taught me to put on tefillin, and I took Hebrew lessons every Sunday for a year from Cantor Melzoff. He spoke with a Russian accent. He had big earlobes. I learned to read Hebrew, but none of it, beyond five or six letters, stuck with me. Anyway, I recited my portion of Torah, but what it was, search me."

Artie was Bar Mitzvahed on Saturday, December 7, 1946, the date Mom wrote on the flyleaf of *Bulfinch's Mythology*,

To my beloved Artie, Happy Birthday.

"They wove bright fables in the days of old,
when reason borrowed fancy's painted wings;

When truth's clear river flowed o'er sands of gold,
And told in song its high and mystic things!"

Leafing through the book, Artie lingered over the sixteen color plates. They knocked him out. Who were Raphael, Veronese, Botticelli, Michelangelo, Delacroix? His favorite painting was *Leda and the Swan* by Michelangelo. A beautiful naked lady lay on her back with her legs wrapped around a huge swan. They were obviously doing it. He looked up Leda in the index. The text said the swan was Jupiter in disguise. There was no sex like that in comics, the movies, or the Mars books by Edgar Rice Burroughs.

Artie read *Bulfinch* from cover to cover in six weeks. His imagination expanded page by page; it spread to Hera, Zeus, Cupid and Psyche, Bacchus, Odin, King Arthur, Taliesin, Charlemagne. He visited the Underworld, filled with the ghosts of boys and girls. He daydreamed about naked water nymphs. Artie copied the reproduction of Edwin Abbey's painting *Galahad the Deliverer* in pen and ink. The best-drawn bit was the horse in profile, including the raised right fetlock—a shape that gave him a lot of trouble.

Mom said, "You're talented."

Artie read about Pan, the god of woods and shepherds, covered with bristling hair, who has curled horns and a goat's cloven hooves. He sketched Pan in pencil dancing among daisies—the easiest flowers to draw. An oversized bee hovered in the air. A poem popped whole into Artie's head. He wrote it on the back of the paper:

Pan is dancing forth and back.
Now and then he stops to snack
On the nectar
From a honeybee's sack.

Where had it come from? Artie looked behind him. The door to his room was shut. I wrote a poem—like Robert Frost. But where did it come from? Somewhere in me. A power in me makes poems.

He showed the sketch and the poem to Mom. She said, "You're a genius."

Artie and Johanna had dinner at eight with Adam and Shirley Jacobson at Roppongi, a Japanese restaurant on 81st and Amsterdam.

Artie put away five little cups of cold sake. Adam downed two Kirins. He was a sixty-five-year-old lawyer who negotiated contracts for Artie's books. Artie wrote and illustrated two books a year. He got between ten and fifteen thousand dollars in advance for each. Twelve of his nineteen books were still in print. Artie's illustrated interpretations of world mythology were cult classics. His readers included Joseph Campbell, who in 1973 wrote him a fan letter: "Like me, you know that myths are shared dreams."

With his royalties, in a good year, Artie made around forty-five grand. He thought Adam was a good man, but he had a narrow, sly face. Adam got fifteen percent of each advance. He didn't represent Artie for the money. He was wowed by Artie's way with words and pictures. He thought, Artie's another Sendak.

Shirley was two years older than Adam but wouldn't admit it. She ran the Armani boutique at Bloomingdale's.

Shirley and Adam congratulated Artie and Johanna on Leslie's pregnancy. Shirley picked up a piece of California roll with her chopsticks. My son will give me a grandchild, after all. He and Hal talk about adopting. Jerry's very maternal. He loved dolls as a kid.

They caught up on their sick friends. Five years after a colostomy and chemo, Elsa was free of colon cancer. Roger had terminal bile-duct cancer; Helen, congestive heart failure. Jake was in remission from multiple myeloma; Jenny was going in for a triple bypass; Phil had a second heart attack. Fred, at seventy-six, was just diagnosed with Alzheimer's.

Shirley: "He told me, 'I have a disease. I can't remember its name, but it can't be cured.'"

Johanna thought, a colostomy and chemo. Artie thought, a colostomy and chemo.

He said, "They're calling our class."

Adam said, "They're calling me. My melanoma's returned. It's local to the same area as before, on my lower back. The doctor can remove it in his office. It won't be the major surgery I had back in February

1999. No lymph node removal or skin graft. The PET scan I had last Wednesday shows everything else is clear."

Shirley: "You've a grain of rice on your lower lip."

Adam licked it off. Artie switched the subject to the raid in Nablus. He found that the bloodstains of the two dead Arab kids had faded from his mind. He was now in favor of the Israeli attack.

He said, "Those Hamas guys are Jew-killers. Israel's at war to the death. Innocent kids get killed in war. What can you do?"

Adam said, "This grilled eel is delicious." He put down his chopsticks. "I see the oncologist next week."

Artie said, "Good luck."

"I can use it."

Johanna thought, You and me both.

She walked Muggs in the mornings. He awakened her every day on the dot of seven by resting his shaggy white muzzle just below her shoulder blades. Johanna often wondered how he knew it was seven o'clock. Every morning was the same. With her eyes closed, she listened to him exhaling through his big black nose. Then she raised her head from the pillow and he raised his from her back. They looked in each other's eyes. Johanna called this "The Ritual." Muggs had invented The Ritual when he was a year old. Johanna saw in it an incipient religious impulse; she said to Artie, "Religion has gone to the dogs."

Citigroup 51.30, Intel 32.05, Cisco 19.87, Microsoft 67.30, Johnson & Johnson 53.30.

Leslie was on the phone with a client named Matt Hagen who was a fashion photographer. She had invested his sixty thousand dollars in a large-cap equity fund. He had another five grand he wanted to invest.

She said, "Matt, the market's drifting. My advice is wait till the picture is a little clearer before committing any more money to large caps. Let it sit in a money market for a week or two. We'll get a better pattern once the market turns. Meantime, I'm protecting your asset base and keeping you whole through withdrawals, redemptions, market declines, and transfers. Yes," she said, "Don't worry so much. We'll talk a lot over the next couple of weeks."

The melody of "Hey, Jude" was running through Johanna's head. She said, "I want to do a bear warrant on Japanese yen."

Leslie, scared of speculating on currency fluctuations, said, "Count me out."

The two had been working together for four years. Johanna sometimes worried that her daughter had never cut the cord and achieved an independent life. As far as I know, she's got a good marriage. She's certainly excited about the baby.

Leslie thought, I'm pregnant! ten times a day. I want a girl. We'll be as close as me and Mom. I'm mother-dominated. Chris wants a son. It's strange to think that my kid's surname will be Pendleton—so Waspy! I won't raise her as a Jew.

Advising clients is scary. Managing people's money is a terrible responsibility. Matt has the jitters. Why do clients prefer to buy stocks when they're expensive rather than cheap?

Cisco closed at 20.02. Johanna thought, 2002 will be a good year for me. I'll be sixty-five.

Six and five is eleven—my lucky number. I don't have colon cancer.

Aug. 3, 2001. Fri. Noon. *This morning eked out two paragraphs on the birth of Odin. Poor Odin's been dead a thousand years. His memorial is Wednesday: Woden's Day. What will remain of Yaweh, Allah, Christ in a thousand years?*

Daydreamed that Leslie had a son, whom she had circumcised at a bris & named Sam.

Artie took the downtown local at 79th and Broadway to Times Square. He hated the photo on his senior citizens Metro card. I'm all bulbous nose. Why does the end of your nose swell with age?

He was zonked by the heat in the Times Square station and headed up the stairs to the corner of 7th Avenue and 42nd Street. He walked east to Paul Stuart at 45th and Madison and bought two pairs of khakis for $176 each. Artie barely squeezed into a size forty; the Italian tailor had to let the pants out in the waist. I gotta cut back on the booze. All those extra calories.

Coming out of the air-conditioned store, Artie broke out in a fresh sweat. A twenty-year-old blonde in a yellow T-shirt heading uptown caught his eye; she wasn't wearing a bra. Look at those tits bounce. Her nipples stick out. That was good for you. How was it for me?

Artie took a packed #4 bus up Madison to 79th Street. He automatically scanned the faces. He was constantly on the lookout for a face to draw in the little sketchbook he kept in the canvas Ghurka bag slung over his right shoulder. Sometimes he drew only a mouth, a nose or chin, the shape of an ear.

He worked his way to the back of the bus through a bunch of out-of-towners. Near the rear exit, he brushed up against a young Mayan. His profile might have been painted five hundred years ago on a polychrome Mayan bowl: slightly slanted eyes, small, receding chin, a hooked nose and sloping forehead. Artie had drawn features like that in 1983 for his book about Quetzalcoatl. This guy's ancestors drowned little girls in cisterns to propitiate the Rain God.

Artie got home pooped. He turned on the air conditioner in the living room and poured himself a stiff Absolut on the rocks. He drank another and took a nip from the bottle before putting it back in the freezer.

Johanna returned from work at six thirty. She sat on the living room sofa with a glass of chilled Sancerre in her hand and put on Brendel's recording of the Waldstein. Artie watched Muggs give her his nightly hug. He raised himself between her knees on his hind legs, placed his front paws on other side of her waist, and pressed his chest against hers.

Artie said, "I'm jealous. Muggs never hugs me."

Johanna skipped the CD to the rondo. The first statement of its theme spirited her away from colon cancer, from Artie, smelling of vodka, and the panting dog—even from thoughts of Leslie's pregnancy. She entered a space in which she longed to live alone for the rest of her life. She went blind in her mind's eye; she dropped out of her own sight. The melody returned twice; she vanished again into the music.

Later on, in bed, Johanna said, "I'm going to insist that Leslie take at least a year off when she has the baby. I've a feeling it's a boy. Mark my words! Are you really going to ask the kids to have a bris? With a mohel and wine? The Hebrew prayers nobody understands? Why does having a bris mean so much to you?"

"I want it done in memory of Dad. I feel very close to him lately. He'd be pleased to know that his great-grandson isn't altogether lost to the Jews."

"Did you remember to buy pants?"

"This afternoon."

"Can you still get into a size forty?"

"Easily."

"You lie! Where'd you shop? Paul Stuart? You could

use some short-sleeved cotton shirts. But don't buy them at Paul Stuart. I went looking there for you Wednesday. Their short-sleeved cotton shirts cost a fortune. Go to the Gap."

Artie saw Dad's ghost in broad daylight at 83rd and West End. Dad was wearing his gray pinstriped double-breasted suit and needed a shave. He had a three-days' growth of white whiskers. Dad looked alive, but Artie knew he was a ghost. The hairs bristled on Artie's forearms. Then he said to himself: Hey, how about that? Death isn't the end.

"Dad," he called out. "You're invited to the bris."

Dad's ghost looked at him with bloodshot eyes. Artie stepped forward and stretched out his arms to embrace him, but the ghost gave off a blast of cold air. Artie staggered back and awoke.

Subj.: Bris
Date: 8/4/2001 10:23:55 AM Eastern Daylight Time
From: Artjo
To: Lespen

Dear Leslie,
If you have a son, would you & Chris consider giving him a bris? It would mean a lot to me. A way of honoring my fathers.
Daddy

Subj: Re: Bris
Date:8/4/2001 10:32:35 AM Eastern Daylight Time
From: Lespen
To: Artjo

Dear Daddy,
Went to a bris once—Alice Schwab's baby, Shawn—& looked away when the guy picked up a little curved scalpel. Alice almost fainted from the blood. I think a bris is barbarous Jewish hocus-pocus. You honor your fathers by offering them a blood sacrifice—a snip of your grandson's penis. Men!

If a bris is so important to you, it's ok with me. Chris is another kettle of fish. He's got a thing about circumcision. You better speak with him yourself.

Love you.
Leslie

PS. Mom says don't forget, buy short-sleeved cotton shirts from Gap. Get 4 assorted colors.

After breakfast on Saturday, Artie got a call from Chris, who said, "Let's meet this afternoon and talk about circumcision." They arranged for Chris to come uptown between two and two thirty. He showed up with Leslie at a quarter past two. Johanna and Leslie set out to shop for maternity clothes at Bloomingdale's.

Johanna said, "We'll stop off at the Armani boutique and say hello to Shirley."

Artie and Chris strolled down to the 79th Street Boat Basin. They sat on a shaded bench that faced the yacht *Clover* moored at the end of a dock. A moist wind blew over the Hudson from the west; the river was choppy. Little waves lapped against *Clover*'s white hull that reflected sunlight off the water. *Clover* rocked sideways. Two ducks, bobbing up and down, swam passed her stern.

Chris said, "I'm not circumcised. My brother and I are practically the only members of our generation of Americans whose pricks are intact. My Dad abhors circumcision—with good reason. Circumcision desensitizes the prick's tip—the glans. Now the glans is the sexiest spot on a man's body—his greatest erogenous zone. The foreskin preserves that exquisite sensitivity. A circumcised prick exposes the glans to the air—it also rubs against clothing—and it becomes desensitized.

"This truth is not widely known. I discovered it by accident at the age of eleven in summer camp. I noticed that my bunkmate Georgie Markle never wore underpants. He ran around naked under his jeans. Now Georgie was circumcised. As I said, most guys my age are circumcised. I tried an experiment. I pushed my foreskin back, exposing my glans, and put on my own jeans. I couldn't walk. The chafing was excruciating. I sat under a weeping willow. There I had a revelation.

My glans, protected by a foreskin, was far more sensitive than Georgie's because he was circumcised.

"If I have a son, he won't be circumcised. His prick won't be mutilated; his foreskin will be preserved to protect his precious glans."

Artie watched a woman, with thin white hair, on a nearby bench feed cracked corn from a jar to a pigeon perched on her knee. He thought, Is it true? Is my glans desensitized?

When Artie got home, he read his mail:

Dearest Friends,

We look forward to sharing the High Holidays with you at Etz Chaim. Rosh Hashana begins this year on September 17th. Rabbi Meir says, "We are all judged on Rosh Hashana and our fate is sealed on Yom Kippur." These are the Days of Awe in which we Jews must examine our hearts, communally confess our sins, and turn in repentance to God.

In the Mishnah (the earliest legal code), Rabbi Akiva said: Israel, how fortunate you are! Before whom do you purify yourselves and who purifies you? Your Father in heaven! As Ezekiel prophesied: I will splash water upon you; and you will be pure. And as Jeremiah prophesied: God is Israel's ritual pool (*Mikveh Israel Adonai*). As a pool purifies, so the Blessed Holy One purifies Israel. (Yoma 9.8.)

During the ten Days of Awe, we at Etz Chaim shall turn inward together and examine our stained hearts.

Then we will bathe them in Mikveh Israel Adonai, the divine pool, while praying that they be cleansed.

May we be renewed together on the High Holidays, and may it prepare us for another year of doing Mitzvot of Torah study, worship, and kind deeds.

Best wishes for a sweet year, inscribed in the Book of Life.

David Klugman, Rabbi

Artie thought, Yom Kippur—those lovely melodies. Kol Nidre, Vidui, the Confession.

That night in bed, Johanna said to Artie, "I'm having my colonoscopy Monday morning."

"I know."

"I can't eat anything except Jell-O all day tomorrow. I made myself a batch this afternoon. Lemon. Do me a favor. Eat dinner at Leslie's tomorrow night. She's invited you. I'll be starved by then. I don't want to watch you eat a pepperoni pizza. Which is what you'll order in, I know."

"So there won't be a bris. That makes me sad."

"What on earth are you doing?"

"Testing the sensitivity of my glans."

"Your what?"

"The tip of my cock. I'm testing its sensitivity to touch."

"Whatever for?"

"Chris says that circumcision deadens it."

"Here, let me do that."

"Rub the top."

"How's that feel?"

"I hardly feel a thing. I never noticed before. I'll be damned. The price of being Jewish is a numb glans."

Artie took Muggs for a Sunday afternoon walk up West End to 96th. There, on the south corner of the wide cross-street, in the hot sun, he overheard one black woman tell another: "He's paralyzed on his right side and has seizures every day. Every single day! And he's ten years old."

On the way back, Artie checked in with Leslie by cell phone: Dinner was at seven thirty; her brother-in-law Sutton would be there.

Johanna logged on to her personal investment account. She had fifty thousand dollars in New York munis coming due on the fifteenth. She thought about rolling them over, but interest rates were so low. She decided to talk on Tuesday to Harry Morgan, her fixed-income specialist, to see if he had any alternative suggestions.

She switched to their Chase account. She paid the Con Ed, Verizon, and Visa bills and moved two thousand dollars from the money market to the checking account.

Artie has no head for figures. He hasn't paid a bill or balanced the checkbook in over thirty years. I'm starved. A bloody stool again this morning. A colostomy and chemo. If I die, he'll have an unearned income from investments of about one hundred and twenty-five thousand dollars. Leslie will have to manage it for him.

Artie nursed an ale in the living room. Snip, snip. My pal Johnny Havistraw's asshole was sewn shut, his intestines rerouted. He crapped through an open wound in his left side into a bag around his waist. He lost sixty pounds. All skin and bones. Like a prisoner in Auschwitz. And always cold; wrapped in a quilt in July, the month he died at home.

For four days at the end, he was unconscious from morphine. He creaked—like the rigging of a sailboat. The creak came from deep in his throat. Artie was reminded of the ten-year-old boy, paralyzed on his right side, who had seizures every day. It's a darkness.

At one point in the evening, Sutton Pendleton—Leslie's brother-in-law—spoke with a catch in his voice. "So Judy moved out on me. We lived together seven months. She moved in with Guy Stewart from the office—my projects manager. I still love her. She's the love of my life.

"She met me before dinner up at Hotspur Associates at the beginning of May. It was a rainy day. Guy invited us into his office for the view. He has a window that looks out over midtown. On a clear day you can see the East River and the Hudson, with the Empire State Building smack in the middle of the island. That day, as I say, it was raining. So the office was in the clouds. The three of us watched glistening raindrops form just beyond the glass. Judy told Guy she taught kindergarten at Trinity.

"He said, 'You're kidding! My mother taught kindergarten in Philly for thirty years.'

"They swapped stories about catching colds from the kids in class.

"Judy said, 'I'm a compulsive hand washer.'

"Guy said, 'So was my mother!'

"They talked five minutes. Then I took Judy up to dinner at Windows on the World.

"Yesterday, she says to me, 'Guy and I have been seeing each other since the first week we met. We're in love. We fell in love at first sight.'

"So I said, 'Are you getting married?'

"Judy said, 'Guy hasn't asked me.'

"I said, 'There was a time you would've married me.'

"And she said, 'You never asked me either.'

"I'm not ready to get married. I want to know what to do with my life. My job bores me. I write thousands and thousands of lines for software applications for banks. Where's the challenge in that? Chris and Dad want me to go in with them. What's the challenge in real estate? I need a purpose in life. But what? I know you all laugh, but I'm waiting for a sign from God."

Leslie pulled at her right earring. Artie picked up the signal: she was lost in thought. I'm pregnant! Sutton looked Leslie up and down. Her tits have grown. He lit a cigarette to go with his second brandy.

Leslie and Chris owned the ground-floor apartment of a brownstone on West 22nd Street between 9th and 10th. They sat with their guests on the teak deck in back. Artie said to himself, It's neat the kids are rich. He looked down at the garden in the moonlight: two pear trees, a young oak, an evergreen, a flower bed planted with a rosebush, impatiens, marigolds, petunias. A big gray tomcat with a scarred nose prowled between the stems.

Sutton turned his head on the pillow. I shouldn't have had two brandies. My shins will ache in the morning. I need to piss. I need a favor, Lord. For Your sake. Get Chris and Leslie to ask me to be their baby's godfather. Incline their hearts to me, Lord, and I will bring their baby to You.

Before going to bed, Johanna called up "colonoscopy" on the NIH website:

> Colonoscopy (koh-luh-NAH-skuh-pee) lets the physician look inside your entire large intestine, from the lowest part, the rectum, all the way up through the colon to the lower end of the small intestine. The procedure is used to look for early signs of cancer in the colon and rectum. It is also used to diagnose the causes of unexplained changes in bowel habits.

Colonoscopy enables the physician to see inflamed tissue, abnormal growths, ulcers, and bleeding.

You will be given pain medication and a mild sedative to keep you comfortable and to help you relax during the exam. The physician will insert a long, flexible, lighted tube into your rectum and slowly guide it into your colon. The scope transmits an image of the inside of the colon, so the physician can carefully examine the lining of the colon.

If anything abnormal is seen in your colon, like a polyp or inflamed tissue, the physician can remove all or part of it using tiny instruments passed through the scope. That tissue (biopsy) is then sent to a lab for testing. If there is bleeding in the colon, the physician can pass a laser, heater probe, or electrical probe, or inject special medicines through the scope and use it to stop the bleeding.

Bleeding and puncture of the colon are possible complications of colonoscopy. However, such complications are uncommon.

Colonoscopy takes 30 to 60 minutes. The sedative and pain medicine should keep you from feeling much discomfort during the exam. You

> will need to remain at the endoscopy facility for 1 to 2 hours until the sedative wears off.

Doctor Gunning said to Johanna, "I've got good news and bad news."

"What's the good news?"

"Your colon is clear. You have bleeding hemorrhoids. Get yourself some over-the-counter Anusol, either suppositories or cream."

"What's the bad news?"

"Your blood pressure is quite high. Did you know that?"

Johanna was still sleepy from the intravenous combination of Valium and Demerol that Gunning had given her for the colonoscopy. She yawned.

"I had no idea."

Artie asked, "How high?"

"182 over 110."

Artie thought, That's very high.

Johanna focused on the shiny chrome endpiece of the stethoscope around Gunning's neck and was suddenly wide awake.

She said, "The last time my blood pressure was taken, it was normal. Noah Garfinkel, my gynecologist, told me so. I remember distinctly what he said: 'Your blood pressure's normal.' That was in January. Only six months ago."

Gunning said, "How old are you Mrs. Rubin?"

"Sixty-four."

"The sudden onset of hypertension in a person your age is fairly common. I won't pull my punches, Mrs. Rubin. Hypertension is a serious disease. It can cause heart attacks, kidney failure, strokes."

"I know. Artie has hypertension."

Artie said, "Mine's under control."

Gunning asked him, "Who's your doctor?"

"Abe Raskin."

"At Columbia-Presbyterian. I know Raskin. He's a good man." To Johanna: "Make a date to see Raskin immediately. And before you go, Mrs. Rubin, I want a sample of your blood."

"My blood? What for?"

"Lab tests. They'll tell us about your liver function, measure your blood electrolytes, your blood sugar, your good and bad cholesterol. Things Raskin will want to know. I'll fax him the results. Leave his number with my secretary."

After dinner, Johanna hit the computer.

> Hypertension, or high blood pressure, the most common and most easily treated of the diseases affecting the kidneys, ensues only when the kidney's usual regulation of blood volume and blood vessel wall tension fails. The "tension" in hypertension describes the vascular tone of the smooth muscles in the artery and arteriole walls. Blood pressure is measured in millimeters of

mercury (mm Hg). The American Heart Association considers blood pressure less than 140 over 90 normal for adults. Primary hypertension, or high blood pressure, affects millions of Americans. It accounts for over 90 percent of all cases of hypertension in the U.S. and develops without apparent causes.

Hypertension is a major health problem, especially because it has no symptoms. Many people have hypertension without knowing it.

If left untreated, hypertension can lead to the following medical conditions:
arteriosclerosis (atherosclerosis)
heart attack
stroke
enlarged heart
kidney damage

Cause
The cause of hypertension is not known in 90 to 95 percent of the people who have it. Hypertension without a known cause is called primary or essential hypertension.

In bed, Johanna said, "Hypertension! Cause unknown. Scary. I didn't know it was a disease of the kidneys. Did you? We both have diseased kidneys. We're in the same leaky boat."

Aug. 7, 2001. Tues. 1 p.m. *Primed the pump with an ale after breakfast & managed 3 (!) pages. Odin killed Ymir; made the earth from his dismembered body: the sea from his blood, the sky from his skull, clouds from his brains, etc. Then Odin created first man (Ask) & woman (Embla) from ash & elm trees fallen on the seashore.*

"Odin said to Ask, 'Why worry? The day of your death was decreed ages ago.'"

Johanna now takes her blood pressure on my digital monitor first thing every morning. Today: 180/100. Abe will see her next Tues. He's waiting for fax from Gunning with results of blood tests.

Johanna's jumpy: "Why can't Abe see me sooner than a week?"

An obit in today's Times: *Glickstein, Leah (nee Solomon) On August 6th. 79 plus. Loving wife, mother, great-grandmother. A lousy cook, she ordered in every night of her life. We loved her.*

Artie said to Muggs, "You have bad breath."

Muggs cocked his head left and right.

That evening, Artie called Adam, who said, "I'm

pretty good. Work keeps me busy. I don't have time during the day to think about my cancer. Nights, though, are tough. I'm not sleeping well. How's the book going?"

Aug. 8, 2001. Wed. 2 p.m. *Today's ale after breakfast gave me the oomph for another 3 pages. Yggdrassil, The Cosmic Tree, whose branches spread above the heavens. It will survive Ragnarok and give birth to new life.*

Writing has temporarily subsumed my desire to draw. Waiting for an illustration to bubble up—just as I waited for all those poems as a teenager. Some weren't bad. They stopped coming when I was 18.

Johanna called Gunning's office this morn. for results of her blood test. He'll call her back at her office this afternoon.

Gunning said, "As you know, I don't pull my punches, Mrs. Rubin. I have bad news again."

"Tell me."

"Your total cholesterol is 285. Way too high. Your triglycerides are 180. Not too bad. But your low-density lipoprotein cholesterol is 160. Too high."

"Meaning what? Don't pull any punches."

"Your cholesterol count and your high blood pressure put you at real risk for a heart attack. You may have coronary artery disease. I faxed Raskin."

Leslie, reading the preliminary prospective on New

York State Series 2001 A Revenue Bonds, caught sight of Johanna's face, and asked, "Mother, what's the matter?"

"I'm at real risk for a heart attack."

"Mommy!"

Leslie saw tears in her mother's eyes. Johanna called Artie and told him the news. She said, "It was a short trip."

"A short trip?"

"In the same boat."

Artie hung up. Coronary artery disease! Jesus!

Johanna said to Leslie, "I want my family around me tonight. Come to supper."

"I'll tell Chris."

Leslie called Chris, and Johanna called Artie again with shopping instructions. He ran around the corner to Zabar's and bought a pound of coleslaw, a pound of Nova Scotia, four onion and garlic bagels, and a container of low-fat cream cheese. It's low-fat everything for Johanna from now on.

Johanna and her family ate the Nova in silence. Finally, she said, "Cheer up! I'm not dead yet."

She and Artie each took an Ambien before going to bed; they were asleep within twenty minutes. Muggs woke Johanna at seven sharp. She was groggy from the pill. It took her a moment to remember that she was at risk for a heart attack. What exactly is coronary artery disease? She Googled it.

> Coronary artery disease is the most common type of heart disease, affecting some seven million Americans. It results from clogged arteries.

Clogged arteries! The fucking thing's a killer.

Johanna spent the morning pitching municipal bonds on the phone to reluctant clients. "Charlie, the most important thing in understanding yield to maturity is that when you invest in a bond and receive interest semi-annually, you assume that during the life of the bond each semi-annual interest payment will be reinvested at the same rate as the stated yield to maturity. For example… Listen, Charlie. Can I get back to you?"

Sludge…cellular sludge is clogging my coronary arteries. My brain's clogged. I can't think straight.

Artie said to Muggs, "I need a hug." Muggs cocked his head to the right and left.

Aug. 9, 2001. Thurs. Noon. *One ale after breakfast, another an hour ago. They worked. Rewrote description of Yggdrasil, the Cosmic Ash Tree that nourishes all life. Its cooked fruit eases childbirth. The myth of a life-sustaining tree is universal. My shul is named Etz Chaim—Hebrew for the Tree of Life, which is what pious Jews call the Torah & the handles with which you lift the Torah scrolls.*

Johanna's my Tree of Life.

Her cholesterol 285.

Ella came in at twelve thirty. Artie told her Leslie was pregnant.

She said, "My baby a mama! God be praised!"

Ella was the only black person Artie and Johanna knew. She'd been their housekeeper since Leslie's birth. Ella was a month older than Artie, but only admitted to sixty-two. She was being treated for high blood pressure and late-onset diabetes. Her eyesight was going.

Last spring Johanna had tried to get Ella to retire on full pay—three hundred fifty dollars a week—but Ella said, "What would I do at home by myself every day, Mrs. Rubin? I'd go crazy. You is family. Working here is my life."

Johanna said to Artie, "We've got a servant problem. The apartment's dusty. Things are not put away right. I find bread crumbs and grease on the kitchen floor. The mirrors are dirty. Ella forgets to water the plants. I saved my azalea in the nick of time. This place needs a thorough going over at least twice a week. We gotta figure a way to get Ella to retire. She'd be OK with her Social Security, her Medicare, and the money we promised her. After all these years, I still think she doesn't trust us to continue her salary. She likes you better than me. Talk with her. Ask her to quit."

"You ask her."

Ella put in a four-hour day, three or four days a week. First off, she drank a cup of instant coffee and ate a slice of buttered toast while reading a chapter from the King James Version of the Holy Bible, Giant Print Edition, with the Words of Christ in Red. Today, as she read Thessalonians 1, her mind was on Leslie as a baby. Her first word was "Ella." The missus was jealous. She didn't say nothing but I could tell. I taught Leslie "Mama" next. That went over big. At one thirty, Ella changed into her housedress in the hall closet. She set up the ironing board in the dining room and ironed one of Artie's white shirts. She got a call from Joyce Ingram, who served with her on the usher board of the Ebenezer Baptist Church.

Ella said, "Good news! My baby is pregnant!"

"She ain't your baby."

Ella came from a Greensboro, North Carolina, family of six; her Mama was a spry eighty-six. Her favorite sister, who lived in Albany, was a nurse; her favorite brother worked as a security guard in Rhode Island. Twenty-five years ago, Ella married Sterling Harper, who worked in a sporting goods store on Broadway and 134th Street.

She once told Artie, "You can't trust mens, Mr. Rubin. I caught Harper cheating on me and throwed a bread knife at him in the kitchen. Pity I missed. I hit his girlfriend with a brick on 125th Street."

Artie was ashamed of loafing around while Ella worked; he went for a walk. He ran across a one-legged youngish woman, with reddish gold hair, tooling up 80th Street in a wheelchair. She was pushing herself backward with her muscular right leg in the middle of the street toward Broadway. Her left leg was amputated just above the knee; she tied her empty pant leg in a knot around the stump. Artie had seen her begging on Broadway with a paper cup and dozing under the green awning of Le Bistro, the restaurant next to the Baptist Church. Where does she go to the john?

Artie said, "Can I buy you lunch?"

"You mean it?"

"Be my guest."

"Thanks."

"You're welcome. My name's Artie. What's yours?"

"Molly."

"How'd you lose your leg, Molly?"

"This guy I knowed slashed me with a machete. He raped my girlfriend and shot her in the stomach. Then he cut out her beating heart and held it in his hand. I seen it. So help me God! On West 145th Street. His hand dripped blood. I was a witness and started to run. He come after me and slashed my leg as I was heading up the basement stairs. The doctors had to cut it off."

She wheeled herself by his side to Le Bistro, where Artie asked her, "What's it to be?"

"What can I have?"

"Anything on the menu."

"Anything?"

"You name it."

She read the menu chalked on a slate by the door, then pointed and said, "That one."

"The fettuccine with vegetables?"

"Fettuccine. Yeah! With vegetables. Vegetables are healthy. And a diet Coke."

The meal cost Artie twelve bucks. Molly waited under the awning to be served by a bald Palestinian waiter, who was nervous about working in a Jewish neighborhood. He was pleased to take part in an act of charity—even by a Jew. God favors the compassionate—even Jews.

Molly said to Artie, "I'm gettin' over a bad summer cold. It was on my chest six days. My doctor gave me Robitussin for my cough."

"Who's your doctor?"

"Dunno his name. He's at Roosevelt Hospital. He told me to come back if my cough didn't clear up in a week. I was lucky. It took six days."

"How do you get from here to Roosevelt Hospital?"

"By bus. It don't cost me nothing."

"Can I ask you another personal question?"

"Shoot!"

"Sure you don't mind?"

"I like talking about myself. I'm all I got."

"Where do you go to the john?"

"Starbucks or McDonald's."

"Well, I gotta get back to work. So long, Molly. Enjoy your meal."

"Yeah. Thanks, Artie. Thanks for everything. What do you do?"

"I'm a writer."

"That's why you're so nosy!"

Artie said, "You're right."

"Nora Roberts is my favorite writer. I read romance novels. They're my escape."

"Well, so long."

"So long, Artie. And thanks again for your kindness. I hope things go better for me."

"I hope so too."

For a moment, Artie didn't recognize the homely old Jew peering at him in the elevator mirror.

Aug. 9, 2002. Thurs. 7 p.m. *A second shift today fueled by vodka. Intro, the gods & goddesses, Odin's children, who will die at Ragnarok. The gods die—unique to Norse mythology. Poor Odin. My beloved Odin. I've also a thing for Thor, the stupid mighty Thunderer, for whom Thursday is named; it'll be tough portraying Loki, the Shape Changer, sly and ambiguous. That's it! Individuate him with a leit motif: a sly narrow face—like Adam's.*

Leslie leaned over the teak railing; a cricket chirped in the flower bed. She said to Chris, "Mom's gone back to exercising. She eats sensibly. She'll be all right. They have medicines to control high blood pressure and cholesterol. Why am I so scared? I got a bad feeling about her health. I can't shake it. Something terrible is going to happen."

Chris said, "You're all in a sweat. Take a swig of my iced tea."

Artie turned off the air conditioner and opened the windows. A breeze off the river blew the pull chain of the rolled-up shade against the side of the bookcase: the chain clicked. Johanna thought, Tick-tock. I'm a walking time bomb. I could have a heart attack any minute.

From the *New York Times* Friday: A Palestinian suicide bomber took the Middle East conflict to the core of downtown Jerusalem on Thursday when he blew himself up in a crowded Israeli restaurant. He killed at least fourteen people besides himself and wounded about one hundred thirty others. Six children were among the dead.

Artie, who'd missed last night's news on TV, put down the paper and called Dani Yellin at his studio in Wallingford, Connecticut. He left a message—"call me"—and tried Yellin's home. Another machine answered.

Artie said, "Are your folks OK? Give me a ring."

Yellin's parents owned a flower shop on Ben Yehuda Street in downtown Jerusalem.

In Israel, Dani'd been in a special commando recon unit that fought in southern Lebanon against Hezbollah and against terrorists in the Territories. Then he'd won a scholarship to the Bezalel Art School in Jerusalem. He painted Jerusalem's building stones, clouds, the Judean Mountains, an old Hasid waiting for a bus in the late afternoon light. But representational art was out among his fellow students; field color painting was in. Dani imitated Ad Reinhardt. After graduation, he worked for three years in the art department of a Tel Aviv ad agency. He painted at night and on Shabbat but couldn't get a gallery to show his work.

On the last day of July 1989, he picked up Alice, who was bumming around Israel, at a sidewalk café on Dizengoff called The Swan. Dani's English, learned in high school, had enabled him to pick up lots of American girls over the years. This girl was different; she shared his passion for Poussin. Alice spent the night in his two-room apartment on Arlozoroff. They spent every night together for a month. At the end of August, Alice returned to New York, where she was going for her master's in French Literature at Columbia. They spoke on the phone six times in one week. The seventh time, Dani asked Alice to marry him.

She said, "Yes, but I won't live in Israel."

I want to be an artist. Why not in New York, the art capital of the world?

He said, "No problem."

Dani flew to New York in the middle of October. He and Alice were married at City Hall; they lived in Queens. Dani worked off the books for a moving company owned by two Israelis from Haifa. In the evenings, and on weekends, he painted large, flat abstractions in broad brush strokes. Again, he couldn't find a gallery. His paintings were well composed; Dani had a feel for arranging shapes on a two-dimensional surface.

In the spring of '92, Alice got a job teaching French at Choate. They moved up to Wallingford and lived in a faculty house on campus. Dani converted the guestroom on the third floor with a southern exposure into a studio and painted full time. He was twenty-nine and felt it was now or never for him to become an artist.

One chilly March evening, he decided to paint in a completely different technique. He began an oil of Alice relaxing on the living room sofa. She posed for him every evening for two weeks. He was exhilarated by contemplating a real object in space, illuminated by real light. He remembered how to light a face from his class in portraiture at Bezalel. He positioned Alice's face at a three-quarter angle to the light from a lamp on her left. He found he could easily capture her likeness by slightly exaggerating her most prominent features: luminous, wide-set, hazel eyes and pouty lips. He painted the light passing through her amber irises and making halos around her pupils; it gave them the illusion of depth. Highlighting the pupils with a flash of white brought her portrait instantly to life. Getting the color of her lips right was a problem till he learned to add a touch of blue to the flesh tones. He used tiny brush strokes made with a sable brush that cost forty bucks.

Dani felt compelled to paint every crease in Alice's blue blouse, every blonde hair on her head, the stitching on her black leather watchband, the coffee stain on the rust colored sofa cushion. He thought in Hebrew, I've found my style. Then he said to himself in English, I'm a Detailist.

Dani won a number of commissions to paint portraits of academics and CEOs all around New England. Artie admired Dani's portrait of a retired Yale historian in a group show at the Studio Gallery in SoHo. The historian gazed at a globe with puffy eyes on the verge of tears. Artie introduced himself to Dani, who raved about his sixteen illustrations in the style of folk art for *American Myths and Legends*. Artie was flattered. They became friends.

Artie returned to work:

"Loki the Sly One gave Odin a gray, eight-legged stallion named Sleipnir, that could carry the High One to Niflheim, the Land of the Dead, and back."

The Land of the Dead. Members of those Orthodox Israeli burial societies wearing surgical gloves, who scraped up gobs of flesh, fragments of bone and gristle with spatulas after a bomb explosion and buried them according to Jewish law. Six kids scattered in chunks among the scorched tables, smashed plates, bent knives, glass shards. Bits of brain, a shattered pelvis, a seared lung, an eyetooth in a common grave. Or were the pieces buried separately? Do they try to match body parts? This tooth in which jaw? Goddamn fucking Arabs.

Dani called in the early afternoon. He, Alice, and Zvi were at a B&B on the Cape for a long weekend. "I spoke with my father on the phone. My parents heard the explosion in the restaurant—the Sbarro Pizzeria on Jaffa Street. It's five blocks from their shop. Their windows rattled. My mom dropped a vase. Three blasts of the air raid siren—a bomb. Ambulance sirens. My dad ran outside and saw a column of black smoke in the sky. He smelled burned flesh. It reminded him of Auschwitz."

It was lovely growing up in Jerusalem. I slept naked on summer nights. Grandma is buried on the Mount of Olives. The sun setting on the Jaffa Gate. My landscapes of the Judean Mountains. I once ate ripe figs off a tree near a dark cave.

He remembered one spring morning on the road north of Jerusalem. A flock of storks circled above the Jordan Valley on black-tipped wings. I'm in exile.

Artie thought of the two dead Arab kids in Nablus.

Johanna felt August 11 would be a lucky day. Too bad the market was closed. Eleven was her lucky number;

she had been born on December 11, married on June 11, and had conceived Leslie on March 11.

Artie showed up for breakfast in a white shirt, brown tie, and his brown summer suit.

"I'm off to shul."

Johanna spread strawberry jam on half a toasted English muffin. Eleven is my religion.

Etz Chaim was on 90th Street—between Broadway and West End. Artie walked the ten blocks uptown among young Orthodox Jews and their kids heading for various Orthodox shuls. He gave a family of three the once-over. A lot of the men had beards; this guy was clean-shaven. But he was dressed like the rest in a black, wide-brimmed fedora, black suit, and white shirt without a tie. He can't be more than thirty-five. Who would have thought, when I was his age, that one day many young Jews...Why do they turn to god?

The guy's wife, like the other Orthodox women, hid her hair under a straw hat that reminded Artie of an overturned basket. And like the other women, she wore a long-sleeved, ankle-length dress. A long-sleeved dress in this heat! Their ten-year-old daughter's skirt covered her thin calves.

Look at them all! Where do they come from? They've turned West End into an Orthodox ghetto.

Artie crossed 89th against the light; a cab driver honked at him. Orthodox Jews! They suck up to their god in hopes...in hopes of what? Catch this pimply kid in his baggy black suit. Why only black? Which commandment is that? Thou shalt dress like an undertaker.

He went in Etz Chaim's side entrance between West End and Broadway. Artie had joined the Conservative congregation the day he turned sixty-five. He picked Etz Chaim because Adam and Shirley belonged.

He said to them, "You're cultural Jews, like me. Going to shul once in a while is part of our cultural heritage. I feel old. Sixty-five! My Dad died of lung cancer at seventy-three. He said, 'I die, you die, everybody dies. But *Am Yisroel Chai:* the People of Israel live.'"

Artie mailed his check for eleven hundred bucks to the admissions office of the shul in hopes that he would come to feel a part of the Eternal People. He attended almost every Saturday morning service and celebrated the High Holidays for a year. He wrote in his journal:

Sept. 30, 1998. Wed. 8:30 p.m. *Au revoir, Yom Kippur. My delight in your melodies, particularly Kol Nidre & Vidui (Confession) Jewish love songs to God. Etz Chaim has no cantor. Rabbi Klugman leads the prayers in a pleasant baritone.*

The melodies remind me of the High Holidays of my childhood—the stuffy shul in Brooklyn, my annual prayer that God would write me & Mom & Dad in the Book of Life for the coming year.

At each Saturday morning service, Artie read the weekly portion of the Torah in English. He took it as a collection of myths portraying the personality of the central character—the god of Israel. Artie thought, He's as capricious as Zeus. And, as Aristotle says, only a fool would love Zeus.

In 1999, Dad's Yarhzeit, which was April 3, fell on Shabbes. Artie followed the suggestions he received in a letter to mourners from Etz Chaim. He bought a Yahrzeit memorial candle at Fairway and lit it just before sunset on Friday night. The flame flickered in the jar filled with wax on the stove. Artie recited kaddish in transliteration from Aramaic during the morning service; because he couldn't read Hebrew, he had to turn down the honor of reading aloud a portion from the Torah, but made a hundred-dollar contribution to the shul in Dad's memory.

That was the first time Artie had done these things. The flame in the jar stayed with him. It lit up the back of his mind, where he still hoped to feel a part of the Eternal People. Come May 14th, the anniversary of Mom's death, Artie didn't say kaddish for her or light a memorial candle. He respected her wish that she had expressed to him when she still had all her marbles: "No kaddish for me. No rabbi at my funeral. I'm a godless Jew."

It takes a year to read the Torah from beginning to end. Artie caught bronchitis in the fall of 1999 and missed Simchas Torah, the service that celebrates the end and the beginning again of the cycle of Torah readings. He watched TV in bed with a fever of 101. It's no use. I don't feel part of anything eternal.

Artie cut back on going to shul. Nowadays he averaged one Saturday morning a month, plus the High Holidays.

Today's service had just begun. Artie put on a yarmulke and a tallis. This always made him think of the graceful way Dad tossed the fringed ends over his shoulders. Artie sat in the third pew facing the bimah.

Most of the congregation was away for the weekend on Long Island, in Connecticut, upstate New York, and Vermont. Adam and Shirley were at their place in Columbia County. Artie figured that fewer than twenty people were seated in the air-conditioned sanctuary beneath the five stained-glass windows. He glanced up at the inscription etched in yellow on the first blue and red window. In loving memory of Celia Novack. Who was Celia Novack? What was her life like? How did she die? Who remembers her? The ancient Egyptians believed if you pronounced the name of somebody dead, his or her spirit returned from the underworld for a while to the earth.

Artie said, "Celia Novack." The woman seated to his left gave him a look.

Rabbi Klugman, standing on Artie's right, in the first row, was going bald on two fronts—his forehead and crown; he used Rogaine. His thinning blond hair was lighter than his bushy beard. Eight years ago, on his first date with his wife, Anne, she had looked at him and thought, What beautiful baby blues!

Klugman's eyes were closed. He faced the bronze doors of the Ark and chanted in Hebrew, "If song could fill our mouth as water fills the sea, and joy could flood our tongue like countless waves...we could never express our gratitude for one ten-thousandth of the lasting love which is Your precious blessing, dearest God, granted to our ancestors and ourselves."

Artie followed the service in English on the left-hand side of the page in the Conservative Prayerbook.

Rabbi Klugman said, "Our prayers this morning prepare us to recite the Sh'ma—our affirmation of God's unity. The Sh'ma is the core of our service. My teacher at the Seminary, the great Talmudic scholar, Rabbi Solowitz—may he rest in peace—used to say, 'The Sabbath morning prayers surround and protect the Sh'ma like a glass chimney surrounds and protects the burning wick of an old-fashioned kerosene lamp.'"

Then the rabbi said, "Don't go through a prayer, let the prayer go through you. Pray in English or pray in Hebrew! But concentrate on the meaning of the words you read. Become their living conduit to God."

Artie chanted the Sh'ma with the congregation. It was one of the few Hebrew phrases he knew by heart: "*Sh'ma Yisrael! Adonoi Elohenu Adonoi, Echod.*" "Hear O

Israel, the Lord our God, the Lord is One."

Dad had yanked the oxygen mask from his face and tried to recite the Sh'ma on his deathbed. He didn't have the breath. He fought for every one. Artie watched him struggle to breathe for half an hour. In a way, it's a mercy. He's not thinking about dying. All his thoughts are concentrated on taking another breath.

Lily Edelman over there. Shirley tells me her kid's got stage four lymphoma.

"Love the Lord your God with all your heart, with all your soul, with all your might."

Rabbi Klugman thought, I love You.

Artie thought, The greatest unrequited love in history: the Jews and their god.

Klugman reached the Kedushah and recited, "The whole world is filled with His glory." Even the roach flitting across the bathroom tiles, under the sink, this morning?

Toward the end of the Amidah, Artie read, "May it please You to bless Your people Israel in every season and at all times with Your gift of peace." Lots of luck.

Lily Edelman couldn't wait for the upcoming part of the service in which the congregation prayed for the sick. Dear God, we get the results of Charlie's PET scan on Monday. Please give us good news. Dear God, remember: he's only twenty-three.

Charlie was eight again, dressed up in a baggy clown's costume on Halloween. The top big yellow button came off the front. I put on my thimble and sewed the button back.

Charlie said, "What's that, mommy? A finger hat?"

Klugman prayed, Show me Your glory in a brown roach with long feelers.

The congregation rose again. Two women and two men opened the bronze doors of the Ark. Artie recognized the tall guy who took out one of the six Torah scrolls—Bernie Wasserman, a lawyer, Adam's friend, who was something of a Talmudic scholar. Wasserman held the Torah tenderly against his chest. It weighed the same as his two-year-old granddaughter, Becky. His nose itched.

Artie again chanted, "*Sh'ma Yisrael...*"

Dad on his deathbed groped under the sheet for his dick. He gave it a squeeze. Then he puffed up his cheeks and blew out his last breath.

Wasserman carried the Torah among the congregation. Everybody crowded the left aisle.

Artie joined in the ritual. He wrapped a corner of his tallis around his forefinger, touched the Torah as it was carried passed, then kissed the part of the tallis that had touched the scroll.

Wasserman laid the Torah on the lectern and gently pulled off its cover. He scratched the tip of his nose, unrolled the parchment scroll and thought, The Romans wrapped Rabbi Hanina ben Tradyon in a Torah scroll before they burned him at the stake. The sage said—the words fly up…No. The parchment burns—that's it—the parchment burns and the words fly free. Well, the words are still here. Where are the Romans?

Becky Hitzig, a modern Hebrew literature major at Barnard, had the honor to recite the beginning of today's portion: Deuteronomy, chapter seven, verse one. Artie noticed her black rayon top. Get a load of those big, soft tits.

She chanted in Hebrew:

> "When the Lord your God brings you to the land that you are about to enter and possess and He dislodges many nations before you. The Hittite, and the Girgashite, and the Amorite, and the Canaanite, and the Perizzite and the Hivite and the Jebusite, seven nations much larger than you and the Lord your God delivers them to you, and you defeat them; then you must doom them to destruction. Grant them no terms and give them no quarter."

Becky thought, Genocide.

Bernie Wasserman thought, The Arabs are the seven nations.

Artie thought, It was tough for Dad not to smoke on Shabbes. He went cold turkey at sundown every Friday.

Klugman said, "Now our holy congregation will pray for the sick in our community. We will pray first in

Hebrew. The English translation, on page 145 of your text, goes, 'May He who blessed our ancestors, Abraham, Isaac, and Jacob, Sarah, Rebecca, and Leah, bless and heal blank, May the Holy One in mercy strengthen blank and heal blank soon, body and soul, together with others who suffer illness. And let us say: Amen.'

"Those of you who know someone sick—when we pray, fill in the blank with a name. But first, stand up and when I call on you, share the name with us. May these names ascend with all our prayers to the Holy One, blessed be He."

Nine people stood up; the rabbi pointed them out, one by one, and each spoke in a loud voice.

"Bobby Cohen."

"Susan Friedman."

"My aunt Susan Lefkowitz."

"Jacob Stern and Marvin Blau."

"My brother Harry Ginzburg."

"Paul Serwitz and Helen Frisch."

"My brother-in-law Billy Rubin."

"Helen Klein."

"My son, Charlie Edelman, who's only twenty-three."

A stockbroker named Sol Radam began reading the Haftorah, Isaiah forty, verse one in Hebrew.

"Comfort, oh comfort my people says your God. Speak tenderly to Jerusalem and be clear to her that her term of service is over, that her iniquity is expiated."

It came time for Klugman to deliver his sermon. He laid the nine-page printout on the lectern. I wrote the whole thing in one go. I write sermons too easily. I'm glib.

He said, "Isaiah calls to us from this morning's Haftorah three days after the massacre in Jerusalem. The prophet says, 'Bid Jerusalem, take heart.'

"I bid you. Come with me to Jerusalem for five days during the third week of October in a show of solidarity with our fellow Jews. We'll stay at the Inbal Hotel. Inbal means bellclapper in Hebrew; the hotel is near the Liberty Bell Garden. The garden's named after our Liberty Bell in Philadelphia. We Jews are proud that the Founding Fathers inscribed the Liberty Bell with words from the Torah. Leviticus 25:10: 'Proclaim liberty throughout all the land unto all the inhabitants thereof.'

"We'll be leaving Tuesday, October sixteenth. The whole package, everything included, costs nine hundred and ninety-nine dollars. You'll be expected, however, to make a five hundred dollar contribution to charity—the New York Jewish Federation. Contact me in my office if you're interested.

"This morning I'm going to talk about the two attributes of God. According to our rabbis, God has the attributes of *Rachamim* and *Din*, mercy and judgment. There is a story in the *Midrash* that Abraham explained why God needs both attributes to rule the world. If He ruled only by compassion, life would be chaos—there'd be no law or fear of punishment. If He ruled only by His fearsome judgement, the world would be consumed.

"In this morning's portion of the Torah, God condemns the seven nations to death. Martin Buber says that if the Bible commands us to kill, the Bible is wrong. But there it is, nevertheless, in black and white: God's ferociousness revealed. For He can be ferocious. Chastising Israel for its sins, He declares in Hosea (13:7–8), 'I am become like a lion to them, like a leopard I lurk on the way. Like a bear robbed of her cubs, I attack them and rip open the casing of their hearts. There I will devour them like a lion. The beasts of the field shall mangle them.'

"The Talmud says that God prays to Himself, 'May it be My will that My compassion overcomes My wrath.'"

Artie tuned out.

Back home, he said to Johanna, "Klugman is leading a group from Etz Chaim to go to Israel for five days in October."

"Whatever for?"

"To show our solidarity with the Israelis. I'm tempted to go."

"Why don't you?"

"I'm tempted. The whole deal costs fifteen hundred bucks. Suicide bombers included."

I got a time bomb in me. My ticker. Tick-tock.

Leslie and Chris had his folks and Sutton over for Saturday brunch. Richard and Caroline Pendleton generally drove to their weekend place in Southport on Friday evening, but they jumped at the chance to spend a couple of hours with the kids, whom they hadn't seen in over a week. They ooh'd and ah'd again at the ultrasound pictures of the fetus in Leslie's womb.

Caroline said, "I didn't notice before. His eyes are almond-shaped. Listen to me! I said 'his.' I'm sure it's a he."

Richard said, "Me too." When he's a freshman at Harvard, I'll be eighty-three.

The men hung around the kitchen while Leslie and Caroline made eggs Benedict. Chris served Bloody Marys. Sutton, who was nauseous from a hangover, passed.

Chris drank two, then said, "You guys might as well know. We're not having the baby baptized."

Caroline said, "I'm very sorry to hear it."

Sut said, "Me too."

Richard said, "Me too. I would have liked my grandson to be raised a Christian and come to love Jesus. Mind you, it wasn't love for me at first sight. My first sight of Him was nailed to a cross in Grandma Claire's illustrated Bible when I was six or seven. His bleeding head, crowned by thorns, flopped to one side. Grandma Claire said, 'This is God,' and I thought, there must be some mistake."

Leslie served scones with the eggs Benedict—Chris

preferred them to English muffins. Their eyes met above the hollandaise sauce.

Sut said, "I guess that means I won't be the baby's godfather."

Leslie asked, "What's a godfather do?"

Sut said, "He's responsible for seeing that the child is brought up in the Christian faith and life."

Chris said, "Our baby won't need a godfather, or a God."

Sut slept through his alarm set for seven fifteen and awoke with a start at eight thirty. He lit a cigarette. Fuck. Another hangover. I'm late for church. He made it to Heavenly Rest at Fifth and 90th at nine fifteen, just in time to join in the prayer: "Grant us therefore, gracious Lord, so to eat the flesh of thy dear Son Jesus Christ, and to drink his blood, that we may evermore dwell in him and he in us. Amen."

Sut swallowed the wafer and the wine. Dad and Mother believe they're only symbols of Your flesh and blood. Give me the faith that they're the real thing. So I won't be the baby's godfather. Well, Thy will be done.

Sut went back to pew fifty-seven in the rear, knelt toward the altar on his left knee, crossed himself, sat down, and thought, the baby must be baptized. Baptism is a prerequisite for Paradise.

He looked up baptism in the Book of Common Prayer, page 313: "In case of emergency, any baptized person may administer Baptism according to the following form..."

He shut the book. I'll baptize the baby in secret.

Artie, setting the dining room table for supper, heard Johanna ask in the kitchen, "Do you want a carrot?"

"Not now, thanks."

"I wasn't talking to you. I was talking to Muggs."

Some ragweed pollen, blown through the open window on the evening breeze, made Artie sneeze. Muggs rushed into the dining room and barked at him. Artie put down a fork and sneezed again. Muggs barked back. Johanna came in to watch the fun. Muggs always barked when somebody sneezed. It was another one of his unique quirks, like cocking his head and hugging Johanna.

She kissed his big black salty nose and said, "Sweet doggie! We've never had a dog like you. You're an original. But you've only got seven or eight years to go. Then you'll be old and sick and we'll have to put you down. So live it up! Have another carrot."

Johanna shook Artie's right shoulder; he stopped snoring. You sound like a buzz saw. She thought about the white roots of her hair that needed dyeing, the wrinkles above her upper lip, the hole under the left armpit of Artie's T-shirt that she wore to bed. Artie snorted. Where's the handsome boy I married?

Johanna met Artie on a blind date set up by her former roommate at Vassar. She had just turned twenty-two and was going for her master's in economics at Columbia. She aimed to be a securities analyst. Artie was twenty-eight—the recent author of his first book, *The Illustrated Myth of Orpheus and Eurydice Retold*, that Colin Harris reviewed in the Sunday *Times:*

> This brief book of sixty-four pages is illustrated by the author with fifteen line drawings in the style of Attic red figure vase paintings. The sexy illustrations and vernacular text compliment each other. They compose a contemporary interpretation of the myth of Orpheus and Eurydice. Rubin's book is a parable of the artist's precarious relationship with his talent. Rubin represents Orpheus's wife Eurydice as his muse—his inspiration—the personification of his musical gift, his very song.
>
> Rubin writes, "Eurydice was Orpheus's tangible vision of the beautiful." Nervous that she might desert him, Orpheus won't let her out of his sight. He checks on her whereabouts day and night. Eurydice becomes a nervous wreck. Bitten by a snake, she dies, and Orpheus descends into the Underworld to retrieve her. Eurydice longs to return to the sunlight but begs Orpheus

> to lay off her. "Get it through your head that I won't desert you."
>
> Orpheus says, "I got it." He charms Hades and Persephone with his singing and they agree to allow Eurydice to follow Orpheus to the upper world on condition that he not look back at her until they leave the realm of the dead. As he climbs the steep stone steps, Orpheus can't hear Euydice's footsteps or her breathing behind him.
>
> "His old fear that he had lost his song made him turn around." Eurydice's not there. She's returned to the Underworld forever. The artist who obsessively doubts his talent will lose it. He must keep faith with his "vision of what's beautiful." Despondent, Orpheus stops singing, and is torn to pieces by the Maenads—who Rubin writes "are Orpheus's passions, loosed from his art."
>
> Arthur Rubin, 28, a recent graduate of Pratt, animates—and reinvigorates—mythology in words and images. To paraphrase W. H. Auden's poem, "Progress?" Rubin beautifully pictures the absent and nonexistent.

On their second date, Artie said to Johanna, "I need a muse."

"Try me."

They were married in the spring. Artie dedicated all his subsequent work the same way: "For my muse, Johanna."

He wrote and illustrated book after book for the joy of making pictures with words and turning words into pictures. He lived in his imagination with his childhood pals: gods, heroes, demons, and monsters. He reworked myths, polished by the flow of centuries, and illustrated them in appropriate graphic styles: Greek, Egyptian, Aztec, Japanese, Indian. Sometimes he culled three or four books from a body of myths. He published four books based on Greek mythology alone.

Now he was studying reproductions of Viking carvings and reinterpreting Norse myths from Snorri Sturluson.

Aug. 13, 2001. Mon. 5 p.m. *My ophthalmologist Seth White just returned my call; gave me details on plucking out an eye, which I need to write next Odin scene.*

White said, "I once had a patient in my ER with one of his eyes in each hand. He tore them out so he couldn't look at his heart's desire—naked men."

Johanna sees Abe tomorrow at ten.

3 obits of men in their early seventies in today's Times.

Johanna said, "Doctor, please! Don't pull any punches with me."

"Punches! You caught that from Pete Gunning. His fondness for that figure of speech is contagious. No, Mrs. Rubin, I won't pull any punches with you."

Abe Raskin read over the fax of her lab report: Total cholesterol, 285. Triglycerides, 180. High-density lipoprotein, 30.

He said, "Your total cholesterol is dangerously high. I'm putting you on 40 mg. of Lipitor daily to reduce your cholesterol. It'll start working in about a month."

"Any side effects?"

"Constipation, nausea, gas. They'll pass. Why the long face? Lighten up. Lipitor, regular exercise, and a low-fat diet will definitely reduce your cholesterol. Do you exercise regularly?"

"I'm lazy. I used to work out four or five times a week on my stationary bike."

"Get back to it. Come on. I said lighten up! Such a long face!"

"Artie tells me you believe that prayer facilitates healing."

"I do. I definitely prescribe prayer."

"Any side effects?"

"Gas. Praying promotes flatulence. It passes."

Johanna burst out laughing.

Abe smiled. "That's better. Now stretch out on the gurney. I want your blood pressure."

Johanna looked at the florescent light above her head. Relax. Gas passes. He has a sense of humor. The gap between his upper front teeth. What's the word for that? Lauren Hutton has one. I know the damn word. What is it? My soundtrack's playing *Hello, Dolly!* Total cholesterol, 285. This time of life sucks.

When Johanna felt the cuff removed from her right arm, she asked, "What's the score?"

"185/100."

"What do we do?"

"I need your average pressure over a twenty-four-hour period. I'm sending you to a good friend of mine—Ralph Keir—a cardiologist who specializes in assessing hypertension. Ralph will fit you with an ambulatory blood pressure monitor that'll give us the information. Then come back for a chat with me about medication.

"Here's the prescription for Lipitor. It might give you gas. Take Beano. You can buy it over the counter. And remember—a low-fat diet and regular exercise. Also aspirin. One aspirin every day."

Why are you smiling? Your smile is smarmy. Phony as a three-dollar bill. What the hell's the word for the gap between your teeth?

Johanna called Keir's secretary in the cab on the way to her office. A patient had just canceled an appointment for tomorrow at twelve thirty. Johanna made the date. Diastema! That's the word for that gap in his swarmy smile: Diastema.

Leslie filled her in on the market. "Johnson and Johnson dropped three points since yesterday."

"My blood pressure's up five."

Aug. 15, 2001. Wed. Noon. *Blocked. Writing about Odin's eye this morn. brought back getting panned in the Sunday* Times *last year for my rewrite of* The Ghost of Oiwa, *an early 19th century kabuki play, based on an ancient Japanese legend. Oiwa is poisoned; one eye swells shut. Her disfigured face haunts her murderer.*

Grossman's review hit the mark. My version of the tale adds nothing to the original, and my illustrations, based on Hokushu's woodcuts, are imitative and uninspired.

Johanna, following Ms. Miceli down the hall, glanced in the office to the left. A handsome Wasp—salt and pepper hair—in a white coat, on the phone behind a metal desk. Doctor Keir, I presume.

Ms. Miceli led Johanna into a small green room. She took Johanna's blood pressure—184/100—and fitted her out with an ambulatory blood pressure monitor that would automatically take her blood pressure every fifteen minutes for the next twenty-four hours.

The monitor was a sealed plastic box, the size of a thick book, in a peeling leather case that hung from a strap over Johanna's right shoulder; it was attached by wire to a blood pressure cuff wrapped around her left arm, above the elbow.

Ms. Miceli: "When the box beeps, the cuff inflates. The beep stops at night."

After the cuff deflated, Johanna had to note the time, her location, bodily position, activities, and emotional states in a five-page Ambulatory Blood Pressure Diary. She looked it over. *Mood Codes:* Happy, Sad, Angry, Anxious. Place a number from 1 (low) to 10 (high) in the appropriate box. Skip if mood is neutral. Ms. Miceli turned the machine on.

The box beeped, the cuff inflated and squeezed Johanna's upper arm much tighter than she had expected. Her forearm swelled; she felt her pulse beat in her wrist. It was a relief when the cuff deflated. Johanna wrote in the Diary: Time: 1:15 p.m. Location: Keir's office. Position: S (sitting). Mood: Anxious (3). Activities: none.

She crossed out 3 and wrote 4.

Ms. Miceli: "Return the monitor and the Diary to me tomorrow at twelve thirty and I'll average out the blood pressure readings of the last twenty-four hours. I'll fax the results to Dr. Raskin."

Johanna took another look at Keir on her way out. He was reading at his desk. Lean, handsome, forty. Mood: turned on.

She gave Leslie a ring and told her she was taking the day off.

"You haven't taken a day off in years. Are you OK? What did the doctor say?"

"I didn't speak with him. A nurse fitted me out with a ridiculous box that beeps and then takes my blood pressure every fifteen minutes. I don't want to wear it around the office."

Leslie read her the numbers: Citigroup 46.90, Intel 27, Cisco 16.04, Microsoft 60.60, Johnson & Johnson 54.40. No significant changes since yesterday.

Johanna called Artie, who said he'd take the rest of the day off too. "We'll spend it together."

"Lovely."

Two thirty. The box beeped. Happy (7).

Artie stared into space. Johanna said, "I thought we were going to spend the rest of the day together. You're not with me. Where are you?"

"I'm second-rate."

"Let's go to the magic place. We haven't been to the magic place in ages."

> There is in New York...a magic place where the dreams of childhood hold a rendezvous, where century-old tree trunks sing and speak, where indefinable objects watch out for the visitor, with the anxious stare of human faces, where animals of superhuman gentleness join their little paws like hands in prayer for the privilege of building the palace of the beaver for the chosen one,

> of guiding him to the realm of seals, or of teaching him, with a mystic kiss, the language of the frog or the kingfisher. This place…may be seen daily from ten to five o'clock at the American Museum of Natural History. It is the vast ground-floor gallery devoted to the Indians of the Pacific Northwest Coast, an area extending from Alaska to British Columbia.
>
> Claude Lévi-Strauss, *The Way of the Mask*, translated by Sylvia Modelski, The University of Washington Press,1982.

Artie read Lévi-Strauss in 1983, while researching a book about Northwest Indian mythology—*The Cannibal Spirit and Five Other Northwest Native American Myths Retold and Illustrated.* He spent every working day for a month drawing the Kwakiutl, Haida, Bella Coola, Tlingit and Tsimshian masks displayed in glass cases at the museum.

Artie made Johanna read Lévi-Strauss. He took her to the museum on three consecutive Sundays in March. He led her in the dim light among carved and brightly painted beech and alder masks: a ghost, the spirit of the sea, owner-of-southeast-wind, born-to-be-head-of-the-world, cannibal raven. Huge, carved eyes, with abalone pupils, closed lids, sunken sockets, hollow cheeks, yellow and green hooked noses, long black beaks that could be opened and snapped shut, hanks of hair, eagle feathers, tufts of otter fur, crimson protruding tongues, sharp white teeth.

This afternoon, Johanna lingered over the Bella Coola echo mask that had five red mouths.

She said to Artie, "The invisible made visible. You do that in your work."

"Is that true?"

She rewrote a verse by Auden: "Talkative, anxious,
Artie can picture the Absent
And non-Existent."

Then she said, "I never bullshit you."

"No, you never do."

Four fifteen. Beep. Happy (9).

Aug. 14, 2001. Tues. 1 p.m. *Johanna restored my self-confidence yesterday with a customized quote from Auden's "Progress?"*

Grossman's review of The Ghost of Oiwa *now seems to me full of shit. My version enhanced the story for American readers because I wrote it in a matter-of-fact, contemporary vernacular that heightens its horror. And my illustrations, ala Hokusha, ain't bad.*

Grossman has it in for me. I became friends with his fourth wife after their divorce. He used to get drunk & beat her up.

Worked all morning. Mimir the wise beheaded by warring faction of gods.

Johanna's short hair, which needed a trim, made nurse Lisa Miceli think of her Mama's short hair, also due for a cut. The two had argued over the phone that morning about Roy, Lisa's new boyfriend, who was black. Mama had said, "Don't do this to me!" Lisa had slammed down the receiver. Now I feel guilty. Poor Mama! Asthmatic and all alone in the world except for me.

But Lisa couldn't bring herself to call Mama back and apologize. She decided instead to be nice to Johanna; why should she sweat out one or two days waiting to hear from Raskin?

"Your twenty-four-hour blood pressure averages out to 185/104."

"You're sweet to tell me. Thank you."

Leslie's client Marvin Spottsworth wanted to convert his portfolio to a more conservative position in the coming fiscal year. Johanna suggested that she investigate real estate investment trusts because they were yielding over five percent.

Leslie asked, "What kind? Apartments? Shopping malls, retirement homes?"

"What you want is well-diversified properties with transparent accounting. I'm worried about the debt level on and off the books of some of the REITs."

"What percentage of Marvin's portfolio should I shift?"

"Let's see first what you can come up with in terms of yield."

My numbers stink! 185/104! To say nothing of my cholesterol. 285! Hypertension, high blood pressure. I'll bet my arteries are clogged.

After work, Johanna went to Citarella's at 75th and Broadway and bought two salmon steaks and half a pound of sautéed spinach with garlic and red peppers for dinner. Crossing 79th, she checked out the bulge in the khaki shorts of a tall twenty-year-old boy on the opposite curb. It was great for me, how was it for you with a sick old broad?

She told Artie, "I got us salmon for dinner."

"Sounds good."

"The trouble with cooking salmon is that the house smells fishy for days."

Artie said, "So it smells. So what? Salmon's healthy for you. Your health is all that counts."

"I don't feel sick. I feel good. I never felt better. Answer the phone for the next half-hour. I'll be on the bike."

Artie snored and pinged. Johanna called it his sonar sound. Ping! Just loud enough to keep her awake. He pinged again. She kicked him in the small of his back. The pinging stopped. But then he blew through his nose like a steam engine. For the next twenty minutes, he lay there on his side blowing off steam.

At breakfast, Johanna said, "Your snores, your pings, your blowing off steam kept me awake half the night. For the second night in a row. Ask the pharmacist if there's anything you can take."

Artie's pharmacist sold him a spray called Snorestop. That night before going to bed he sprayed it once under his tongue and once in the back of his throat. A slightly bitter taste.

Johanna said, "I wish there was something for red spots. I'm covered with red spots. And liver spots. Floppy warts. I got a new one on the side of my neck. Then there's waxy growths. I've got waxy growths all over my legs; my shins, particularly. My fingernails are brittle. The wrinkles on my upper lips smear my lipstick. My gums are receding. I've sprouted whiskers on my chin. My hair is lank."

Snorestop worked wonders. Johanna had a good night's sleep for the first time since the weekend.

Aug. 16, 2001. Thurs. 3 p.m. *Abe's put Johanna on 5 mg. Altace and a diuretic—25 mg. hydrochlorothiazide—daily.*

Wrote Odin's eye.

"Odin preserved Mimir's head from decay by rubbing it with a leaf from the ash Yggdrassil. He held up the head by its long blonde hair, and said, 'I know a secret charm that'll

give you back the power of speech. I'll sing it in your ear.'

"Odin sang the charm in Mimir's left ear. He set the head on the ground to guard the fountain of wisdom that gushes from under the World Tree's third root.

"The head spoke. 'Thanks, All-Father, for my giving me back my voice. What would you like in return?'

"'One sip from your fountain. I want to become wise.'

"'For that, you must pluck out one of your eyes and drop it in the water. But not as a god—for as a god you won't feel pain. Acquiring wisdom is very painful. Pluck out your eye in the guise of a man!'

"'The right or the left?'

"'Suit yourself.'

"Odin dimmed his godhead and assumed the guise of a bearded man in his mid-fifties. He took off his hat and with three fingers of his right hand parted the lids of his left eye, which was his keenest, and would be therefore be the greater sacrifice. Then he dug his right thumb and third finger into the socket. 'So this is pain!'

"He dug his fingers behind his eyeball. He squeezed and

yanked. The eyeball popped into his hand. It was still attached to his brain by the optic nerve. Odin pulled. His optic nerve stretched; one end ripped from his retina and snapped back into his bleeding socket. Odin's head jerked. He tore a strip from the hem of his blue woolen cloak and stuffed it in the wound. The bleeding let up. Odin dropped his left eye in the water, filled up his drinking horn, and took a sip.

"The tear in Odin's right eye trickled down his bearded cheek.

"Said Mimir, 'I see you've acquired wisdom'."

Subj: Surgery
Date: 8/16/2001 8:16:09 PM Eastern Daylight Time.
From: Artjo
To: Adamlaw

How did your surgery go?
Artie.

Subj: Re: Surgery
Date: 8/16/2001 8:30:03 PM Eastern Daylight Time
From: Adamlaw
To: Artjo

No fun, but only six stitches. The tumor was encapsulated. Margins clean. But since this is my 2nd in two years, my oncologist says I should be treated for a year or so with some drug that hikes immune response. It's got bad side effects.

Thanks for your concern. You're a pal.
Adam.

Lily Edelman skipped the Saturday morning service at Etz Chaim. Praying is for shit. What good did praying last week do for Charlie? My poor Charlie. Riddled with cancer.

In the early afternoon, Artie and Leslie crossed Bow Bridge across the Central Park lake toward the Ramble. They strolled on the path up the slope, passed the stand of sassafras.

Near the sour gum tree, opposite a lamppost, Leslie said, "It must be five degrees cooler in the park."

"At least. Thank God for Central Park. I can't imagine life in this town without it."

Artie caught himself staring: her breasts are swollen. He fixed his eyes on the gum tree; it had a double trunk. They walked back over the bridge then west beneath Cherry Hill. At Strawberry Fields, the little white spiky flowers of the sweet pepper bush to the right of the path filled the humid air with their fragrance.

In the shade of the big oak, Artie asked, "Will you raise your kid as a Jew?"

"Was I raised as a Jew? What's that mean? Oh, I knew I was Jewish. We celebrated Passover. But we also had a Christmas tree. You taught me that Passover and Christmas were myths. That God's a myth. You never took me to synagogue; I had no Jewish education. You once said to me, 'I'm a Jew because of the Holocaust and Israel.' So you made me read about the Holocaust and sent me to Israel."

She watched two young squirrels chase each other around the gum tree.

"I read Primo Levi, Borowski, Anne Frank, Etty Hillesum. I'll never forget that one-legged little girl in Borowski's book, the one burned alive. But the Holocaust's history to me. Anne Frank's been dead almost sixty years.

"You can have Israel. I loathed my month on a kibbutz. The Valley of Jezreel is hell in July. The grass is brown. I smoked Lebanese hash, shoveled chicken shit, and fended off the macho Israeli guys hitting on me. Things were quiet, though. Everybody expected peace with the Palestinians. Fat chance. Israeli and Palestinian mothers must now be crazy with fear for their kids. Kids shot and blown up. What's with those people?

"I never deny I'm Jewish, but it's not important to me. What will it mean to my kid? I want a daughter. Chris and I agree: we'll raise our kid an atheist. We think believers are deluded. They're needy and not willing to take responsibility for their lives. They're looking for someone to give them answers instead of making their own decisions. I know you agree. Why do you go to synagogue?"

"It makes me feel close to my father. I'm a sentimental old Jew. The last Jew in my family."

"You're not old."

"I'm pushing seventy. I can't believe it, but here I am."

Leslie pulled her gold earring. He looks seventy in this heat. Sweaty wrinkles.

A robin hopped at the foot of the white pine to the left of the path. Artie noticed two white blossoms in the crown of the mulberry tree on the right. The robin flew away.

Artie kissed Leslie on the forehead and said, "I love you."

"I love you too. You're not old."

The lawn was crowded with kids lying on the grass bordered by elms. Artie smelled pot. Leslie watched a homely blonde, with legs crossed under her, nursing her tow-headed baby boy. He sucked on her left nipple. Artie read the steel plaque set in the big flat stone on the little hill beside the juniper and above the rose bush:

Imagine all the people living life in peace...John Lennon.

The restoration of this part of Central Park as a Garden of Peace, endorsed by the above nations, was made possible through the generosity of Yoko Ono Lennon.

Artie checked the list of nations. Israel was between Ireland and Italy.

A bunch of tourists snapped pictures of the round, black-and-white marble mosaic on the concrete path inscribed with the title of Lennon's song, "Imagine." One of them put five yellow African daisies wrapped in cellophane next to a gutted candle melted on the marble. Artie and Leslie sat on the bench among the dogwood and gingko trees near the 72nd Street exit. They cooled off in the shadows of the leaves.

Leslie said, "I'm worried about Mom."

"She has the farts from Lipitor."

They left the cool park for the hot street. The 8th Avenue subway roared under the grate in the sidewalk at their feet. An empty tour bus was parked near the corner. The Dakota across Central Park West was Artie's favorite apartment building in New York. He could pick out German Gothic, French Renaissance, and English Victorian styles mixed together in its facade.

They crossed Central Park West toward the Dakota. Leslie thought, Lennon was murdered in the entrance there, in front of that spiked iron gate. I was ten. I love New York. But it scares me.

The day after Christmas, when Leslie was sixteen, she and her date, Josh Lautman, went out for a walk in the fresh snow on Riverside Drive. They saw a taxi driver's corpse sprawled in a puddle of slushy blood in the middle of the street between 81st and 82nd.

Josh said, "The blood's so red. And there's so much of it."

The driver, on his back, arms outstretched, was surrounded by cops. He had been shot in the right side of his head. The left front door of his cab was wide open. The bullet had knocked him into the snow.

Leslie drove out the memory. Crossing Columbus, Artie thought of being bathed at eight or nine by Mom. He felt her soapy hands slither up his back. Her brown cloth coat had a beaver collar; it had once glittered with snowflakes. That was in a snowstorm on Kings Highway. Wet, cold feet. My right hand in Mom's palm was warm. A falling snowflake melted on the tip of my tongue. Her soft hand. It's now bone.

Johanna: "I was thinking today. Our fortieth anniversary is coming up in February. Where do you want to go to celebrate?"

"Venice. We haven't been to Venice in fifteen years. Venice in February. Remember? Let's stay at the Monaco again. Can we afford it? Can we afford both my trip to Israel in October and a fancy trip to Venice in February?"

"We haven't taken a trip since last August. We can afford to spend ten grand a year on vacations. Twelve, in a pinch. We'll splurge for our anniversary."

Artie repeated, "Venice in February."

Their thoughts met on their twenty-fifth anniversary among red and green traffic lights reflected at night in dark canals, the top of the Campanile hidden by mist, the black gondolas crammed with Japanese tourists.

"Let's fuck at the Monaco on the night of February twenty-seventh."

"You're on."

Sweet Jesus! It's eleven o'clock. I slept through the alarm and missed communion. My poor head!

Aug. 20, 2001. Mon. Noon. *This morn. the newly wise Odin broke a limb off the World Tree and made a shaft from it for his spear Gungnir. The Tree feels pain.*

Today is Mom's birthday. She would have been 91.

My remorse at letting her die alone. She was in a coma. Soon as her death rattle began, I fled the room. Waited 20 minutes in the corridor, by the nurse's station; when I returned, she was dead.

Artie's arthritis in the first joint of his right big toe was kicking up. He limped walking Muggs on West End at three thirty. He thought of Thor, wrestled to the ground by Old Age disguised as a withered crone named Elli. Old age is getting me down.

Johanna felt gassy from the Lipitor. The Beano she took with lunch hadn't worked. She was ten minutes late for the six o'clock meeting of the Admissions Committee of the board of her co-op. It was at 575 Madison in the conference room of Douglas Elliman, the managing agent for the building. She went up in the elevator with Fred Blair, the committee chairman, who was a senior partner and specialist in trusts and estates at Simpson, Thacher.

He said, "I'm reading Proust for the first time in twenty years."

"In French?"

"No, no. The old Scott Moncrieff translation."

"What's Proust like? I haven't read him since college."

"He's very funny."

"I don't remember Proust as funny."

"Well, he is. He's a great satirist. Sometimes he makes me laugh out loud."

Johanna said, "I could use a laugh."

The candidates for the apartment, Noah and Esther Levin, were seated in the anteroom. Johanna took them in at a glance. A yarmulka. They're Orthodox. Where did she buy that hideous black straw hat? If they're accepted, they'll be the first Orthodox Jews in the building. Why does that bother me? Shame on me.

Johanna and Fred went into the conference room. They apologized for being late and sat down at the mahogany table with the two other committee members: Bruce Cohen, a law professor at NYU, and Patsy Grey, in human resources at Verizon.

Each committee member had already studied what

they called the Packet: papers that detailed the Levins' qualifications as candidates for admission to the building. Each had perfunctorily read the five letters of recommendation from Levin's former landlord, his lawyer, two people who worked with him, and Harvey Weintraub, who had lived in 12C for fifteen years. Then each had carefully gone over the financial statements. Levin was a partner in Thomas Futures, a small but well-regarded firm that traded commodities on the New York Mercantile Exchange. Esther had been a lawyer, an associate at Hughes, Hubbard, and Reed, until she quit four years ago when Ari, her second son, was born.

The Levins hoped to buy 2D. They had agreed to pay the asking price of $1.2 million. The building required that they put down forty percent. Johanna figured they wouldn't have trouble covering the mortgage, plus the monthly maintenance that together came to a little over $2,000. For the last six years, exclusive of his bonus, Noah averaged about a million a year. Johanna liked that; she black-balled candidates who relied on their bonuses. Then why don't I want the Levins in the building?

Patsy: "What's so hot about 2D? It's got three dark bedrooms and a dark maid's room; only the living room gets the morning light."

Johanna: "It's accessible by stairs on the Sabbath, when Orthodox Jews are forbidden to use an elevator."

"Is that so? Live and learn."

Fred: "I think we agree the Levins' finances are in

good shape. I, for one, have no objections to them as candidates for admission to the building on that score. Johanna?"

"They're okay with me." On that score.

"Patsy?"

"Fine with me." Patsy, who lived in 1B, hoped that some other Orthodox Jew would pay a good price for her dark, noisy four-room apartment in the back on the ground floor.

"Bruce?"

"No objections." 1.2 million smackeroos! That means my five-room apartment on the fifteenth floor, with two bathrooms and an eat-in kitchen, is worth a fucking fortune!

Johanna toted up the value of her seven rooms on the twentieth floor: a million and three quarters!

Fred invited the Levins into the conference room. They sat facing each other at the end of the table opposite the door. Fred introduced them around. Esther didn't shake hands with the men. Fred was taken aback. Then he remembered that Orthodox women won't touch men. It's amazing how much I've picked up about Orthodox Jews by living on the Upper West Side. The men are polluted by touching women having their period. They must purify themselves. I hear they bury themselves to their necks in the earth. For twenty-four hours! No wonder their women are trained to keep their distance.

Noah was sweating. He poured himself a glass of cloudy water from the open carafe on a tray.

Fred said, "The committee has reviewed your personal and financial statements. Is there anything you want to add?"

Levin said, "Four nineteen's location is perfect for us. Our synagogue—the Carlebach shul—is right around the corner.

"Two D was made for us. You know we Orthodox Jews are forbidden to take the elevator on the Sabbath. Don't get me wrong. We can afford to live on a higher floor. But we don't like to pester our Gentile neighbors to work the elevators for us on the Sabbath."

Fred: "Very thoughtful."

Patsy: "Do you know another Orthodox couple who'd be interested in buying my four-room apartment on the ground floor?"

Levin: "I'll ask around."

"I'd appreciate it."

Johanna said, "You have three kids, I believe."

Levin said, "Yes, Seth, five, Ari, four, and Miriam, who's eighteen months."

"We have a strict rule against kids playing in the lobby. Our doormen are not to be used as babysitters."

"We wouldn't hear of it."

Johanna's snotty tone embarrassed her. She mollified Levin with a smile. He smiled back. I didn't catch her last name. She looks Jewish. The worst. A Jewish anti-Semite.

Esther said, "Our friends the Weintraubs who live in 12C say that 419 West End is a friendly building. They've made many friends here. So have their kids. My husband and I would be pleased to live in such a community. I want to become involved. Adele Weintraub tells me you have a house committee that meets with the super a couple of times a month. I was on the house committee in our present building and would welcome the chance to join yours. I hope you give us the opportunity to make our home here at 419. Thank you."

Fred told the Levins that Dennis Azzarella, the building's managing agent, would inform their real estate agent tomorrow of the committee's decision. Johanna farted. Everyone pretended not to notice, except Levin. He looked at her with amusement. The Levins left. The committee voted unanimously to recommend to the Board that their offer of $1.2 million be accepted for 2D.

Aug. 22, 2001. Wed. 12:30 p.m. *Spent the morning with Odin in Valhalla, among his dead heroes, who every day strap on their armor, go into the courtyard, kill each other, and are resuscitated.*

I'm not writing this book in my usual vernacular style. Its melody is stately—the way I feel sagas should be expressed.

Appointment tomorrow at Etz Chaim 3 p.m., with Rabbi Klugman re Oct. trip to Israel. Last time I was there was spring of '98, promoting Hebrew translation of Jewish Myths & Legends *(illustrations a la Chagall) at Jerusalem Book Fair. A bunch of us—writers, publishers, agents—were stoned by Arab kids near the Jaffa Gate. Two Israeli soldiers with M16s chased them off.*

Citigroup: 46.69, cholesterol: 285, blood pressure: 155/110. Tick-tock.

Thursday morning, Rabbi Klugman wrapped his tefillin strap a third time around the middle finger of his left hand while reciting in Hebrew, "'I will betroth you to Me forever, and I will betroth you to Me with righteousness, justice, kindness, and mercy, I will betroth you to Me with fidelity, and you shall love the Lord.'"

As he put the tefillin away, he smelled coffee brewing and heard Anne feeding the boys in the kitchen. "Michael, put that plate down!"

August coincided with the Hebrew month of Elul, the thirty days before the Days of Awe. Elul is a propitious time for repentance. The Hebrew letters that make up the word Elul are taken by the rabbis as an acronym for "I am my beloved and my beloved is mine," from The Song of Songs (6:3), Klugman's favorite sacred text. He shut his eyes in the kitchen doorway. Beloved, make me yours.

Klugman set aside half an hour after morning service

each day this month to meditate on the prayer from the service on Yom Kippur eve:

> As stone in the hand of the mason, to be broken or preserved as he wishes, are we in Your hand, Master of life and death.

Artie met Klugman in his office on the second floor of Etz Chaim at three.

"Nice to see you," Artie said. "It's been a long time since we talked."

"About a year. Our last conversation was about Ginzberg, if I remember. *The Legends of the Jews.*"

"You've a good memory."

"For some things. I forgot the cauliflower for last night's dinner. I bought the potatoes, but forgot the cauliflower. My wife damn near killed me. You said over the phone that you wanted to sign up for the trip to Israel."

"Here's my check for nine hundred and ninety-nine dollars. I've sent five hundred bucks as a contribution to the Federation."

"Only five others have signed up so far."

"People are scared to go."

Klugman said, "I'm scared too."

"I'm a little nervous myself. Who're we kidding? Israel's at war. It's at war with the whole Palestinian population. And vice versa. They're killing each other's kids."

The remark stuck with Klugman like a grain of sand

in a oyster. A sermon began accreting around it. For the second day of Rosh Hashana.

Hotspur Associates had moved in May from Park and 47th to a fourteen-room suite in the northwest corner of the 102nd floor of the north tower of the World Trade Center. Sutton wrote code for software applications in a windowless cubicle. Guy, his project manager, kept tabs on him and six other engineers from the cubicle to the left that had a narrow window. Guy called it, "My lucky window." It had brought him and Judy together for a look at raindrops forming in a cloud.

They had watched the raindrops and sized each other up out the corners of their eyes. Each thought: you're the one for me.

Judy called Guy at the office for a date the next morning. She lived with Sut on East 23rd Street. Guy had an apartment to hell and gone up in Morningside Heights. They had a quick fuck in a borrowed apartment on Third Avenue on Sunday morning while Sutton was at church.

Judy figured, Why feel guilty? Guy's a great lay. And what a body! Solid muscle. Sut has thin arms and narrow shoulders; one is higher than the other. And he doesn't want to marry me. He wants to find himself first. Well, I'm thirty next November. My biological clock is ticking.

Guy said, "Let's do it again."

"First wiggle your finger up my ass. Ow! Which one are you using?"

"The forefinger."

"Well, the nail is too long. Try your middle finger. That's good. Wiggle! And don't forget my thighs. Stroke the inside of my thighs. Lightly! I adore having the inside of my thighs lightly stroked."

They fucked their brains out the next three Sunday mornings in July. Sut didn't suspect a thing.

On the twenty-ninth, when he got home from church, Judy said to him, "I'm in love with Guy. He loves me. It was love at first sight. I'm leaving you."

"Guy Stewart? My projects manager? I introduced you."

"That's when we fell in love."

"In those few minutes?"

"Soon as we looked at each other."

"I don't believe in love at first sight.

"I do. Oh, Sut! I've lost my heart!"

Sut said, "I wish you the best of luck."

Judy moved in with Guy at the beginning of August. Guy and Sut just talked business at the office. Guy was on Sut's ass about finishing a customer account reconciliation module. After work Thursday, they silently shared the local and then the express elevator down. The trip took six minutes.

Sut spoke to Guy in the lobby: "You and Judy

betrayed me. But you couldn't help yourselves, so I forgive you."

"Up yours."

Sutton backed off. He was scared of getting into a fight. It was a sensation out of childhood: eating shit from a bigger, stronger boy. Guy had the broad chest, the thick neck, the muscular shoulders and arms of a heavyweight high school wrestler.

Guy went out to the plaza, passed the fountain, and called Judy on his cell phone: "Sutton says he forgives us for betraying him. I gave him the finger."

"Well, get it back. It's my favorite."

He didn't laugh. The vast, crowded plaza beneath the twin towers shrank his self-esteem. He said, "Would you have left Sutton for me if he'd been willing to marry you?"

"I left him because I fell in love with you at first sight."

"Then marry me."

The woman, on his left, hurrying toward the Cortlandt Street station, overheard him and smiled.

Judy said, "Is this a proposal?"

"Yes. You're the best thing that's ever happened to me. So? What's your answer? If I were rich like Sutton you wouldn't hesitate."

"I'd love to be rich. Well, why not? I teach kindergarten, for Christ's sake. I earn $35,000 a year. Try living in New York on $35,000 a year!"

"Marry me."

"What's that? I can't hear you. You're breaking up."

"I said, Marry me."

"I hear you."

"Well?"

"Why not?"

"What kind of an answer is 'why not'?"

"A bitchy answer. From the witch in me. A bitchy witch. I'm your bitchy witch if you'll have me. Oh! My cunt is wet. I love you, Guy. Make me your wife."

I must tell her about my balls. Do I have the balls?

Aug. 25, 2001. Sat. 1:15 p.m. *The first Sat. I've worked in months. Odin's names are paradoxical: Pleasant One, Terrible One, Life-Giver, One-Who-Blinds-with-Death, Far-Sighted One, One-Eyed One. He's two faced—like Yahweh.*

Johanna constantly grooms me; in preparation for our dinner party tonight, she cut the long hairs from my ears with blunted nail scissors. My right ear is hairier than the left. She calls them Esau & Jacob.

Adam poured over the obits in the *Times*.

Sumner, John S. of Harrison, New York, aged 63, died Thursday, August 23, 2001, of melanoma.

Johanna prepared an herbal mustard coating for lamb. She blended mustard, soy sauce, garlic, rosemary, and ginger in a bowl. She beat in olive oil drop by drop;

the mixture turned into a mayonnaise-like cream. Gigot à la Moutarde was a crowd pleaser; it was an old recipe from Julia Child. Johanna knew zilch about cooking when she married. She taught herself to become a good cook. She enjoyed pleasing her family and friends. Most of all, she got a kick out of mastering the skill.

It was a nuisance to carve a whole leg of lamb, even partially boned. Johanna bought two shank ends that were easier to manage. She smeared them with the mustard sauce and set them on the rack of the roasting pan. Muggs sat in front of the stove. His nose twitched. The smell of the raw lamb made him salivate. Artie sipped a vodka on the rocks. Johanna bent over the sink. He caught sight of the white roots of her dyed hair. Her white hairs fill me with tenderness. Does my bald head do the same for her?

Johanna let the lamb sit two hours before she turned on the stove. Ella, who was serving tonight, set the dining room table for eight: Johanna and Artie, Dani and Alice, Shirley and Adam, Leslie and Chris. Shirley was allergic to dogs; Artie shut Muggs up in the bedroom.

Adam swallowed a spoonful of cold cucumber and yogurt soup and said to Alice on his left, "We met here New Year's Eve."

"So we did."

"You teach French at Milton."

"I'm head of the Romance Language Department at Choate."

"Choate, of course."

"And you're Artie's accountant."

"His lawyer."

"Lawyer, of course."

Dani said to Shirley on his right, "I remember you from New Year's Eve."

"You're the Israeli sculptor. I remember. Artie adores your work."

"I'm a portrait painter."

Leslie smiled at Johanna, on her left, seated at the end of the table near the louvered doors to the kitchen. Mom looks worn out and old.

Artie fingered the stem of his wine glass. My first illustration will be Odin's face—a brownish-red beard, one eye. Johanna called to him down the length of the table, "Open more wine."

She put down her soup spoon. I'll only eat the potatoes and the salad. Red meat is poison for me.

Artie went into the kitchen for a corkscrew. Shirley smelled the roasted lamb. It's too hot for meat. I would've poached salmon steaks in this heat. Wait. Chris doesn't eat fish—like Hal. Only two more weeks till Jerry and Hal get married. My son married to a man! It's a good thing my parents are dead.

Johanna: What's with Adam and Alice? They're not talking to each other. The silence between them had spread to their whole side of the table.

Artie said to Adam: "What's up?"

"The pathology report was good. I start chemo after Labor Day. September fifth. No more golf for me. Not for a long while. I get 2 cc's of Interferon administered intravenously up at Columbia-Presbyterian five days a week for the next month. Then injections of half that dose three times a week for two years. I give myself the shots."

Chris, on Adam's right, made conversation with Alice. "I went to Choate."

Adam said to Chris, "Alice is head of Romance Languages there." Alice smiled at him. Johanna caught the exchange. My party's back on track.

Artie returned to the dining room with an uncorked wine bottle. Ella cleared away the bowls. She said to Leslie, "Congratulations, baby."

Ella's legs ached. She'd been on her feet since one. She wished she were in bed. She served dinner and cleaned up after a day's work for the extra money—sixty-five dollars, plus cab fare home—145th and Lenox Avenue.

Artie wrote in his head: *"Odin's wife was Frigg, first among the goddesses. She foresaw the future, but refused to prophesy."*

Ella served the lamb and roast potatoes; Artie downed his third glass of wine. He heard Adam say to Alice, "The French are anti-Semites." Chris heard him too. There they go—the obligatory discussion of anti-Semitism. Israel's next. Then the Holocaust.

But Adam said, "What do you teach besides Fr ench?"

Leslie to Johanna: "I've gained six pounds."

Artie forgot Adam's last name. I know it like I know my own. For God's sake! The God of Abraham, Isaac, and Jacob. Jacobson!

Adam: "A black minister, a rabbi, and Pat Buchanan are playing golf. Poof! The ball turns into a genie. The genie says, 'What's your wish?' The black minister says, 'Bring all my people back to Africa and make Africa into a Garden of Eden.' 'Done,' says the genie. The black minister vanishes. The genie turns to the rabbi. The rabbi says, 'Bring all my people back to Israel and make it into a Garden of Eden.' 'Your word is my command,' says the genie. The rabbi also vanishes. The genie turns to Pat Buchanan. Pat Buchanan says, 'Wait a minute. You mean to tell me all the blacks are back in Africa and all the Jews back in Israel?' 'I do,' says the genie. 'In that case,' says Buchanan, 'Gimme a Diet Coke.'"

Chris thought, Now Israel.

Dani said to Artie, "I've come to the conclusion that Israel should expel the Palestinians from the occupied territories. Either that, or…"

Shirley: "Please! Let's not discuss Israel."

Chris: "My brother believes that the Palestinian suicide bombers are possessed by what Dostoevsky called 'the spirit of self-annihilation, of non-being.'"

Shirley: "Which spirit is that?"

"The devil."

"Your brother believes in the devil?"

"He most certainly does."

Ella, from the kitchen doorway, said, "Smart boy."

Shirley pictured Jerry in a white wedding dress. Puff sleeves, a veil over his bearded face. She brushed her right hand across her forehead. Can't get the image out of my mind. Broad-shouldered Jerry in an old-fashioned, white satin wedding dress with a train. Lace, hairy-backed hands. What's gotten into me? She thought of a grinning face, horns, a forked tail, cloven hooves.

Johanna said to Artie, "Good night. Sleep well."

"I had a senior moment during dinner. I couldn't remember Adam's last name. He's starting chemo on September fifth."

"Shirley told me he's depressed."

"He doesn't act depressed."

"Well, he's on Prozac. Jerry and his boyfriend are joining us next weekend. Labor Day! The summer's flown. Time speeds up with age. Have you noticed? It passes faster and faster. I wonder why."

"How about some hanky-panky?"

"Not tonight. My vagina's irritated."

Alice brought four sesame bagels from H&H Bagels at Broadway and 80th Street back to Wallingford for Sunday breakfast. Seven-year-old Zvi, whose upper front teeth were loose, had trouble taking bites. Alice tore off little chunks for him and smeared them with cream cheese. She liked babying him, though he resented it. After breakfast, Dani posed Zvi in the studio on the blue stuffed chair in front of a TV with a VCR playing *Pinocchio*—Zvi's favorite movie.

Zvi watched Geppetto tell the goldfish in her bowl, "Cleo, meet Pinocchio. Say how do you do," while Dani set up his toned canvas. Zvi had Alice's wide-set eyes. He was named after his maternal great-grandfather, gassed at Treblinka. Alice had qualms about giving Zvi an Israeli name. My kid's American. But she gave in to her mother-in-law out of guilt. The old lady had such a tough life!

Dani's mother Dora was born in Krasnik, Poland, in 1936. She often told Dani how she was saved during the war by Wanda, her family's Polish maid, who hid her for four years in a carved pine wardrobe, painted with pink roses, on Wanda's father's farm outside Lublin. The Germans shot Poles for hiding Jews. Wanda's father wanted to turn Dora in.

Wanda said, "If you do, I'll tell the Gestapo that you sell eggs and cheese on the black market in Lublin."

Dora told Dani as a kid, "Wanda taught me, don't trust anybody. It's good advice."

"You trusted Wanda. I trust you, Mama."

Dani's father, Jacob, said, "Listen to what Mama tells you. You can't trust anybody. Even us. In Auschwitz I saw a father steal a moldy crust of bread from his starving son. The boy grew so weak he fell into the latrine and drowned."

Dani mixed an inch of turpentine and a dab of burnt umber in a jelly jar, then vigorously tapped the metal ferrule of his number eight brush against the rim.

"Shhh, Daddy! I can't hear Jiminy Cricket sing."

The turpentine stank. Zvi held his nose. Dani stared at the blue-and-gray toned canvas. He thought about his mother. Four years—from four to eight—buried alive in a dark cupboard—an upright pine coffin—sleeping hunched in a corner, arms about her knees. One shaft of light through a knothole. Her hair and nails grew and grew; she was half-blind from the dark. Pissing and shitting in a soup tureen. The stench. To this day, she sleeps on a bed in the corner. She's never hugged or kissed me—not once. Nor my father, either. And never once, from either of them, "I love you."

Zvi squirmed, the Fairy Godmother told Pinocchio, "Prove yourself brave and truthful." The studio was stifling. Dani opened its four windows; the air smelled of roses. A bee flew in, bumped against the ceiling and flew out again. Zvi relaxed, with his left arm on the left arm of the chair.

Dani dipped his brush in the turpentine wash and rapidly drew the shape of an egg—Zvi's head—slightly left of center, two inches from the top edge of the canvas. He established the position of the eyes with a lightly brushed-in horizontal line one-third of the way down the egg.

A dark pine wardrobe, a moldy crust of bread. My childhood drowned in a latrine before I was born.

He said, "I love you."

"I love you, too, Daddy. Now shh!"

Pinocchio asked Geppetto "Why?" three times in a row.

After church, Sutton smoked a joint at home. I got the munchies. He ate two teaspoonfuls of sugar. Cool! Life is sweet! I'm crazy about grass. It makes me delight in the way things are.

Artie had an early supper of cold lamb and chutney, with two glasses of red, so he could be at Etz Chaim by a quarter to seven. He volunteered once a month to work for two hours in the shelter for homeless men on the third floor. An overnight volunteer—usually a rabbinical student from the JTS—arrived at nine. Up to ten homeless men were referred to the synagogue by the Penn Station Partnership, a social agency in the West Thirties that took care of them during the day then bussed them up to Etz Chaim, where they slept on folding beds in the big third-floor classroom. They were allowed to stay two or three weeks. Some moved on to SROs; others went back on the streets.

Artie took the shelter keys, on a chrome ring, from a nail on the back of the maintenance office door and with the yellow key opened the pantry in the big classroom. He turned on the air conditioner and welcomed a thin, bearded black guy reading the sign Scotch-taped to the wall:

> Two men are needed to carry a single bed down the back stairs from the storage room. The constant dragging of beds downstairs is breaking the wheels off. Don't forget to bring down a bed for the overnight volunteer. Put it in the small classroom.
>
> Put used sheets and pillowcases in the plastic bags on the back stairs. Dry towels too. Put wet towels on railing of back stairs. Put blankets in separate bags. Important!!! Take a shower before going to bed. It's disrespectful to others if you smell.

The bearded black guy, who struck Artie as part Indian, handed him a letter:

Alex Devi (I'm right: he's part Indian) is currently receiving services from the Penn Station Partnership and participating in our program. He has agreed to abide by the rules of your shelter that keep it a safe and peaceful place.

Artie collected letters from the nine other guys and wrote all ten names in the Shelter Logbook on the desk in the volunteer room, the small classroom at the end of the hall. Alex Devi, Enoch Wooten, Eric Knight, Andrew Bella, Harry Grace, Lenford Barnholz, Gilbert Booth, Steven Slaughter, Abner Slates, Frank Gibbs.

Everybody except Devi and Wooten had been here before and knew the ropes. Booth clued the newcomers in. They helped bring down eleven folding beds and set them up. Andrew Bella and Harry Grace rolled a microwave and a TV out of the pantry. Bella turned the TV on; he couldn't find wrestling. Fuck. Hulk Hogan's my man.

Enoch Wooten took out a package of Shabbat Kosher frozen meat loaf and peas from the fridge in the storage room. Look like icy puke. He fixed himself a peanut butter sandwich on whole wheat. Tomorrow, come hell or high water, I call Mama.

Frank Gibbs made up his bed. I'm thirty-five next Tuesday. My life is slipping away. What will become of me?

Lenford Barnholz washed his white cotton socks in the bathroom sink and hung them to dry over the back of a chair. I need a drink. He settled for cold apple juice.

Alex Devi microwaved two packages of frozen veal loaf and carrots for seven minutes and gave the veal loaves to Lenford Barnholz.

Devi bowed his head. Restore me. He ate the carrots with a plastic fork off a paper plate at the metal table in the middle of the classroom.

Eric Knight, a towel around his neck, wanted to shave and shower. He asked Artie for talcum powder. Artie searched in the cardboard boxes on the bottom pantry shelf: combs, toothbrushes, Crest toothpaste, April

Fresh shampoo, Bic razors, bars of Ivory soap, cans of Mennen shaving cream.

Under *Comments*, beneath the names in the Log Book, Artie wrote, "We need talcum powder."

Knight jerked off in the shower. Abner Slates sneaked a cigarette on the back stairs.

Steven Slaughter opened a can of tuna fish. No mayo.

Artie, at the desk, reread Tadeusz Borowski's short story, "This Way for the Gas, Ladies and Gentlemen." He found the passage that Leslie had recalled in the Park.

"Several other men are carrying a small girl with only one leg. They hold her by the arms and the one leg. Tears are running down her face and she whispers faintly: 'Sir, it hurts, it hurts.' They throw her on the truck on top of the corpses. She will burn alive with them."

I smell cigarette smoke.

Devi spoke from the doorway: "Know anybody who could use a man to help around the house? I'd like to live with a family. I'm cheap to feed—fruit, vegetables, nuts. I won't eat meat or dairy; they give me excess mucous buildup. I do windows. But I don't cook. I got excellent references from the Children's Aid Society, East Harlem Branch, and the Department of Social Services.

"I spend my nights in a chair at St. Anne's on Centre Street. It's hard to sleep in a chair. I'm on my feet the whole day. I walk the earth for Greenpeace. It's my spiritual destiny. God laid out this path for me to follow when

I was fifteen. Today is Sunday. The Lord's day. Every day is the Lord's day to me. My father was a Hindu from Jamaica. My first name is really Alak, which is Bengali. Hindus say, 'I worship the God in you.' God lives in us."

Devi pressed his palms together in front of his chest. "I worship Him in you."

Citigroup 29.89, Intel 29.89, Cisco 18.22, Microsoft 63.36, Johnson & Johnson 54.74.

Steve Tobin, one of the fifteen people in investment banking at Barstow and Lee, said to Johanna, "I'll put it to you straight. We hold five hundred thousand shares of Intel we've got to sell. Your pro-rata allocation is five thousand shares to be sold at 29 bucks a share. Which is the price of the last trade."

"Wait a minute! At our meeting this morning with Jack our Intel analyst, he said he thinks the stock is overvalued at the current price. I won't push overvalued stocks on my clients."

Leslie took a deep breath. All three knew that Johanna was risking her job by refusing to contribute to the firm's commissions in the sale of those five thousand shares. Furthermore, she was putting the firm at risk by not unloading them now. If the firm's analyst believed that the stock was overvalued, it was likely to go down.

Tobin said, "Look, I'm conflicted, too. I don't relish pushing stocks we own on our broker's clients. But I've got my orders. Think of your fees!"

Johanna disliked his cold gray eyes. A wife and two kids; can't recall her name. She has MS and smokes cigars. He speaks of her tenderly. "My darling Sally." Sally! That's it. Poor Sally. Stuck in an electric wheelchair. She can't be more than forty.

Johanna said, "How's Sally?"

"The same. She got her hands on a box of Havanas—twenty-five Montecristos. She smokes one a week. It stinks up the house for hours. The kids never complain."

"Steve, I can't do it."

"But the price now is twenty-nine."

"You and I both know it's still overpriced. I won't stick my clients."

"You've got guts, lady. You're the only broker here—one out of a hundred and three—who's refused me. Thanks."

"For what?"

"For restoring my faith in human nature."

That evening, Leslie told Chris what happened and said, "I agree with what Mom did, but I wish she'd consulted me."

Artie took Tuesday off from work. Like last year, he followed the Jewish custom of visiting the dead during the month of Elul. Artie was moved by the symbolism: the inclusion of the dead in the living community of Israel. In the morning, he hired a subcompact from

Avis at Broadway and 76th to visit his parents' graves at Mt. Moriah cemetery in Queens.

Artie crossed the Triborough and took the Grand Central Parkway to the Jackie Robinson Parkway. He noticed an open mausoleum, behind a wrought iron fence, in the big cemetery to his left. Queens is filled with cemeteries; it's the land of my dead.

He made a right on Cyprus Avenue; Mt. Moriah was straight ahead. The woman in the office wore a gold *chai*—the Hebrew symbol of life—around her neck; it seemed to him like an amulet to ward off evil spirits. Artie asked her to locate his parents' graves. She called up their names on her computer and marked a map.

She said, "Their address is Sinai Avenue, Section 1, Block Q."

The cemetery was laid out in grids, bisected by avenues, streets, roads, and boulevards named for places in the Bible. The city of my dead. Artie walked west on Bethel Street, between two rows of marble tombstones, then south on Jerusalem Road toward a huge white oak that he recalled from last year.

His eye caught a tombstone next to a granite bench:

Lt. Richard Klein
Born September 11,1920 Died July 8,1944
In the service of his country

Dad was too old to be drafted. He was an air raid warden. The white helmet and arm band marked CD. Civilian defense. He even served on Shabbes. "Our sages tell us it's permitted to violate the Sabbath to save lives." During the early days of the war, he was scared Brooklyn would be bombed.

Mom was a Gray Lady—a nurse's aide at New York Hospital. Her dove-gray uniform. With gloves to match. I once found a condom under their bed.

Dad's horribly enlarged prostate. Removed at sixty-two. The surgery made him incontinent. Poor guy wore diapers. He was probably impotent as well. What did that do to their marriage? Who knows?

Sinai Avenue. Artie walked north among the graves covered with ivy.

"Our dear father..." "Sheene. Baby Greenburg. Baby Sheene." "Inseparable forever." The crickets in the ivy stopped chirping as he walked by. Where the hell is Section 1, Block Q? Nothing's marked. Nobody around to ask. Why am I here? I'm missing a day's work. Hold it! Over there, straight ahead. My dead.

Rubin

Lea, 1910–1990 Samuel, 1905–1978

Beloved wife, mother, and grandmother. Beloved husband and father.

1905–1978. Seventy-three. I'm going to die at seventy-three.

Johanna said to Leslie, "Forgive me. I should have consulted you yesterday. I put your job in jeopardy without your permission."

"I'm proud of your decision. I agree with it. We can't stick our clients with overvalued stock."

"Nevertheless, I should have consulted with you. We've been working together four years. It's about time we became equal partners. Here you are, Joe! Come in."

Joe Sloan, the office manager said, "You wanted to see me?"

"I want you to tell payroll that from now on Leslie and I split fifty-fifty instead of sixty-five thirty-five. She's my full partner."

"Whatever you say."

Leslie said, "I'm speechless."

"You've earned it."

"Thank you."

"Congratulations, Leslie."

"Thank you, Joe."

"Between us, Johanna, I want to say I admire your decision yesterday. But we're a team here at Barstow and Lee. We pull together. That includes the both of you. From now on."

The edge in his voice was sharpened by its thin, high-pitched tone.

Leslie waited till he left before she said, "I appreciate what you did, Mom. But can you afford it? You and Daddy surely need the money more than I do."

"It's not a question of money. I've recognized you as my equal partner. I've been waiting your whole life to tell you this: think of yourself as my equal in all things. Our relationship has entered a new phase. What's today? August the twenty-eighth. Let's remember this day."

Leslie filled Chris in about what had happened at the office. Then she said, "Oh, my God! The baby just moved. I felt a soft flutter. There it goes again. What a lovely day!"

"I'm going to die like Dad did at seventy-three."

"What makes you think so?"

"The feeling came over me at his grave this morning. I feel it now. I tell you, I'm going to die at seventy-three."

"I'd settle for seventy-three."

Aug. 29, 2001. Wed. 11:55 a.m. *Johanna's blood pressure on waking: 155/100. She sees Raskin next Tuesday.*

One ale after breakfast. My cast of characters is growing: Tyr or Tiw, the phallic war god, who gave his name to Tuesday.

Artie walked to Broadway and bought a honeydew melon and a container of low-fat cottage cheese from the Korean market for lunch. Le Bistro's green awning, to his right, reminded him of Molly. I haven't seen her in weeks. He went looking for her in front of the Baptist Church at 79th. A young guy, with a green knapsack by his side, was reading the *Times* on the steps. Maybe she's in front of Zabar's. I've sometimes seen her there.

The block between 80th and 81st was crowded. No Molly. Artie was woozy from the heat. The glare from the sunlight reflected from the sidewalk made him squint behind his glasses.

All these people: the elderly couple—in their seventies!—wearing identical broad-brimmed Panama hats, the pretty girl with a strand of pearls around her smooth neck walking an Irish setter, the braid down the back of a stocky girl. Molly has broad shoulders. Which one of her legs is missing? Artie visualized her in her wheelchair. The left. Slashed by a machete. Was that true? Had she really witnessed the murder of her girlfriend? The murderer cut out her heart; he held her dripping heart in his hand.

A sweaty blind woman tapped her way along the sidewalk with a long white stick that had a metal tip. A boy said into his cell phone, "I have to see my sister home." There's no heart that drips blood in their lives—or mine. Molly comes from the netherworld. She's gone back down.

Guy asked Judy, "More wine?"

"Just a drop. Whoa! That's too much."

"More chicken?"

"Yeah. I'm starved. I had a doughnut and coffee for lunch."

Guy helped her to two tablespoons of sweet and sour chicken from the plastic container on the kitchen counter. "Judy, I haven't been honest with you."

"About what?"

"My balls."

"What's the matter with your balls? I love your big hairy balls."

Three stories below them an uptown No. 1 train rumbled on the elevated tracks through Morningside Heights. The kitchen window shook.

Guy said, "I should have told you about them before I asked you to marry me. I was scared you'd turn me down."

Another secret. She knew about his father; his father had freaked out on crack with a carving knife at a Thanksgiving dinner. "What's so hush-hush about your balls?"

He said, "I may be sterile."

"Sterile?"

"I had an infection called epididymitis my freshman year at Baruch. My balls got inflamed and swollen. They were very painful. I ran a fever. The pain got worse as the day wore on. Some nights I couldn't walk. Antibiotics knocked the infection out, but my doctor said I could be sterile. I can't bring myself to be tested. Supposing I am sterile? Will that make any difference to you?"

A No. 9 rattled and screeched on the tracks below. The window shook again.

Judy said, "It might. Like most women, I want kids of my own. I don't know how I'd feel if you can't give me any."

"I should have told you before."

"Yes, you should have."

"I was scared you wouldn't marry me. I was right, wasn't I? I see it in your eyes. You have second thoughts."

"Get yourself tested."

Guy burst into tears. He covered his face with his hands. The tears leaked between his fingers. He said, "Don't leave me. You're the best thing that ever happened to me."

Judy pushed the hair from his forehead. She said, "This is the first time I've seen you cry. It's endearing."

"Say you love me."

"I love you."

"Say you don't have second thoughts about marrying me."

"Get yourself tested."

Chris got off the elevator. The hostess said, "Welcome to Windows on the World." He went through the blue glass doors into The Greatest Bar on Earth, where Sutton was on his second Gibson. Sut thought, I never used to drink at lunch. Now I regularly drink two Gibsons. Am I an alcoholic?

He drank up. Over the rim of his glass he followed

Chris's progress along the oval bar toward his table. I'd know his swaying walk anywhere. I tried to walk like him as a kid.

Chris noticed two cocktail napkins on the table. Is Sut an alcoholic? A candidate for AA? His belief in God would stand him in good stead in AA.

Chris said, "Dad sends regards."

"Give him my love. How's the real estate business?"

"Good."

"And Leslie?"

"Good. She sends her best."

"My best to her," Sut said. "Want a drink?"

"No. Let's have a look."

They rose from their brown easy chairs, went to the windows, and stood among the gaping tourists. They were just in time to see a light blue, high-winged Cessna flying below them. Sut made out N438HC on the fuselage. A Cessna. He remembered reading in the *Guinness Book of World Records* that an Frenchman ate a whole Cessna in ten days. He dismantled the plane into little pieces, ground them up, and sprinkled the granules on his food.

Chris had booked a table by the windows in the Wild Blue dining room for twelve thirty. Sut took in some of that view: a crowd opposite, two hundred feet away, on the observation deck of the south tower, the Statue of Liberty's left profile, the northern tip of Staten Island.

Sut ordered another Gibson from a waiter wearing

black pants and a maroon shirt with a black tie. He had a pimple on his chin. Chris ordered a Diet Coke. He said, "Leslie has a girl for you. Her name is Diana Chamberlain. They were in the same class at Wellesley. Interested?"

"What's she like?"

"A knockout. Tall, leggy, blonde. A lovely oval face. Very smart. A clinical psychologist. And a serious Episcopalian."

"I'm not ready to date."

The drinks arrived. The third Gibson worked on Sut's brain like a joint. I'm in paradise.

This world is paradise. I'm ravished—ravished—by everything I see. The wake down there of the Staten Island ferry ravishes me.

The wake lengthened. He said, "Judy and I once had dinner here. The famous roast suckling pig. The crisp skin is the best part. Judy has a big appetite for a small girl. She eats anything you put in front of her. I loved watching her eat. She has a zest for life. It's contagious. I felt alive when I was around her. Yet I wasn't ready to marry her. I have to find myself first. I'm drunk. I hope Judy gets fat. Fat girls turn me off."

Artie wasn't nuts about going to the Jacobsons for the weekend. The double bed in their guestroom was too soft. He awoke Saturday morning with a stiff back. Jerry and Hal arrived at eleven in a borrowed Saab. Artie hadn't seen them in almost a year.

He said to Jerry, "Your beard becomes you."

Hal said, "Don't you just love it? Doesn't he look handsome?"

Artie had pegged Jerry as gay at the age of eight when he wandered into the dining room during a dinner party at the Jacobsons wearing Shirley's beige slip and jade necklace.

After Jerry came out at Harvard, Adam said to Artie, "I can't deal with the anal business."

"Don't think about it."

Jerry had told his therapist in Cambridge, "My homosexuality repels my Dad. He tries to hide it, but I can tell. He's stopped kissing me. It breaks my heart. Dad's my man. I've had the hots for him ever since I can remember."

Hal worried that he reminded Jerry of his father. One, we're both lawyers. Two, we sulk when we don't get our way. Three, we hate the theater. Am I just a reflection of his old man? Is that a solid basis for a relationship—much less a marriage?

Jerry was a deputy director of strategic planning for the MTA. He holed up in his room till lunch making notes on the last Citizen's Budget Commission report:

> "Mayor has not adequately anticipated economy downturn. City and state fiscal situation will

likely not allow them to provide additional assistance to MTA."

Jerry's thoughts drifted from his laptop screen to the fresh five-inch scar on his dad's lower back. Let me kiss it.

Adam said, "I have a green thumb."

He walked Artie to his vegetable garden. Muggs followed at their heels. The garden, protected by a chain-link fence, was halfway between the house and three apple trees at the edge of the south lawn. A doe emerged from the pines beyond; she was attracted to the apples rotting on the grass. Adam unlatched the garden gate. The doe bolted back into the woods. Artie held Muggs by his collar. The doe's white tail vanished in the shadows. Artie admired the rows of peas, tomatoes, lettuce, arugula, broccoli, cauliflower, carrots, horseradish, and chard.

Adam said, "The horseradish is for Passover. I wonder how I'll be next spring. I know how: nauseous and exhausted from the Interferon. It's heavy-duty shit. The side effects are awful. I have to be on it for two years, but there's no guarantee that the melanoma won't return. The odds in my favor are only sixty-forty. Christ, I feel low."

Shirley took the veal she had poached yesterday from the fridge. She said, "Our lives will never be the same. From now on, we'll be living with the possibility of Adam's dying from cancer."

Johanna sliced a tomato. "Well, I'm living with the possibility of dying from a heart attack."

"How do you do it?"

Johanna looked from the tomato to Shirley tearing basil over the sink. Behind her, to the left, through the kitchen window, Johanna saw a hovering hummingbird. It dipped its bill into a pink trumpet honeysuckle blossom on the vine that climbed the outside brick wall.

She said, "Ah, moment, stay!"

Hal, in from the dining room, asked, "Can I help with lunch?"

Shirley said, "Come slice the mozzarella."

"What are we making?"

"Vitello tonnato, and a tomato, mozzarella, and basil salad."

Johanna: "Who said, 'Ah, moment, stay'?"

"Search me."

"Search me."

Adam showed Artie the trees he had planted over the years. "This is a black walnut. It's called a grandchild tree because it grows so slowly. Jerry and Hal talk about adopting a kid. They're being married by a gay Episcopal priest and a lesbian rabbi. You heard me. A gay priest and a lesbian rabbi. It's sad."

"Why sad?"

"I don't know, it just is. It's sad and comical. A parody of a heterosexual marriage ceremony. That's why it's sad. Do you like Jerry's beard? It elongates his face. Jerry has my narrow face. How's your work going?"

"It's like pulling teeth. I'm drinking too much. Writing

gets harder as I grow older. And I haven't come up with any ideas for illustrations."

"Listen to the oriole! Hear it? The shrill whistle is the giveaway. We have orioles, blue jays, nuthatches, hummingbirds, sparrows, chickadees, goldfinches. Yes, and swallows in the barn." I want to live!

Everybody trooped out to the flagstone terrace for drinks. Artie continued his thoughts. I envy Malcolm Woodward. He finished his book. It took eight years. A bio of Darwin. The sun's about to set behind the Heldenberg Escarpment. Heldenberg—hero's mountain.

He said to Malcolm, "Darwin is a hero of mine."

"How so?"

Shirley asked around: "Red or white?"

Artie said, "A vodka on the rocks for me. I'll get it." He stood up. His lower back was still stiff.

Shirley said, "Stay where you are."

Standing gave Artie a glimpse through the kitchen window of a patch of sunlight on the chimney of the cast-iron Vermont stove. He watched the light fade. Another day gone. It makes me blue.

Helen Woodward said, "Malcolm is taking a sabbatical from Yale. He's invited to lecture at Oxford in October."

Malcolm said to Artie, "What do you admire most about Darwin?"

"His courage. It takes guts to tell the truth."

Adam said, "It takes more to face it."

Hal asked, "What's the truth?"

Malcolm said, "Darwin wrote, 'Thus from the war of nature, from famine and death, the most exalted object of which we are capable of conceiving, namely the production of the higher animals, directly flows.'"

Adam thought, I flow from death. Well, so be it.

Dear God, let me love Your world without smoking dope or drinking Gibsons.

Sept. 3, 2001. Mon. 1 p.m. *This morning, Odin & his army of dead warriors galloped in a thunderstorm on the Wild Hunt through the countryside. They stampeded a herd of red deer among some pine trees & gave a farmer named Thorstein Flat-nose a fatal heart attack in his barn.*

Shirley told me Johanna fears same. She's home from work today. Her blood pressure on awakening 157/100. She sees Abe tomorrow at noon. My fear of dying at 73.

"I've had it with Ella, Artie. I asked her Friday to give the apartment a thorough cleaning and spent two hours this afternoon cleaning up after her. Her eyes are no good. She can't see the dirt. The bathrooms were filthy. We'll get roaches! I had to wash the soap dishes and wipe off the guck around the bottoms of the faucets. I found little strings from the mop on the floor in the corners.

"And that's not all, not by a long shot. She can't see

the backs of the shelves in the fridge. The vegetables rot. I threw away a moldy red pepper, a yellow pepper, and two cucumbers. She left a pool of spilled vinaigrette dressing behind the milk on the top shelf. That's because she can't see. Then she's lazy. I asked her to dust the cross bars under the dining room table and behind the lamps in the living room. She ignored me. I have to clean up after her."

"From now on, I'll give you a hand."

"No you won't. You say you will, but you won't. You'll put it off, then you'll forget. Or, you'll do a half-assed job because your mind is elsewhere—on your work. I'll have to clean up after both of you."

The rotten vegetables, the spilled salad dressing, the dusty lamps, the guck on the faucets were all news to Artie. He said, "Thank you."

"For what?"

"For keeping life's dirt at bay."

The tune in Johanna's head switched from "Mrs. Robinson" to "I Don't Know Why I Love You Like I Do." She sang along to herself, I don't know why, but I do.

Intel 27.56. Johanna said to Leslie, "Intel's holding up. Maybe our analysts were wrong. I feel like a fool getting on my high horse over it. I could have jeopardized our jobs for nothing."

"You did what you thought was right. The baby just moved."

"You once kicked me in the bladder during a movie. I peed on the seat."

"We saw Sutton last night. He got drunk. Chris is worried about Sut's drinking. The smell of booze makes me nauseous. My sense of smell has intensified. Touch, too. And taste. I feel so alive. I'm eating like a horse." And fucking like a rabbit.

"Sutton says God is life. What's that mean?"

"I'll tell you a secret. We just decided. If the baby's a boy, we're naming him after Daddy's father. Samuel. Sam Pendleton. It was Chris's idea. He wants to make it up to Daddy for the circumcision. Chris feels guilty about it. He looks for things to feel guilty about. It's how he was brought up. His folks gave him a bad case of Protestant guilt. How does Sam sound to you?"

"Dad has a new thing about his father."

"What kind of thing?"

"He's convinced he's going to die like him at seventy-three."

"Since when?"

"Since last Tuesday. He got the feeling in the cemetery, over the old man's grave. I know these feelings. You can't shake them. I feel eleven's my lucky number."

Abe Raskin told Johanna, "Your blood pressure's still too high. We need to do better." He increased her dose of Altace to 10 mg. daily.

Abe automatically responded with a smile that showed the gap between his two upper front teeth. It was a reflex that he had acquired as a fat kid to hide his rage at being teased. His fat cheeks had long since melted away; his phony smile remained like a scar of his unhappy childhood.

He said, "The last time you were here, you asked me if I believed that prayer promotes healing. And I said, Yes, I do. Well, I'm not alone. In a randomized study at Duke, angioplasty patients around the world were prayed for by members of seven different religions. They had better clinical outcomes than those getting standard therapy."

"Seven different religions?"

"I think that's the number."

"It makes a good case for polytheism."

He smiled again—the phony smile of the fat kid humiliated in a Bronx schoolyard.

He said, "Come and see me again in a month."

Subj: Starting chemo
Date: 9/5/2001 6:17:11 PM Eastern Daylight Time
From: Adamlaw
To: Artjo

Dear Artie,

Started chemo this morning @ Henry Irving Cancer Center, Columbia-Presbyterian. 20 mg. Interferon administered by IV. Needle stuck in back of rt. hand hurt, nurse adjusted it, said it was pressing on vein.

She tried to put me at my ease. "What are your passions?"

"My passions?"

"What interests you the most?"

"Right now? Right now what interests me the most is knocking out my cancer."

The bald young man—very pale—on an IV two chairs from me retched. My nurse drew a curtain around him. Between more retching, behind curtain, the young man said 3 times, "That which doesn't kill me makes me stronger."

Our nurse said to me, "That's his mantra."

Ditto. Best, Adam

Wednesday night, Guy couldn't get it up, so Judy gave him some head.

He said, "Forget it, honey. I'm too nervous. I made a date today with a urologist for a sperm count. I see him on the eighteenth. I'll have to jerk off into a test tube."

A downtown local screeched beneath the bedroom window; the panes shook. Judy rolled her eyes.

When the screech stopped, she said, "My poor darling, I've been thinking. I love you. I want to marry you. If we can't have a child together, I'll be disappointed. I won't pretend I won't be disappointed. I want to experience pregnancy. Of course, with my appetite, I'll have to watch my weight. Maybe I'll be artificially inseminated."

"I couldn't stand it. It would be like having you fucked by another man."

"Then artificial insemination is out. We can adopt."

"Lenny Wolf in my office and his wife recently adopted a baby girl from an orphanage in China. They picked her up last month. I could love a Chinese baby girl."

"So could I."

Guy imagined them living in a quiet apartment downtown, on the top floor of a brownstone, with a plump Chinese baby girl.

He said, "Chinese babies are cute, but grown Chinese women—they're frequently…Suppose our baby girl grows up homely. What then? I'm no racist, mind you, but I mean to say…"

Judy shut him up with a blow job.

Guy woke at three thirty to pee. A car alarm kept him awake. He counted sounds like sheep: rattles, rumbles, squeals, squeaks, two sirens, and this fucking alarm. I'll be here three years in November. Judy's here a month. She must really love me to put up with this noise. We gotta find a quiet place. He gazed at her head on the pillow. That adorable, perky nose. Chinese noses are flat.

The alarm quit. A truck roared. The street sounds sometimes drowned out conversation in the apartment. Guy and Judy invariably rolled their eyes and waited for the racket to stop before talking again. They rolled their eyes at each other in public for the fun of it. Two nights ago the waiter in a West Side French restaurant thought they were stoned.

Guy's father, Ronnie, was a crackhead. Guy didn't know if he was dead or alive and didn't give a shit. Ronnie had been a vice president of marketing at the Campbells Soup Company in Camden, just across the river from Philly, where he lived with his family in a three-bedroom house on Lombard Street.

Ronnie, at forty-five, was still out to experience life. He took his first hit of crack on Memorial Day, 1988, from a street hooker at 13th and Locust. It cost twenty dollars. She taught him to load up on oxygen with two deep breaths; then she stuck the stem of the glass pipe in his mouth and told him to inhale slowly while she burned two matches, one after the other, over the melted rocks in the bowl. "It always takes two matches." The smell was the sweetest he'd ever known. He exhaled and felt dizzy; his heart raced. He forgot how to talk. Ahhh! This—at last—is what life is all about!

Ronnie never again got a rush like that from a hit. He smoked in his parked Saab and behind locked stalls in restaurant johns. He spent three hundred dollars a day on crack for six months. He cleaned out his bank account—sixty thousand bucks. His job was on the line. He slept on the living room sofa.

His wife, Amanda, thought about a divorce, but couldn't bring herself to act. She suddenly saw everything through the wrong end of a telescope: diminished and far away. Guy became remote to her. She once looked at him across the table at breakfast; his face was puffy with sleep. She didn't recognize him. She nearly asked, Who are you? Guy took out his rage against Pop on the wrestling mat at Central High. He became the heavyweight champ.

Ronnie smoked more. One hit and they watched him between the slats of the living room blinds and through the brass keyhole of the hall closet. They watched him from under the sofa. The two in the medicine cabinet watched him reach for an aspirin.

He took a hit in his car parked on 22nd and South just before Thanksgiving dinner. They're watching me from inside the turkey. He stabbed the carcass with the carving knife. The blade struck the breastbone and slid off to the right, knocking a slice of white meat to the floor at Guy's feet.

Amanda said in a distant voice, "Ronnie, drop the knife."

He turned and faced her. "Make me."

Guy told Judy the rest in early June: "I went on automatic pilot. I crouched down and tackled Pop around the knees. He dropped the knife. I remember the thud of the bone handle on the dining room carpet. Pop fell forward on his stomach. He groped for the knife with his right hand. It was just out of reach. Then he tried to get up.

"I was back on the mat in gym. The object in wrestling is to knock your opponent off balance. I grabbed his right wrist with my left hand and pulled him toward me. At the same, I pushed my right shoulder against his left. He fell over on his back with a thump. The breath whooshed out of him. I grabbed his throat with both hands and squeezed.

"Mom screamed, 'Don't kill him!'

"She had it right. I wanted to kill him. I squeezed harder.

"She screamed again, 'Don't do it!' So I let him go. He scrambled to his feet and ran out of the house. That was the last we saw of him."

Thursday morning, Guy said to Judy, "I've had a tough life. But your love for me will make things right."

Sept. 6, 2001. Thurs. 2 p.m. *Slightly drunk on 4 sakis with lunch at Roppongi. The booze dulls my anxiety about being blocked for the last 4 days. According to the myth, Odin sacrifices himself to learn the secrets of the dead. He journeys to the underworld.*

Odin's character, portrayed in The Prose Edda *& Norse poetry, is static; his experience in the Land of the Dead doesn't* *change him. He has no emotions. My Odin must feel—what? I don't know.*

Dinner party tonight at Sandra Grossman's. Jacob Fuchs & wife Myra will be there. She supported him after the war for twenty years by working as a saleslady at Saks Fifth Avenue. Haven't seen Fuchs in four or five years. He & Abraham Sutzkever, who lives in Israel, are the most celebrated Yiddish poets who write about the Holocaust.

I like Fuchs's early poems best, particularly "Ashes." I know Ira Bernstein's translation by heart:

> *"We Jews sowed the ashes of Jews with shovels on the icy paths between the barracks, and along the double rows of electrified barbed wire fence.*
>
> *The paths sown with ashes bloomed with the hobnailed boots of the SS making their rounds.*
>
> *My first shovelful of ashes was blown in midair*
> *Toward the snow clouds by a beat of Michael's wings.*
>
> *Michael is Israel's guardian angel.*
>
> *He gathered my scattered shovelful of ashes and threw it into God's eyes.*

They stayed dry."

Johanna said to Artie, "My hemorrhoids are acting up. The sight of blood in my stool no longer scares me. I'm now scared of what I can't see: what's happening in my arteries."

Sandra Grossman said, "Artie, you know Ann Kahn."

"I'm afraid not."

"Arthur Rubin, Ann Kahn."

Artie waited for Kahn's brown eyes to widen slightly—a sure sign that she'd recognized his name. Her eyes narrowed. She doesn't know who I am. The fact is, in my old age, I hate literary dinner parties. Supposing I'm not recognized. Ah! *The* Arthur Rubin. Rachel Klein, over there on the sofa with Fuchs, once introduced me to Abraham Heschel as *the* Arthur Rubin.

I was once almost famous, thanks to Joseph Campbell's TV series on myths. Mythology was all the rage. The sales of my books soared. Well, not exactly soared. But they topped fifty thousand. I was interviewed by Merv Rothstein in the *Times*. 1988 was my year. Everybody recognized my name at parties. I read it in their widened eyes.

Artie downed a vodka on the rocks and took a second from Sandra, who dropped another ice cube in his glass and Saul Bellow's name in his right ear. "Saul's work is mythic. Jacob's, too. You artists are so obsessed by myth!"

She saw from his smiling eyes that he was flattered

by being implicitly included with the likes of Saul Bellow and Jacob Fuchs. She had done her duty as a hostess and turned to her other guests.

They all know that Lenny married me for my money and regularly beat me up. He once broke my nose. One of our major literary critics! Brilliant! They're all brilliant. Rachel's brilliant piece in last week's *New Yorker* on the poet Yehuda Halevi. Medieval Zionist. He abandoned his wife and kids in Spain and made *aliyah* to Palestine. The legend says he was murdered there by an Arab. *Plus ça change*...Israel's a mistake. This is the Promised Land. God bless America!

She ran in her mind through the verse Lenny—the old Socialist—had taught her:

God bless free enterprise,
System divine.
Stand beside her
And guide her,
Just as long as the profits
Are mine.
Good old Wall Street,
May she prosper;
Corporations,
May they grow;
God bless free enterprise!
The status quo!

She said to Johanna, "I'm worried about the market.

How was it today?"

Myra Fuchs said, "Hello, Arthur," as he approached the sofa.

Fuchs said, "Do I know you?"

Rachel said, "Jacob tells me he's in the early stage of Alzheimer's. He was just diagnosed."

Jacob spoke in a low voice. "Did I say that? I can't remember. I can't remember things that just happened. I can't remember names or faces. Gevalt! I've developed a goyishe kop in my old age."

He asked Artie, "Do I know you? I remember some things clearly. I remember our kitchen drain is clogged. The Irish super. I can't remember. I remember leaving home this evening without my glasses. Myra had to go back and get them. Myra! My poor Myra! Esther Hamalka meine. She cries when she thinks I'm not looking. What's Esther Hamalka meine in English?"

Myra said, "My Queen Esther."

"My English is slipped. You say 'slipped'? I think more and more in Yiddish. I can't write poems anymore. Nu! I can't complain. I've had mazel—a lucky life. I'll die famous, thanks to what's-his-name. My English translator. He couldn't come tonight. I can't remember why. Ira! Ira what?

"His translation of 'Ashes' in the *Partisan Review* brought me to the attention of the American reading public. My eight books are all in print. Nu! I can't complain. I've had mazel—a lucky life. I was lucky to get a job at Brandeis. Yiddish literature in translation. I've always had terrible trouble with names. I could never remember my students' names. They knew it too and resented it. I remember the past like yesterday. No, not like yesterday. I can't remember yesterday. What's today?"

Myra said, "Today is Thursday."

Jacob turned his boney face toward Artie. "Notice my low voice? It's been a couple of months now. My voice goes low in me, real soft. Like now. The SS screamed at us. The kapos screamed at us. I hear them in my dreams. '*Macht schnell!*'

"I was selected with twenty others in my barracks for the gas chamber. The guard marched us out to the truck. It was raining. Thirst in the camp was worse than hunger. I caught the drops on my tongue. Another guard ran up.

"He said, 'Where are you taking this bunch?'

'To the gas chamber.'

'I need them for a work detail at the tracks.'

'Well, they're marked down for the gas chamber.'

'Never mind, I'll fix it at the office. Give them to me for the work detail.'

"Meantime, I'm standing there in the rain at attention, with my cap off, thinking, What's the difference? I die today or tomorrow.

"To make a long story short, we were sent to shlep steel bars across the railroad tracks. Then my detail was transferred to work in a munitions factory in Nuremberg. So my life was saved. Nu! I can't complain. I've had mazel—a lucky life. But my luck's run out."

September 7, 2001. Fri. 2 p.m. *Still blocked. 5 cups of saki at lunch again in an effort to loosen Odin's tongue—get him talking about his journey to the Land of the Dead. Characters have a life of their own. Odin has died on me.*

Fuchs's Alzheimer's has squelched his poetry. He resembles his wife: wrinkled, hairless cheeks, thinning white hair. Myra comes from a rich German-Jewish family; survived the war in Zurich.

Said she's already suffering from caregiver's stress. "If Jacob repeats himself one more time, I'll scream! What happens when he needs more care than I can provide?"

"Arthur, this is Myra Fuchs. Thank you for listening to me kvetch last night."

"You're welcome, Myra."

"I just wanted to add that rereading your books means a lot to me at the present time. They let me escape into other worlds, but also bring me into contact with myself. And your illustrations! They give me great pleasure. There aren't many things that give me pleasure anymore."

"Thanks for your kind words, Myra. I'm deeply moved."

"You'll forgive my association, Arthur, but Jacob hasn't moved his bowels in ten days. The doctor says they're impacted. Forgive me for bringing up the subject. It's very much on my mind."

Jerry and Hal's commitment ceremony at the Second Universalist Church was tomorrow evening. Neither Johanna nor Leslie had gotten around to buying them a gift. They decided Friday at noon to go in together for a hundred and fifty bucks apiece. The boys were registered at Bloomingdale's.

Johanna said, "Bloomingdale's is for bedding, towels, housewares. Let's give them something festive. We'll try Simon Pearce and Chelsea Passage at Barneys. They're a block or two apart."

Leslie said, "Barneys has a bigger selection."

"Barneys it is!"

They shopped during lunch hour. Leslie looked over the straw handbags to the right of the Madison Avenue entrance. "I need one with a shoulder strap."

"I don't see any."

They took the escalator up a flight and turned right into Chelsea Passage. They eyed silver cocktail shakers, Fornasetti plates, and black-and-white pottery designed by Betty Erteman.

Leslie said, "Chris and I are going out to dinner tonight with Sutton and Diana Chamberlain. I fixed them up. They've got a lot in common. She's a big Episcopalian. Judy rarely went to church. I didn't tell Diana about her. Why complicate things? What do you think of this?"

"How much is it?"

Leslie turned over the wooden bowl, inlaid with a leaf, and read off the price: "Eighty-eight dollars."

"That's not enough. You should have told Diana about Judy."

"Maybe you're right. Diana's very masochistic. She'll blame herself if the date doesn't work out."

"Is Sutton drinking?"

"Chris says not as much."

"Dad's drinking too much. He's blocked on his book. Every time he blocks on a book, he's scared it's for good. This has been going on for forty years. I'm sick of it. I told him to work on an illustration. He can't come up with an idea. He's going to his sketch club tomorrow at the Atheneum. Maybe a pretty naked model will inspire him. I'm tired of being his personal cheerleader. 'Rah, rah, rah, sis boom bah. Artie Rubin's not a blah.'"

Leslie said, "I dreamed last night that Chris and I were walking by the Central Park lake. I leaned over the water in front of the boathouse. The baby dropped out of me and drowned."

"When I was pregnant, I once dreamed that you were born with a cleft palate. A bowl is a good idea."

They couldn't find one item that was expensive enough. They settled on four yellow faïence soup bowls from Provence and four matching plates that all told set them back $332 plus tax.

Subj: I'm OK
Date: 9/7/2001 19:20:22 PM Eastern Daylight Time
From: Adamlaw
To: Artjo

Dear Artie,
I'm OK in the mornings and wiped out in the afternoons. I go in for treatment at 1:30. It lasts until 4:30. I stay awake a while, then sleep12 hours. Fatigue and queasiness accumulating. My doctor is giving me 20 mg. time-release Ritalin to keep me alert tomorrow during the commitment ceremony.

Shirley sends love. She's unhappy that the ceremony's being held in a church. She says why not in the gay & lesbian synagogue? The church was Hal's choice. He's pals with the (gay) pastor.

Adam

Leslie said to Chris, "Each bowl and plate has a slightly different floral pattern."

Diana asked Sut, "Where did you go to school?"

"Carnegie Mellon."

"What did you study?"

"Computer science and physics."

Diana said, "My younger brother's a physics major at MIT."

"That so?"

"Leslie tells me you work on the 102nd floor of the World Trade Center. Your view must be something."

Sut said, "My office doesn't have a window."

"What a pity. What is it you do?"

"I'm a computer engineer. I write codes for software applications for banks. It's a bore."

"What do you want to do?"

"I wish I knew. What about you?"

"I just got my PhD in clinical psych at Rutgers. I'm going for postdoctoral training in cognitive therapy."

"So what's cognitive therapy?"

Diana explained; she saw Sut wasn't listening. In the last few minutes, between the appetizers and main course, the lights in the restaurant had dimmed. The lower half of Diana's oval face was now solely lit by the candle in the red-tinted little glass on the table. Her nostrils were pink; her pearl earrings gleamed. She gestured with her right hand as she talked; its shadow flitted across her cheek.

Sut, who had limited himself to one glass of wine with dinner, resisted the temptation to refill his glass.

He heard Diana say, "It gives patients a clear explanation of their emotional difficulties."

A match flared behind her at the bar; he looked at the cigarette smoke, the blue vase on the counter filled with pussy willows, the mirror reflecting a red brick wall, and her pink nostrils. You're beautiful!

Diana read his mind. You noticed!

He said, "Leslie tells me you belong to Grace Church." Judy never went to church. I didn't care.

Diana said, "To tell you the truth, I haven't been in weeks. I always feel remiss when..." He's not listening again. Nor looking at me in the same way. I talk too much. I'm not his type.

Sept. 8, 2001. Sat. 9 a.m. *Off to draw a naked girl at the Atheneum, where I hope to get an idea for a portrait of one of the Norse goddesses—Freyr, Frigg or golden haired Sif.*

Betty Cook got the modeling job at the Atheneum's Saturday Morning Sketch Club through her roommate, Gloria Sternberg, who had posed there last spring. The Sketch Club paid twenty dollars an hour, and you ate a buffet lunch with the artists.

"A huge spread," Gloria said. "You name it. Waldorf salad, poached salmon, filet mignon, curry chicken. I had poached pears for dessert."

Betty skipped coffee at breakfast; coffee made her sweat. The Atheneum was on 38th between Park and Lex. So this is a club for famous artists and writers. Maybe one day I'll belong. The building looks like a bank. There's nothing—no bronze plaque or anything—on the outside that tells what it is. Cool.

Luiz Ramirez, the Head Hallman, introduced Betty to Sue Martin, the watercolorist, who was president of the Sketch Club.

Martin said, "Send Gloria my best. I remember her very well. She told me that she has a recurrent dream that she can't get her clothes off to go to work."

Betty said, "That's my dream! Gloria stole it from me!"

"I'll be damned!"

Betty struck a pose on the platform in the middle of the big studio under the skylight. She felt the morning sun on her raised left arm and the nape of her neck. Her head was turned to the right. Her right hand was on her hip; all her weight was on her right leg. She knew that during the last five minutes of the twenty-minute pose her right hip, her locked right knee, and right heel would hurt. Her left shoulder and arm would get heavy, ache, go numb and cold. A year and a half of modeling had taught her to hold the pose in pain.

She talked in her head with her father in St. Paul, who was against her modeling in the nude. I've toughened up. I'm more disciplined, stronger than before I modeled. I'm more sure of myself. And it shows in my own painting. I've made real progress in the last year and a half. Larry Katz, my teacher at the Art Students League, says so.

Artie drew her with a 2B pencil on a 22 x 30 inch sheet of high-quality rag paper—Rives BFK—tacked to a plywood board he held on his lap. He started drawing her left side down the right-hand side of the sheet. The fine blond hairs on her raised forearm reflected the sunlight on her skin and made it glow. Sif—what luck!—golden-haired Sif—I've found a model for golden-haired Sif. Her weight's on her right foot. I can't feel the flow of the outside of her body. I can't feel anything today.

Artie lifted his pencil from the sheet of paper. Everybody else was working. Their sounds—the squeak of charcoal, the scratch of a pen, a turned page—reproved him. He watched the *New Yorker* cartoonist Jeff Kramer draw in India ink with a sharpened piece of bamboo on a sheet of Japanese rice paper. Sue Martin, seated cross-legged on the floor, was sketching in watercolors.

Artie went back at it. Suddenly his right hand, on its own, repeatedly drew little arcs that turned into the rounded nape of Betty's neck, the tops of her shoulders, her collar bones. Firm tits. I love drawing firm tits. Their soft crescent-shaped shadows on the rib cage. He hatched them in. Now for the nipples and their shadows, then another curved line—the fold of flesh along the bottom of the tits. They don't have enough weight. Think of them as full bags. Yes, sir, yes, sir, two bags full.

Everyone's staring at my naked body. I'm still not used to it, even after a year and a half of modeling. They see all my imperfections—my fat thighs and thick ankles. Never mind. I'm not me. I'm an object for the use of my fellow artists, like their bottles of turpentine. I'm a bottle of turpentine. A jar filled with water. A tin paint box. A stick of charcoal. The board in the old man's lap. His pencil. An expression overheard in her teens from a garage mechanic outside St. Paul came back to her: does the old guy still have lead in his pencil? Don't think about sex. It shows.

Artie hatched in the soft shadows on top of Betty's stomach and below her navel. Shit! The shadows under her tits are too high. He darkened their crease where they met the ribs. That's better. All of a sudden, he saw his sketch with a fresh eye. It's lifeless. It has no movement. The proportions are wrong. Goodbye, Sif.

Betty was talking with her father again. I got your five-hundred-dollar check. The check! I forgot to deposit Dad's check yesterday! It won't clear in time to cover my check for the rent. I've only got $520 in the bank. I'm short almost three hundred bucks. Gloria will kill me!

A drop of sweat from her left armpit rolled down her left thigh. Artie, with his pencil in his mouth, saw her break out all over with beads of sweat. Her sternum glistened. A faint mist gathered around her nipples; their tops were wet.

Her skin's dewy. It's got a yellowish cast. Bluish over the veins in her groin. The different shades of pink! I never realized: strawberry-blonde hair is actually very light green—yes, like corn silk; light yellow-green. The tuft under her armpit, in the shadow, is a darker green. It vibrates with light inside the shadow. Sparse reddish hair on her rosy cunt. The damp curl beside her left ear; her moist throat. I see the pulse in her throat. Oh, that I were young again and held you in my arms.

Jerry got back home at noon.

Hal asked, "How's your dad?"

"Fatigued, nauseous, pale as a ghost. But he's coming tonight. He's taking Ritalin to stay awake. He's so pale—the color of a candle. He was always tan in the summers when I was growing up. Such white teeth! He played badminton with me on the lawn with his shirt off. Turns out, all that exposure to the sun didn't do him any good. He's got a hairy chest. I imagine it's now grey. After the badminton, we showered together. I loved his naked body streaming with water. I thought every boy loved his daddy's naked body. When I was twelve, I fantasized sucking him off. I wanted to be his sex slave.

"My therapist in Cambridge was amazed that I didn't repress such thoughts. He said my repressive mechanism is defective. I'm grateful. Dad's naked body turned me on to other boys in the locker room. It set me on the path that led to you.

"Don't interrupt! Let me finish! You sometimes remind me of dad. Particularly when you sulk if you don't get your way. But that's not why I love you. I love your sweet tenor. Your long fingers. Your compassion. The way you do pro bono work—Dad never does pro bono work. I love your love of family. How you want us to build one together. I first loved you the night you told me that you often babysat for your sister's four-month-old and changed his Pampers. I finally found a guy who loves babies as much as me."

The Rev. T. E. Shaw said, "Dearly beloved, we have come together in the presence of God to witness and bless the joining together of this man and this man in Holy Union. The union of two people in heart, body, and mind is intended by God for their mutual joy; for the help and comfort given one another in prosperity and adversity. Therefore such a union is not to be entered into unadvisedly or lightly, but reverently and in accordance with the purposes for which it was instituted by God."

The Ritalin gives me palpitations. But I'm not sleepy. It's stuffy in here. The priest is sweating. He's got faggoty mannerisms—a sibilant S, swishy hands. He presses his fingertips to his chest like a woman does, between her boobs. At least he kept Jesus out of the service. Am I the father of the bride or the groom? Jerry washed his beard since I saw him this morning; it shines. Like his eyes. He's happy! Let him always be as happy as he is tonight.

Shirley is sniffling. She always cries at weddings. A commitment ceremony's not a real wedding. It has no legal validity. This is a parody of a wedding. Who were those adorable little black flower girls? Their lilies, and the ones on the altar, cost me five grand. I don't begrudge it. Hal's a Senior Associate at Harmon, Lewis, and Gewirtz. He must make a hundred and fifty thousand a year. He and Jerry are spending the night at the Tribeca Grand.

The anal thing. Artie says don't think about it. Easy for him to say. My muscles ache. I'm nauseous. A metallic taste in my mouth. Pain behind my eyes. And these chills! On this warm September night. I've got years yet. The slender rabbi with short hair and a yarmulka—she looks like an adolescent boy. Now what? The exchange of rings.

Rabbi Ellen Berger said, "'Set me as a seal upon thine heart, as a seal upon thine arm: for love is as strong as death.'"

She wrapped the boys face to face in a tallis. "This is a symbol of being enveloped by God's presence."

Ugh! They're kissing on the mouth in public! So what? Jerry's happy!

Let their love outlast me.

Judy asked Guy, "How about Sunday, June second?"

"Sounds good."

"Or is a June wedding a cliché? What do you think?"

"I think a June wedding is just fine."

"Cool!"

Maybe I'll go to Grace Church this morning, and make nice to Diana. "I had to see you again." Leslie didn't tell her about Judy. I'll tell her. Diana's a psychologist. She'll understand. I'll take her to lunch. The shadow of her cleavage in the candlelight. She kept rubbing her bare upper left arm. The smell of Judy's bare arms around my neck. Judy! Come back to me and I'll marry you. The hell with Diana.

Sept. 10, 2001. Mon. Noon. *Tore up the 6 sketches I made at the club Sat., though my observation that yellow, light green, with orange highlights are the colors that compose strawberry blonde hair will find its way into my description of Sif's gorgeous locks, which Loki cuts off.*

Meanwhile, Odin still stymies me. What happens after he leaves the Land of the Dead? Pouring through Sturluson & Norse Poems, *translated by W. H. Auden & Paul B. Taylor—particularly the mythological poems.*

4 p.m. My $780 El-Al round trip ticket to Israel for Tues. Oct. 16th has arrived in the mail. The Jewish god doesn't die & come back to life—like Odin or Christ—but we Jews did, in Israel, after the Holocaust.

Daniel, with whom I spoke, asked me to deliver 2 pairs of new Adidas sneakers to his mom & dad, who are on their feet in their Jerusalem florist shop all day long. Sneakers are very expensive in Israel.

Guy walked in on Sut debugging a particularly elusive exception thrown by his C code.

"You're busy. Forgive me. And forgive me for being so rude to you that day in the lobby."

"You're forgiven."

"I wanted you to hear this from me first: Judy and I have set the date. We're getting married in Philly, where her mother lives, on June second."

"Congratulations. Congratulate Judy for me."

"You bet."

Sut scrolled his screen through five pages of if-then loops, print f statements, and mallocs without seeing anything.

After work, he steered away from the Wild Blue Bar; it reminded him of having a drink there before dinner with Judy in May. He went to the Tall Ships Bar on the ground floor of the south end of Three World Trade Center. The wall on the right, as he entered, was covered with thick ropes.

Sut drank four Gibsons, then caught a cab home. He polished off half a bottle of Absolut and passed out on his bed while pulling off his right shoe.

Next morning, at 8:50, Johanna called Artie from the office: "Turn on the TV. A plane just hit the North Tower of the World Trade Center. Chris hasn't heard from Sut."

Caroline Pendleton got the news on *Good Morning America*. Sut's dead. My baby!

"Judy?"

"Guy? What's up?"

"I called to say good-bye."

"Good-bye?"

"A plane's crashed into my building."

"A plane? What plane?"

"A jetliner. A Boeing 767. I heard its engines—they were too loud—and looked out the window as it barreled past the Empire State Building. It hit below us. I'm in my office. I'm trapped on the 102nd floor. The south stairwell's a huge hole. The door to the east stairwell's blocked by some gypsum boards that are on fire. The fire's spreading. I love you."

"I love you too."

"The office is filling up with thick, black smoke. It's hard to breathe. Hang on! Lenny Wolfe broke my window with a computer terminal. He cut his hand on the glass. Some smoke's streaming out. It looks beautiful in the sunlight. We're getting air. I can breathe easier. Four or five more people have come into the room. We're all on cell phones."

"You're breaking up."

"Is this better?"

"I can't hear you."

"How about now?"

"That's good. I love you."

"Oh my God! Something—or someone—just passed the open window. Judy, you're the best thing that ever happened to me. It was love at first sight. I fell for your nose. I hope Pop's dead. I can't bear him outliving me. Now we'll never know if I'm sterile. Thanks for wanting to marry me whether I'm sterile or not. June second will be tough on you. Tell mom I love her."

"Guy, are you there? I can't hear you again. There's static on the line."

"Tell mom I love her."

"I hear you now. I will."

"Sut's not in the office. He's missing all the fun. Lenny's on the phone with his wife. He's looking at pictures of their new baby. Phew! I smell jet fuel. When the plane hit, the whole building swayed back and forth. It groaned and creaked. So help me, the steel moaned. The door frame ripped off the wall. The ceiling tiles are down."

"Is that screaming? Who's that screaming?"

"Some guy in the doorway. I can't make out who. A woman in a floral dress just fell past my window. I hear explosions below me. The floor's buckled. It's getting very hot in here. Some papers blown off my desk near my face are singed. I feel heat on my cheeks and forehead. Like from an open oven. The sprinkler system doesn't work. I love you."

"And I love you."

"The smoke makes it hard to see in here. Lenny? Yes, that's Lenny. He's knocking out the pieces of glass left in the window. He's got one leg over the sill. Now the other. Lenny's got a big ass. It's a tight squeeze. He jumped. I fell in love with you staring out that window at the raindrops. Remember? I think of it as my lucky window."

"Don't jump, Guy."

"It's jump or burn."

"Then jump, darling. Jump into my arms, where I'll hold you close for good."

Guy dangled his legs out the narrow window. The heated air shimmered around him; it was filled with rising soot, glowing cinders, sparks, and scraps of colored paper—red, yellow, green, blue. He couldn't see down through the black smoke. Fuck this shit. I finally had it made. Like Mom always says, life's a joke.

The inner soles of his shoes felt warm. A burning scrap of lined yellow paper from a legal pad rose near his knees. The north wind momentarily carried away the smoke roiling beneath him. My last look at the Empire State Building, the East River, the Hudson. He pushed off with his right hand under his thigh on the sill. He fell feet first, his arms and legs spread. He shut his eyes. He felt the cool air against his face. Funny! I don't feel I'm falling. I feel like I'm floating in one place. He heard a roaring wind. Don't look! Keep your eyes closed!

His earliest memory returned to him: a red plastic fire engine with black wheels. He remembered the first time he tied his shoelaces. It was my right shoe. I suddenly grasped the principle of how to tie a bow. Mom taught me. He thought of her smearing Vaseline on the bulbous end of a thermometer when he was in bed with the chicken pox. She was so young! Not a wrinkle. Light brown hair. Her hair's getting thin on top. Mom'll miss me.

He smelled her frying eggs and onions. Don't look! Don't look! How come Sut didn't show today? He'll marry Judy. I don't care. I'm done with them. I'm done with everything.

One last look around. What street is that down there? All those people running. The roof of a cop car. How come I never noticed the roof of a cop car before? Flashing red and yellow lights in a V shape. They alternate. Mommy! The sidewalk's coming up at me so fast!

"Hello?"

"Mrs. Stewart? This is Judy Murray."

"Where are you?"

"I'm at school. I just spoke with Guy at his office."

"I saw what happened on TV. I just tried to get him. There was no answer."

Judy said, "He sent you his love."

"What else did he say?"

"He said good-bye."

"I'll come up to New York tomorrow. I can't come today. I'm having root canal done this afternoon. I have an infected molar. I'm in excruciating pain. It's killing me. I can't stand the pain."

"Don't worry yourself. I don't even know whether

you can get into New York today. I hear everything's closed off. I'll expect you tomorrow."

"I'm grateful for my pain. I won't take a painkiller. The pain keeps my mind off Guy for minutes at a time."

"Chris?"

"Sut? Is that you? Thank God. Where are you?"

"Back home. I just got back home. I'm covered with gray ashes. I overslept twenty minutes this morning. I remember hitting the snooze button twice, then waking up at eight fifteen."

The three vodkas in him set him talking without a pause. "So I skipped coffee and rushed to work. At the World Trade Center station, some guys with World Trade Center on their shirts directed a crowd of us to exit from the mall, right across from the Banana Republic. I saw bright orange flames shooting out of a hole in the North Tower. And people falling. This guy with a red tie that stood straight up in the air beside his head. I looked away. I still see that red tie.

"Then—let me think—I saw a jet flying low overhead bank to the left. Was it to the left? Yes. The left wing was below the right. I'm sure of it. The plane was way too low. The pilot leveled the wings. I heard him gun the engines. Like in a dream, I watched the jet close on the South Tower. There was a tremendous platinum and gold flash and a gigantic ball of fire. I'll never forget the colors—platinum and gold.

"Chris? Listen! The truth is, I overslept because I passed out last night. I have a terrible hangover. Hear what I said? I was twenty minutes late to work. I'm alive because I got drunk last night. I got drunk because Judy's getting married. Or was. Guy's dead. I feel it in my bones. What about the others? We have thirty-one people working at Hotspur. Everybody's at work by eight thirty. I'm always at work by eight thirty. Except today, because I passed out last night and overslept. Today of all days. Why? Answer me that. There must be a reason."

Then jump, darling. Jump into my arms, where I'll hold you close for good. Then jump, darling. Jump into my arms, where I'll hold you close for good. Then jump, darling. Jump into my arms, where I'll hold you close for good.

I'm going crazy.

Caroline, Richard, and Sut went to Leslie and Chris's brownstone on West 23rd Street for dinner. They sat out on the back deck. The cool air smelled of scorched steel.

Caroline said to Sut, "I thought you were dead for three hours and twenty-three minutes this morning, and then Chris called and told me you were alive. Understand what I'm saying? You were dead and then came back to life. What's her name—Lazarus's mother? She has nothing on me. What's her name?"

Sut said, "We don't know. It's not mentioned in the Bible."

"Call her Caroline."

Sept. 11, 2001. Tues. Midnight. *Took the day off from work. Watched CNN's coverage of the attack on the World Trade Center.*

My urgent need, after supper, to get back to my book. With 2 vodkas, wrote Odin's journey to the underworld in 4 hrs.

"Odin thought, 'I'll sacrifice myself to myself to learn the secrets of the dead.'

"He stood with his back against the trunk of the ash Yggdrasill and drove his spear through his left chest. The iron point pierced his chest wall, his sixth rib, his left lung, his heart, and went out again between his ribs, through the muscles of his back and deep into the wood.

"Then he died.

"He mounted Sleipnir, his eight-legged horse, and galloped north for nine days and nights though a dark valley that wound under the earth. Then Odin heard flowing water. He rode across the river Gioll on its crystal bridge.

"At the far end, a dead woman in rags grabbed Sleipnir's

reins and asked Odin, 'Why are you riding on the road to Hel?'

"*'I want to learn the secrets of the dead.'*

"*'Keep heading north and down.'*

"*Odin rode on till he came to the open gate of Hel. He dismounted from his horse and greeted Hel, the Queen of the Dead, seated on her throne made of dead men's fingernails. Her right side was a radiant naked young woman; her left, a rotting corpse, swarming with maggots. She gave off the sweet stink of decay.*

"*Hel said to Odin, 'You will rise from this death, but the next will be forever.'*

"*'The next?'*

"*'An axe-age is coming, a sword-age, when shields will be shattered. It will be the age of wind and wolves. Brothers will kill each other for gold, mothers and sons, fathers and daughters, siblings will lie with each other. There will come a triple winter, with no summers in between.*

"*'The whole human race will walk the road to Hel. The chains that bind the ravening wolf Fenrir will snap. Surt, the frost ogre, will come up from the south waving his flaming sword. Hordes of fiends, giants, and trolls will follow him. You gods will arm yourselves against them. You, Odin, will put on your gold helmet and a new coat of mail. Then you and your enemies will annihilate each other in the battle of Ragnarok.'*

"Odin asked, 'How will I die?'

"Hel said, 'You'll be eaten alive by the wolf Fenrir, whose jaws gape from heaven to earth. When all you gods and your enemies have slaughtered each other, Surt will set fire to the world. Clouds of ashes will blot out the sun, moon, and stars. The blackened earth will sink into the sea.'

"Odin asked, 'What will happen afterwards?'

" 'A new green earth will rise out of the waters. Fields of grain that were never sown will grow. Yggdrassil, unscorched by the fire, will put forth sticky buds and from its heartwood, a man and a woman called Lif and Lifthrasir will emerge. They will eat the morning dew, and people the world. They will worship new gods.

" 'Now you know the secrets of the dead.'

"Odin heard laughter behind him. He whirled around and found himself standing before Yggdrassil, with his spear in his right hand.

"To calm himself, Odin went for a walk in the guise of a man. He came across nine farmers mowing wheat in the hot sun and asked, 'Would you like me to sharpen your scythes?'

"The tallest of the farmers, a man named Thorolf, said, 'Why, yes, sir; that would be very kind.'

"Odin took a whetstone from his belt and sharpened the nine blades that flashed in the sun. Olaf, the richest farmer, offered to buy the whetstone.

"Odin said, 'It's not for sale. But I'll tell you what. I'll toss it up and whoever catches it can take it home.'

"Thorolf said, 'Since I'm the tallest one here, that's fine with me.'

"Odin threw the whetstone into the air, high above the farmer's heads and Thorolf, standing on tip-toe, caught it on the way down in both hands. Olaf cut Thorolf's throat to the neck bone with his scythe and bent over to pick up the whetstone. A bald farmer named Helgi plunged the point of his scythe into Olaf's back, between his shoulder blades, screaming, 'The whetstone is mine!'

"Leaning on his spear, Odin watched the six remaining farmers slash each other to death with their sharpened scythes for possession of the whetstone. Then he picked up the whet-

stone, slippery with blood, wiped it off on a sheath of wheat, and stuck it back in his belt. The nine slashed corpses were already buzzing with blue-bottle flies.

"Odin remembered that he too was going to die. He thought, What have I done? For the second—and last—time in his life, a tear trickled down his right cheek, into his brownish-red beard."

"Is this Sutton Pendleton?"

"That's right. Who's this? What time is it?"

"Ten o'clock. Did I wake you?"

"That's all right. Ten o'clock? Time to rise and shine! Though I don't know why. I've no place to go."

"That's why I'm calling you. This is Bruce Pietch. The vice president of business development at Hotspur."

"I know who you are. I thought you were dead."

"That's what I thought about you."

Sut asked, "So, where you calling from?"

"Boca Raton."

"Boca Raton?"

"In Florida. I came down here Sunday to be with my dad. He had a heart attack Saturday night."

"I'm sorry to hear it. How's he doing?"

"So-so. But hey, look at it this way: his heart attack saved my life. What saved yours?"

"I was late for work. I overslept."

"Lucky you. I'm glad you're alive."

"I feel the same about you."

"I'm calling everybody who worked at Hotspur. I've called seven people this morning They're all missing. I spoke with their families or friends. I called Roy Hamilton, Jake Goldstein, Hank Glick, Larry Starkie..."

"Who's Larry Starkie?"

"One of the four guys in quality assurance."

"I remember now. The new black guy. Tall and handsome."

"That's the one."

"So did you call Guy Stewart?"

"I just spoke with his girlfriend, Judy Murray. Guy called her from the office to say good-bye."

"Guy said good-bye to her?"

"That's what she said."

"Who else did you call?"

"Billy Hixon."

"Who's he?"

"One of the guys in sales."

"I don't know him. Who else?"

"Let's see. Rose Hirsch. The receptionist."

"Poor Rose."

"Her husband told me she was two months pregnant. Talking to him was a toughie."

"Poor Rose. Let's keep in touch. Let me know if anybody else made it. What's your cell phone number?"

"I turn it off in the Coronary Intensive Care unit at

the hospital. Call me here at my dad's condo after 9 p.m. (561) 445-4536."

"Hang on a sec. Let me write it down. What was it again?"

"(561) 445-4536. Do you think anybody else who was in the office survived?"

"No."

"Neither do I," Pietch said. "We're the last of the Mohicans."

Sut burst out crying in the shower. Later he called Judy on her cell phone. "It's me."

"Sut! Is it really you? I'm so glad!"

"I overslept on the eleventh because I got drunk the night before. I got drunk because Guy told me you and he were going to be married."

"It's funny how things work out."

"Pietch told me Guy called you and said good-bye."

"Yes, his last words were over the phone."

"How can I help you?"

"You're sweet to ask. I can't talk now. I'm expecting his mom. Gimme a ring in a week or so and we'll talk. I need a friend."

"You can count on me."

"Rabbi Klugman?"

"Speaking."

"This is Fred Levy."

"How are you, Mr. Levy?"

"Call me Fred. I'm not so hot, Rabbi. Which is why I called you. You don't know me well. I only come to Etz Chaim on the High Holidays with my father. He died yesterday in the South Tower. I worked on the sixty-ninth floor of the North Tower. I could see his office window from mine. His office was on the seventy-ninth floor. I was looking at his window when the plane slammed into it.

"I want him to have a real Jewish funeral. The whole works. He didn't go to shul much, but in his own way, he was a believing Jew. Would you officiate?"

"Of course. God be with you. Let's get together and talk. Come to my study, or I'll go to your home."

"Your study will be fine. But give me a couple of days. I'm enmeshed in the process of getting a death certificate. You can't have a funeral without a death certificate, and it's tough to get a certificate without a body."

"Yes, I know."

"You got a text for me, rabbi?"

"A text?"

"Words to help me through."

Without having to think, Klugman said, "Psalm Fifty-one. 'A broken spirit is the acceptable sacrifice to God.'"

"'A broken spirit.' That's me."

"That was me, too, Fred. My spirit broke in half when my mom—may she rest in peace—when Mom was dying of bone cancer at fifty-two. I was at the Seminary. One year from becoming a rabbi. Even with morphine, Mom was in terrible pain. She couldn't bear to be touched. I forgot myself and sat for a moment on the edge of her hospital bed. Her scream broke me. I thought to myself, it's all a darkness. I lost my faith.

"Then one afternoon, a month or so later, on an impulse, while riding the downtown Broadway bus, I recited those words from Psalm Fifty-one. I prayed, Master of the Universe, take my broken spirit as a sacrifice. I had a distinct physical sensation. I felt my prayer lift up the two pieces of my broken spirit, from my guts, and fuse them back together inside my heart. That's the only way I can describe it. The two pieces of my broken spirit were fused together again by prayer. I burst out crying. The bus stopped at 86th. I was crying tears of joy. My spirit was whole."

Levy said, "Whole, eh?"

"Pray, Fred. Lift yourself up."

"I'll give it a go, rabbi. I'll give it a go."

Sut had lunch with Chris at the Harvard Club. They had a choice of tables in the nearly empty main dining room. Chris chose to sit against the far wall to the right of JFK's portrait.

A gaunt Monsignor, class of '55, with cropped white hair, looked up at them from the near corner and said to the waiter, "More coffee, please."

Sut had a turn. The waiter's dark crimson jacket

verged on the maroon. And he wore a black tie. Maroon and black—like the shirt and tie of our waiter at Windows on the World. That waiter's face came back to him with appalling vividness: he had a pimple on his chin. He couldn't have been more than twenty-five. He was bald. Is he dead?

Sut said, "I wouldn't admit this to anyone else. But when I heard that Guy is missing, I felt glad—glad and guilty at the same time."

"I almost always feel glad and guilty at the same time."

"That guy with the red tie flashed through my mind in the shower this morning. I cried. You think God saved me for a purpose? Out of all those people? Not bloody likely. And yet, what happened to me Tuesday morning gave me an inkling—an intimation—of something about God that had never, never, occurred to me before."

His voice carried to the near corner in the quiet room. Monsignor Robbins pricked up his ears.

Sut said, "I saw a head on top of a car in the middle of Church Street. The hair was burned off. Where was God? I'll let you in on a secret. I felt Him in the guy with the red tie, the blackened head on the car. I felt His face shine on me with a black light. I saw it: a burst of black light. My teeth chattered. I glimpsed His darkened face—the face He showed when He had His only begotten Son tortured to death to redeem us.

"I knelt down, crossed myself, and kissed the sidewalk.

It was covered with papers, dust, big chunks of concrete, and sharp pieces of metal. I pulled one out of my shoe. Then I ran north. The North Tower collapsed behind me. I was caught by a rolling cloud of black dust and ashes. I couldn't breathe."

"Have a drink."

The Monsignor, a Professor of Canon Law at Fordham, envied Sut's sallow skin and the dark rings under his eyes. Show Yourself—for once—to me!

Amanda Stewart arrived at Guy's apartment a little after two thirty wheeling a black carry-on behind her. Judy, caught off guard by the luggage, nevertheless said, "You'll stay with me, of course, as long as you like. I'll sleep on the living room sofa."

"I wouldn't think of it. I'll take the sofa."

"No, I insist. How's your tooth?"

"Much better, thank you. I was scared of the root canal surgery. I had root canal work twenty years ago and it was excruciatingly painful. I remember very well. The doctor stuck a pin in my tooth and hit the nerve. Now it's easy. I hardly felt a thing. Dentistry has made real progress over the years. Guy neglected his teeth at college. It cost him a fortune to have them fixed."

"Did you have lunch?"

"I ate a ham sandwich on the Metroliner."

"Train food is awful. Are you sure I can't get you anything? A cup of tea?"

"A cup of tea would be nice."

Judy said, "I've got a perpetual lump in my throat. I can't swallow solid food. I live on canned soup."

They drank their tea at the kitchen table. It was the third time they'd met, and the first without Guy. They both expected him to walk into the room, pour some boiling water from the kettle into a cup, and drop in an Earl Grey tea bag. He was partial to Earl Grey.

A No. 9 train rattled the window. Judy was struck by the silence of the street. There's hardly any traffic. Amanda stirred her tea; her spoon clinked against her cup. Her back gum, on the lower right side, was sore. I still can't make out why Guy fell in love with her at first sight. She's pretty, yes, but conventionally so; big brown eyes, an upturned nose. Her nose is bright red.

Amanda said, "You think Guy's dead?"

"I know it."

"How can you be so sure?"

"I was going to lie to you, but I can't. I haven't slept in two nights. I gotta get it off my chest. I'm going crazy. I told Guy to jump. Yes, it's true. He said it was either jump or burn. I said, 'Jump, darling. Jump into my arms, where I'll hold you close for good.'"

Amanda asked, "And what did he say?"

"The phone went dead."

"You did the right thing."

"I hope so."

"I gave birth to him, woke up in the middle of the night to nurse him and sing him lullabies. I raised him, taught him right from wrong, and then, at thirty-two, he has to jump from the 102nd floor of the World Trade Center. What's it all for?"

Judy said, "Hold me. Please hold me."

"Come into my arms."

All afternoon, Amanda spoke to Judy about Guy in short bursts: "He was eight pounds, six ounces at birth. A baby Hercules! His first word was 'Crabgrass.' He got it off some commercial on TV. He was physically very well-coordinated and walked before he was a year old. On the other hand, he was a late reader. I worried that he was dyslexic, but he was just late. I taught him phonics. He started reading at eight and never stopped. He read *A Hundred Years of Solitude* when he was thirteen. I don't suppose he felt any pain, do you?"

"I don't imagine so."

"Guy worshiped his father when he was growing up. And Ronnie was a good father till he became a crackhead. Not a good husband, mind you—he played around. But a good father. Proud of Guy's athletic prowess. Guy excelled at pitching. Ronnie took him out to practice every Saturday. Guy once pitched a ball so fast, it caught on Ronnie's thumbnail and ripped it off. Guy was horrified. How long do you suppose it takes to fall 102 floors?"

"I don't want to know."

"I do, and I don't."

"You know what happened between Guy and his father. After that, Guy quit wrestling. He kept in shape, though."

"I loved his shape. I fell in love with his shape. The first thing I saw of him, out of the corner of my eyes, was his broad shoulders and slim hips."

"Guy enjoyed being projects manager. The day he was promoted, he said to me, 'Mom, I've got ten software engineers under me!' I suppose they're all missing."

"All except one."

"Could I talk with him?"

"Sut's the one I left for Guy. "

"How awkward for you! Don't worry. I won't call him. How come he survived?"

"He was drunk the night before and overslept. And he got drunk because Guy told him he and I were getting married."

"So Guy saved him."

"In a way."

Amanda said, "That's a laugh. Life's a joke."

Sept. 12, 2001. Wed. 10 p.m. *No work today. Spent more than 7 hrs. with Johanna trying to volunteer our services in the emergency. The stock market's closed; she joined me at the NY Blood Center on Amsterdam and 67th where we waited on line to give blood for 4 hrs. before being turned away. Next, on a tip, we waited on another line for 3 hrs. outside the Javits Center to give our names to a cop at a table.*

The kid ahead of us told the cop he was studying mortuary science. The cop said, "We'll be in touch."

Almost no traffic in the streets, and no planes overhead. Fall is in the air. It's cool enough for a light sweater.

Dinner at a crowded little Italian restaurant at 80th Street and Amsterdam. We ate outside. Amsterdam was jammed with people strolling in the clear, crisp air. Said Johanna, "We all feel a need to be together."

The breeze shifted, and we got a whiff of an acrid smell. A murmur ran up and down the avenue.

I'm proud of the American flags hanging from all the awnings on West End. Goddamn fucking Arabs. America attacked. Unbelievable. A new era in our history. We're vulnerable to be attacked on our own soil. I take it personally. "You may not be interested in history," says Trotsky. "But history is interested in you."

Johanna stopped flossing her teeth over the sink and called into the bedroom to Artie, "I'll tell you one thing. I've lost faith in eleven as a lucky number."

Sept. 13, 2001. Thurs. Noon. *This morn. Loki, the mischief maker, hid behind a tapestry hung in Sif's bedroom & when she turned on her side in her sleep, cut off her golden* *hair that reached her waist. "The mass of hair Loki dropped on the stone floor shimmered in a patch of morning light with different colors: yellow, orange, green."*

Johanna's blood pressure on awakening: 150/100. She's having a check-up with Abe next Fri. morn.

At Zabar's, Artie bought six loaves of sliced onion rye, four pounds of sliced Black Forest ham, two pounds of sliced Swiss cheese, and a large jar of Dijon mustard while Johanna picked up a large jar of Hellmann's mayonnaise and a box of fifty Ziploc sandwich bags at the Westside Market. Then they laid out ten pieces of bread at a time on the kitchen counter and made fifty ham and cheese sandwiches. It took them an hour and three quarters.

Artie smeared half the slices with mustard and half with mayo. Johanna covered each of them with one slice of cheese and two of ham. Once in a while, she tossed Muggs a bite. I've never worked side by side with Johanna in the kitchen before. It's a first in almost forty years. Artie's right hand, as he raised the butter knife loaded with mayo, grazed Johanna's left elbow. She smiled at him. Artie would remember thinking at that moment, this is happiness.

They took the fifty sandwiches, wrapped in sandwich bags, by cab to the Javits Center on 11th Avenue between 36th and 38th, where they turned them over to a cop for the volunteers combing the smoldering rubble downtown. Johanna read one of the photocopied posters plastered all over the walls:

Missing. Melissa Trevor. Five feet five. 30 years old. Blue eyes. Dirty blonde hair. Beauty mark on left cheek, beside mouth. Worked for Cantor Fitzgerald, 103rd floor. Please help us find our daughter Melissa.

Please call (516) 746-3351

Johanna said, "If Leslie died before me, I'd kill myself."

Sept. 14, 2001. Fri. 12:30 p.m. *Rewrote scene, Loki & Sif.*

Leslie having ultrasound 1 p.m. that should reveal baby's sex. She invited us & Pendeltons to dinner tonight for the news.

Johanna heard in the lobby that the neighborhood firehouse, Hook & Ladder 25 on 77th Street between Broadway and Amsterdam, was missing six men. She cooked two three-pound meat loaves, wrapped them in foil, and ran them over to the firehouse with Artie at three. Thirty or forty people were milling around the entrance with food and flowers. Johanna smelled corned beef and lilies. Lilies! Yuck! She held her nose. Artie squeezed inside, to the right of the parked fire engine, and put the loaves on the concrete floor next to three other offerings: a plastic rose, a plastic angel, and a red card written in a kid's hand.

September 14, 2001
Dearest Daddy,

Last night I looked up at the stars and matched each one with a reason why I miss you. I was doing great, but then I ran out of stars.

I hope you have a super birthday today.
XXX
Alice

Judy read in the *Times* that the 69th Regiment Armory on Lex between 25th and 26th Street was the designated central processing center for missing people. "Particularly important are hair samples for DNA testing." She plucked some brown hairs from Guy's brush and sealed them in an envelope.

She and Amanda stood in the long line that stretched beneath the Armory's barrel-shaped walls. They were stunned by the pale faces, the tears, the runny noses, the screams, the woman behind them who sobbed, "I wish I was dead!"

Judy got used to it all. Within an hour it seemed perfectly natural that a weeping stranger came up to her and said in a deep voice, "I have no hope."

Afterwards, Judy couldn't recall to whom she gave the envelope in the Armory. One of the queries on the seven-page missing persons questionnaire stayed with her: "Toenail characteristics: Deformed ( ) Dirty ( ) Decorated ( ) Other ____"

Leslie poked her head between the sliding glass doors to the deck and said, "It's nippy outside. We'll have drinks in the living room."

When the six of them were settled in front of the red brick fireplace, Chris said, "It's a boy!"

He passed around three ultrasound pictures. Caroline asked, "How can you tell from these?"

Leslie said, "This little thing here is a penis."

"I take your word for it."

Chris said, "We've chosen his name. We're calling him Samuel Richard."

Richard asked, "Who's Samuel?"

Chris said, "Artie's Dad."

Artie said, "I don't know what to say."

Johanna said, "Say thank you."

"Thank you."

Chris said, "You're welcome."

Richard thought, Why not Richard Samuel?

Caroline thought: Well, Samuel's an old American name. Sam Adams wasn't Jewish. Artie and Johanna took a cab home about eleven. All up and down West End Avenue, huddled outside the entrances to the buildings, people held flickering candles. Johanna spotted Fred Blair shielding a flame with his hand. The candles reminded Artie of the Yahrzeit lamp burning on the stove in Dad's memory. What would he have made of his great-grandson—and namesake—who wasn't going to be circumcised?

In bed, Johanna asked, "When Leslie said, 'this little thing is a penis,' what did you think of?"

"Sag Harbor. What else?"

Artie rolled over on his pillow; their foreheads almost touched. Each smiled in the dark at a memory shared for thirty-seven years. They were at a drunken weekend party in Sag Harbor. Some guy they didn't know, reeking of Scotch, had staggered up to Johanna, unzipped his fly, whipped out his cock, and said to her, "You know what this is?"

And Johanna had said, "It looks like a penis—only smaller."

Next morning, over Leslie's second cup of coffee, she said to Chris, "Your father was disappointed we didn't name the baby Richard."

"I know."

"Your mother was too."

"Tell me about it."

"I don't remember my grandpa Sam very well. I was only eight when he died. He smelled of stale cigarette smoke. Dad was pleased we named the baby after him."

"I'm glad."

"It was nice of you to suggest it."

"I'm a nice guy."

"True, but you suggested it because you felt guilty because you won't allow the baby to be circumcised."

"That's true, too."

"It's strange to think that when my grandpa Sam died, he was only five years older than Dad is now. Dad is scared he's going to die at the same age—seventy-three."

"That's in only four years."

"Five," Leslie said. "Dad'll be sixty-eight in December. That's old. Nearly seventy. He told me in July, before he started his new book, that it would be his last. He said, 'I'm winding down.'"

"Well, I'm all wound up."

"About what?"

"Sut. I'm anxious about Sut. He's in bad shape. He had a kind of vision on 9/11."

"What kind of vision?"

"A religious vision. Cuckoo."

Leslie: "Well, he went through a lot."

"He saw a burned head on top of a car."

"In his vision?"

"No, on Church Street."

Leslie: "I once saw a bloody corpse on Riverside Drive."

"What a world! What in the world will Samuel Richard Pendleton see?"

"I don't wanna think about it."

Artie said to Adam, "I thought I smelled pot."

"Come in. Come in. Shut the door. Good to see you. Sit by me. Bring the chair nearer the bed. Want a drag? It's courtesy of Jerry and Hal. Three hundred bucks an ounce. I smoke a joint a day. Sometimes two. This is my second today. Two joints a day keeps my nausea—and depression—away. I have suicidal thoughts. At the same time, I want desperately to live. Go figure. I'm on Interferon, Prozac, and pot. After the IV drip in the mornings, I spend the rest of the day stoned in bed. Have a drag."

Artie took two.

Adam said, "Watch your ashes! I already burned a hole in one sheet. When's the last time you smoked pot?"

"At my sixty-fifth birthday party."

"Yes, of course, I remember. You were really stoned. I'm stoned all the time. It's the way to spend old age! I watch the rescue workers on CNN. I lie here wondering if the Interferon will knock out my cancer. That's all I think about these days. I'm in a rut.

"Rosh Hashana starts Monday night. I won't be in shul for the first time in fifteen years. You and Shirley can pray for me."

He laughed. Artie joined in.

Adam said, "I grew up Orthodox in the Bronx. I went to a yeshiva on the Grand Concourse. The Days of Awe scared me shitless. Even as a teenager, I believed that in the ten days between Rosh Hashana and Yom Kippur, God decides who lives and who dies in the coming year. I sweated them out.

"Well, I'm sixty-five. With cancer. Now every day is a day of awe. I wonder every day: will I die in the coming year? Or the year after that? Do I have five years left to live? A question you tell me you often ask yourself. The days of our years—where's that from? I tell you: these are our days of awe."

"I'll buy that."

"Save your money! I can get it for you wholesale."

Adam laughed again and so did Artie, without knowing why.

At dinner, Artie ate three helpings of Shirley's spaghetti and eggplant plus a big dish of Coffee Heath Bar Crunch ice cream. Jerry and Hal cleared the table.

Jerry said to Artie, "Johanna tells me you couldn't get connected at the Javits Center. Go to Pier 94. Safe Harbor is looking for volunteers. Say I sent you from the mayor's office."

"What's Safe Harbor?"

"A victims' assistance agency."

"I'll go down tomorrow morning. Is there any more ice cream?"

Johanna said, "You've had enough."

"I'm still ravenous. Pot makes me eat like I've got two assholes."

Hal said, "I wish I had two assholes."

Back home at eleven, Artie popped a Viagra. Three quarters of an hour later, he said to Johanna, "That was good for you. How was it for me?"

"Thought you'd never ask."

After walking Muggs in the morning, Johanna said to Artie, "I feel crummy. I think I'm coming down with the flu. I'm going back to bed."

Artie felt her forehead. "You're cool as a cucumber."

"I'm not feverish. But I ache all over. My hair hurts. And I'm nauseated. Do me a favor. Fix the bed."

Artie straightened the sheets and fluffed up the pillows. Johanna stripped to her bra and panties. "I'm gonna take a nap. You go volunteer at the Pier."

"I'll wait for you to wake."

"What for? Go."

"Did you take your blood pressure this morning?"

"It was down a little. 150/95."

"I'll wait for you to wake up in case you need something."

"I won't need anything. Make yourself useful. Go volunteer!"

Artie said, "Call me when you wake up."

His bald scalp brushed the American flag hung from the end of the awning. Another perfect fall day: a few leaves on the pear tree at the curb had turned brown. The white impatiens planted in the tree bed were drooping. Artie took a cab to Pier 94 at 54th Street and 12th Avenue. He glanced at two of the hundreds of homemade picture posters fastened to the chain link fence: "Where are you?" "We miss you!"

The cop on duty let him through the door to his left when he said, "I was sent here to volunteer by Jerry Jacobson at the mayor's office."

Artie talked himself onto Safe Harbor's volunteer list and pinned his ID card to his shirt, but the young woman in charge, swamped with work, left him on his own in the crowded, cavernous hall. He latched on to another Safe Harbor volunteer named Isabella Levinson who showed him the ropes and explained the organization's financial policies.

"We're giving away money, up to ten thousand dollars, to victim's families, and people who lost their livelihood—delivery men, dish washers. One guy—an illegal Mexican—made a good two hundred bucks a week shining shoes in the North Tower. On 9/11 he walked down seventy floors. I'm working on his case.

"Help people fill out these forms—someone in the victim's family must fill out the New York State Crime Victims Board Affidavit. One bit of advice. Don't say to anybody, 'I know how you feel,' because you don't. Start with the top folder. Here—Joseph Sanseli. Call his name out over there. Then find two empty chairs, and you're in business."

"I'm Artie Rubin. Please sit down, Mr. Sanseli. How can I help you?"

"My son Ed is missing. He worked at Thorpe and Fletcher on the 102nd floor of the South Tower. Ed maxed out on his Visa, so two weeks ago, I lent him mine to buy two round-trip tickets to Hong Kong for him and his wife, Tess. Their tenth anniversary is on November sixteenth. They have no children. Up till Tuesday, that was my chief sorrow. Little did I know!

"The two tickets come to $2,370. Mr. Rubin, I'm a retired car salesman. My wife has diabetes. We live on a strict budget. Two thousand three hundred seventy dollars is a lot of money for me at this time. I understand you might be able to reimburse me that amount. Is it possible? Can you help me?"

"I'm sorry, Mr. Sanseli. Safe Harbor gives awards up to ten grand—but only to make up a loss of earnings or support. We're not allowed to reimburse you for those plane tickets. I'm so sorry."

Sanselli said, "Well, it's a damn shame. Do you have any grandchildren?"

Artie answered "No," and let it drop.

Sanselli said with satisfaction. "That's too bad."

My uncontrollable crying in the shower! Every single morning! It's got me down. Maybe I should see a therapist. What do You think? But above all, tell me this: why did You spare me?

Johanna called Artie on his cell phone at one forty. She said, "I had a good sleep but I still feel crummy."

"I'm coming right home."

"That'd be great. My nausea's gone—thank God.

There's nothing in the house to eat. I didn't have breakfast. I need something in my stomach. I'm a little light-headed. I don't wanna get out of bed. Pick me up an assortment of vegetable salads and a pita at Zabar's. As a matter of fact, bag the pita. Get me one croissant for lunch and one for tomorrow. I'll have a fat, flaky, buttery croissant smeared with honey for breakfast. Forget the calories! Let's live it up!"

Tick-tock.

In the late afternoon, Chris took his dad to hit some balls at Tennis Port in Long Island City. Chris borrowed a basket of balls from the pro and fed them to his dad for an hour. Richard worked up a sweat. He was getting in shape for next Saturday's senior doubles match at the Meadow Club in Southampton, where once upon a time, hour after hour, he fed Chris balls on the grass court.

Why doesn't he name his son after me? He's under some obligation to Rubin to name the boy after Rubin's father. What could it be? Rubin wants the boy circumcised! That's it—I'm sure. Circumcision's big with Jews. Chris feels like I do about it. He's naming the boy Samuel to make up for not circumcising him. Jews and Muslims cut themselves off from us—ha! ha!—by circumcision. Damned contentious Semites! Their war's spread here!

The big gray tom cat with the scarred nose rubbed up against Sut's right ankle as he looked down from the deck into the garden and said to Leslie and Chris, "Your marigolds are lovely this year. All yellow and gold! Beat it! I'm allergic to cats."

The tom leaped off the teak deck and disappeared in the dark beyond the marigolds.

Sut said to Chris, "Those nineteen hijackers were possessed by what Dostoevsky called 'the spirit of self-annihilation—the spirit of non-being'—the cleverest spirit of them all, says Dostoevsky. I know you don't believe it, but this spirit exists. Satan is, I think, only mentioned once in the Book of Common Prayer. During the baptismal service. 'Do you renounce Satan and all the spiritual forces of wickedness that rebel against God?' My question is—what's Satan's relationship to his Creator?"

Chris: "You got me."

My brother and the hijackers come from the same place—a world with a god and a devil, a heaven and a hell. I haven't lived there since I was thirteen.

Johanna said, "I feel fine. Absolutely fine. Whatever I had yesterday—obviously some kind of a bug—is completely gone."

She went for the bread box. "And now for my croissant smeared with honey."

Artie said, "I ate it."

"You ate my croissant?"

"With honey."

"You're kidding."

"I never bullshit you."

"Then go buy me another."

"I didn't eat it. I was kidding. I'm glad you're all better."

"Know what? You have a sadistic streak. It shows in your work. When do I get to read *Norse Myths*?"

"When I've finished a complete draft. That way, you can judge its structure. Be warned! It's not written in the vernacular. I can't come up with a single illustration."

Johanna said, "One will come to you," marveling as always at his compulsion to make pictures out of words and turn words into pictures. "You're an alchemist. No, not an alchemist. I know what you are! You're a sorcerer! You change dead trees into live books." She kissed his lips. "Floss your teeth, sorcerer! You have bad breath."

Sept. 17, 2001. Mon. Noon. *This morn. Thor, Sif's pissed-off husband, made Loki swear to replace her shorn hair. Sif is a fertility goddess; her hair symbolic of grain. "Her cropped head looked like it was covered with the stubble left on a harvested wheat field."*

Johanna wore her shoulder-length auburn hair up when she was young.

Her flu-like symptoms yesterday all gone. She almost never gets sick & had me worried. She said, apropos of nothing, "I love this town! It's the capital of the world. What a privilege to be able to afford a comfortable life here! Here's to New York! Tough old New York! Ever new!"

Rosh Hashana begins at sundown. Services 6:30.

Citigroup 38.25, Intel 23.50, Cisco 13, Microsoft 52.80, Johnson & Johnson 55.65.

Johanna said, "Quite a morning! First the Fed cuts its interest rates and now the European Central Bank lowers its lending rates. I'm amazed stocks haven't fallen much, but if you ask me, we could be in for a hell of a recession. Six days ago, the economy was stagnant. Now, my guess is that it's going to contract, maybe by as much as one percent annually."

Leslie said, "The Holland brothers are both missing."

"Jean Miller told me."

"When the World Trade Center was bombed in '93, Johnny Holland carried a complete stranger down more than a hundred flights of stairs. I agree about the economy. You look tired, Mom."

"I had a bug over the weekend. I don't think it's completely out of my system."

"Why don't you take the rest of the day off?"

"No, I feel fine. Really I do."

Leslie said, "Do you think we should call all our clients?"

"Not yet. Let things settle down a bit. So we know more about what we think is happening. By the way, I notice there's no more talk in Congress about preserving the Social Security surplus. Jean lives in Brooklyn Heights. She says that the wind from Lower Manhattan smells sickeningly sweet."

"Sweet? Why sweet?"

"Because of the corpses rotting under the ruins."

Artie made himself two scrambled eggs and bacon for lunch. On his way out of the building, he gave Lawrence the handsome black doorman five bucks to walk Muggs at three, then took a cab to Pier 94. The cop outside checked his ID, and Artie went in the door to his left.

He heard a grey-haired man say to Isabella Levinson, "Why would anybody want to kill my daughter? Nancy didn't have a mean bone in her body. She never harmed a soul. I want revenge. That's not like me. I'm a good Catholic. I don't like what I've become."

Artie's first client said to him, "I have four kids—two boys and two girls—all under twelve. My husband Bill is missing. He was a sales manager for Harbinger ATL. I have no idea what I'm going to do. None at all. I can't think."

Next was a couple in their early sixties. The pasty-faced wife said, "We only had this one son, and he was our world. And he was handsome. And he was good to us. He paid our rent. And now he's gone."

After them, Artie cared for another couple around the

same age. This time the husband spoke up, "Kevin was our chief financial support. Here are his tax returns to prove it. He was thrilled he was recently hired as an emerging markets manager at Vitro Intercapital on the ninety-second floor of the South Tower. Monday, September tenth, was his first day of work."

Artie's last client said, "I'm a widower with bad arthritis. Look at these fingers! I can't bend them more than this. I lived with my daughter Amy, who was a government bond broker. She was married to Ken, a derivatives broker, also at Webster and Kling. We know their office caught fire. Amy was five months pregnant. I know in my heart that they're dead. I lost the three of them."

Artie helped all his clients fill out New York State Crime Victims Board Death Affidavit. He skipped two questions: "Are there unreimbursed burial expenses as a result of the victim's death?" and "Before the victim's death was medical treatment received as a result of the crime?"

He said to Johanna over the phone: "I gave nearly forty thousand dollars this afternoon to six people who really need the money. If only I could do more for them. I feel that in the abstract. Actually, I can't feel anything. I'm numb."

Artie got home at five and read his mail:

Dear Mr. Rubin,

As the result of the terrorist attack on the Twin Towers on 9/11, Congregation Etz Chaim has cancelled its trip to Israel on October sixteenth. Your check in the amount of $999 will be fully refunded. We hope that conditions will allow us in the near future to demonstrate in person our solidarity with our Israeli brothers and sisters.

May I wish you a better New Year than this last, and inscription in the Book of Life.

Rabbi David Klugman

Subj: Cancelled trip.
Date 9/17/2001 3:01:52 PM Eastern Daylight Time.
From: Artjo
To: Danik

Dear Dani,
You'll have to find another way to send your folks sneakers. My trip to Israel has been cancelled. I'm relieved. Israel has become a strange land to me—an occupying power, partly possessed by belief in its tribal god who gives it license to oppress a subject people in the name of a covenant Abraham made with him in the Bronze Age. The ideal of a secular, humane, social democratic Israel of my youth is all but gone, replaced by a new messianic religious nationalism that resembles resurgent militant Islam.

Even our secular nationalists have made a religion out of a "Greater Israel," their new god. O, my people–you break my heart.
Love to Alice & Zvi

Happy New Year!
Artie

Subj: Re: Cancelled trip
Date: 9/17/2001 3:10:34 PM Eastern Daylight Time
From: Danik
To: Artjo

Dear Artie,
Your heart breaks easy. Israel must smash the Intifada—whatever it takes. My parents regularly take the number 20 bus on Jaffa Rd. in Jerusalem. Let them die in bed.

I've got an Israeli friend flying home next week who'll deliver the sneakers. Thanks anyway.

Happy New Year!
Best to Johanna.
Dani

Though Rabbi Klugman couldn't afford it, he celebrated the coming of the New Year by handing a twenty-dollar bill to the black bag lady who hung around Broadway and 86th.

She said, "You Jews are filthy rich. Don't get me wrong. I'm grateful. I'd starve if it weren't for you rich Upper West Side Jews."

Klugman was running late. He didn't get to the mikveh on 110th Street until three thirty. He followed the custom of pious Jewish men who purify themselves for Rosh Hashana in a ritual bath.

A bunch of bearded Jews taking showers together creeps me out. Can't help thinking: gas chamber. We're an ugly-looking lot. How about the one with a hooked nose and pale skin—'a shade away from the morgue.' Who wrote that? Get a load of his huge dick! Klugman switched thoughts. Philip Roth wrote that in *The Counterlife.*

Klugman stepped naked into the small blue tile pool that smelled of chlorine. He bobbed in the chest-high tepid water ten times, for the ten Cabalistic attributes of God: crown, wisdom, intelligence, love, judgment, compassion, lasting endurance, majesty, foundation of the world, diadem. The crown is Nothingness; the diadem is the Shekhinah—the feminine Divine Presence, identified with the Oral Torah, the Sabbath, the Community of Israel, the Mother of souls, who intercedes for her children, the Jews.

One. Rav Kook says we can identify with the forces through which God acts, but not with God as He is in Himself. Two. You once acted on me, while riding a bus, with some words from Psalm Fifty-one. Three. I must take stock of my sins during the Days of Awe and repent. Why don't I visit Mom's grave? I keep postponing it. Four. I said to myself, I'm too busy writing my four High Holiday sermons, worrying about how to make ends meet on my salary, getting ready for the opening of Hebrew School, patching up marriages, visiting the sick, burying the dead. Five. My mind's a blank.

Six. I must call Fred Levy. Seven. Who am I kidding? I know why I don't visit Mom's grave. I'm still pissed at her for dying on me. That was nine years ago! I'm going on thirty-seven! Get over it! Eight. Forgive Mom and visit her grave. Nine. Those are my tasks—with Your help—for the Days of Awe. Ten. Why the hell did Dad marry again?

Klugman said, "I wish you all a happier New Year than the one just passed. Terror and desolation have come to our city, and we are gathered today..."

This is my first Rosh Hashana in shul without Adam. It's like being a widow. God forbid! Artie's bored stiff. He's leafing through the prayer book. I'm bored too. The evening service of Rosh Hashana is a crushing bore, apart from the blowing of the shofar. A ram's horn. The ram caught in a thicket. Isaac bound on the altar. I always picture old man Abraham holding a butcher knife. Nobody asks Sarah's opinion about sacrificing her son. Judaism's a male religion. Yet Mama was the observant one in the family. She wouldn't wind her wristwatch on the Shabbos. I come here on the High Holidays in your memory, Mama. If Adam dies, I hope I'll have the strength to go on like you did after Daddy died.

Artie was left with something Klugman said: "Rosh Hashana is the only Jewish holiday that begins with the New Moon. During the ten Days of Awe, as the moon waxes and its light is renewed, the soul in darkness turns to God for illumination and renewal."

Fred Levy squirmed in his aisle seat.

Time to get up. Today's the eighteenth. The day Guy would have had a sperm test. Do you get the results right away? We might have known by tonight whether he could have been a father. I would like to have been gotten pregnant by him and had a boy with his brown hair and brown eyes. Maybe, in a parallel universe last Tuesday didn't happen, and the parallel me rushes home tonight after work and learns that the parallel Guy's not sterile. The parallel we get married on June second and have a son with brown hair. Or maybe a daughter with a nose like mine.

This is the only world there is. I don't believe that Heaven crap. I'll never see Guy again.

Where's his gorgeous body? The last morning of his life—the imprint of his thumb on a new tube of Colgate toothpaste. I'll keep it forever. Guy had such thick fingers! He gently pulled my nipples. Amanda saved him from strangling his father. I'm sorry I gave her Guy's hairbrush. She so wanted it. What am I going to do with his clothes? I've got to go through all his things. Can't face it. I can't afford to stay in this apartment. It's too noisy, anyway. That's the second siren in less than a minute. The traffic's back—worse than before 9/11. Can't stand it. Got to find a quiet place to live before the end of the month. I'd like to go home to Paterson and have my mom take care of me.

Artie read to himself from the *Mahzor*—the prayer book for the Days of Awe, "Praised are You, Lord our God, King of the Universe...who made me in His image, who made me a Jew."

Ergo, God's Jewish. Made in our image. All these Jews packed together for Rosh Hashana. Faces I haven't seen in a year. The fellow with the sad black eyes. And his mousy wife. Their twelve-year-old daughter has his sad, Jewish eyes and her mother's small chin. The kid looks something like Anne Frank. The father looks bored. Still, he brings his family here on the High Holidays. Why? I'm bored too. Why do I come? Because of the crowd. I get a charge out of being in a big crowd of Jews doing what we've done this morning for thousands of years. You gotta give us credit. We hang in there.

A while later, he read, "Three score and ten our years may number, Four score years if granted the vigor."

Amen!

Then jump, darling! Jump into my arms, where I'll hold you close for good! Then jump, darling! Jump into my arms, where I'll hold you close for good! Then jump, darling! Jump into my arms, where I'll hold you close for good!

When the Ark was opened, Artie had a vision of Odin in the Land of the Dead at the moment that he learns from Hel that he must die. He saw his bared teeth, his empty left eye socket and bright blue right eye, his bony cheekbones and bristling eyebrows like those on what's-his-name there blowing his nose. But what about Odin's beard and hair?

The service went on and on. Artie yawned. What's this? Shirley, on his left, was standing beside him. She called out Adam's name for inclusion in the communal prayer for the sick. Artie was astonished to hear her pray:

"May He who blessed our ancestors, Abraham, Isaac, and Jacob, Sarah, Rebecca, and Leah, bless and heal my husband Adam. May the Holy One in mercy strengthen him and heal him soon, body and soul, together with others who suffer illness. And let us say: Amen."

Shirley caught Artie's look and said, "What have I got to lose?"

Artie perked up again at the beginning of Klugman's sermon. "This morning's Torah portion, Genesis 21, is—like much of Torah—great prose. Precise, concise, and visually evocative. 'Sarah saw the son Hagar the Egyptian had borne to Abraham, playing. She said to Abraham, "Cast out that slave-woman and her son, for the son of that slave shall not share in the inheritance with my son Isaac."'

"Playing! The verb brings the scene to life. I imagine little Ishmael, with the hot sun behind him, trying to step on his shadow like I used to do as a kid.

"'The matter distressed Abraham greatly, for it concerned a son of his. But God said to Abraham, "Do not be distressed over the boy or your slave; whatever Sarah tells you, do as she says, for it is through Isaac that offspring shall be continued for you. As for the son of the slave-woman, I will make a nation of him, too, for he is your seed."'

"Abraham is interested in one thing and one thing only—the continuance of his line through Isaac. For only those descendants, of all nations, will serve God. He obeys his wife.

"'Early next morning, Abraham took some bread and a skin of water, and gave them to Hagar. He placed them on her shoulder, together with the child, and sent her away. And she wandered about in the wilderness of Beersheba. When the water was gone from the skin, she left the child under one of the bushes, and went and sat down at a distance, a bowshot away; for she thought, Let me not look on as the child dies. And sitting thus afar, she burst into tears.'

"Notice the homey details—early next morning, bread, a skin of water. Abraham loads the bread and water on Hagar's shoulder, along with their son. What does Abraham feel as he watches Hagar walk away? We haven't a clue. Kierkegaard calls Abraham the Knight of Faith. The kabbalists said the faith of Abraham was described by the prophet Isaiah (41:8) when God calls him, 'Abraham, My lover.' I imagine him trembling in an ecstasy of submission to the will of his Beloved. Abraham submits, and Hagar wanders with Ishmael in the desert around Beersheba.

"I hiked there one summer. The stones are cracked by the heat. The parched grey-green bushes are covered with tiny white snails. When Hagar's waterskin runs dry, she puts Ishmael in the shade of a bush, encrusted with snails, and sits at a distance, a bow shot away. How far is that? I can't say. Our ancestors knew. We're heirs to a haunting archaic phrase that still connotes the distance that separates the weeping mother and her abandoned child.

"'God heard the cry of the boy, and an angel of God called to Hagar from heaven and said to her, "What troubles you, Hagar? Fear not, for God has heeded the cry of the boy where he is. Come lift up the boy and hold him by the hand, for I will make a great nation of him."'

"God heeds the cry of the boy—not his mother's tears. Ishmael is the hero of this story, plotted by God, and the phrase 'A bow shot away' now serves another purpose; it presages his destiny.

"'God opened Hagar's eyes and she saw a well of water. She went and filled the skin with water, and let the boy drink. God was with the boy, and he grew up;

he dwelt in the wilderness and became a bowman. He lived in the wilderness of Paran; and his mother got a wife for him from the land of Egypt.'

"And their descendants became the Arabs—a great nation, but not the servants of God. Isaac's descendants—we Jews—are."

Artie glazed over. I wonder how Myra Fuchs is making out? Sooner or later, she'll have to put Jacob into a nursing home. I know Myra. She'll feel guilty because she's honest enough to acknowledge that she'll relish her freedom—not having to care for Jacob anymore.

I'm short of breath. Or is it my imagination? It's my imagination. Still, I'm glad I'm seeing Abe on Friday.

Shirley read from her prayer book, "On Rosh Hashana it is written and on Yom Kippur it is sealed: How many shall leave this world and how many shall be born into it, who shall live and who shall die, who shall live out the limit of his days and who shall not, who shall perish by fire and who by water, who by sword and who by beast..." and who from a metastasized melanoma.

Sept. 18, 2001. Tues. 8 p.m. *Glimpsed Odin's anguished face in the Land of the Dead this morning during services at shul & stayed home after lunch from the afternoon service to make a charcoal sketch in the style of a Viking carving. It didn't work. Maybe something realistic would do the trick. In what medium?*

Want to portray Odin at the moment that he learns from Hel that he will die at Ragnarok. But how?

Johanna begged off dinner tonight with Leslie & Chris. Says she's tired. She looks haggard, aged. She has permanent bags under her eyes, the skin sags from her neck. I've never loved her more.

Artie arrived at services late the next morning; he hadn't intended going at all, but had made no progress with a realistic pencil sketch of Odin and thought that maybe an idea would come to him while he was wool-gathering in shul. Maybe the evocation of one god would again bring another to mind.

He grabbed a seat in the last row in time to hear Klugman talk about today's portion of Torah. Klugman spotted Artie coming in. Rubin! My inspiration! Your remark in my office back in August gave me the theme of my sermon.

Klugman looked around. Not an empty seat in the house. Must be fifteen hundred people here. Most of them won't like this.

"Rashi says that we read about the Binding of Isaac in Genesis 22 on the second day of Rosh Hashana to remind God during the Days of Awe that our fore-father Abraham was willing to sacrifice his beloved son to prove his devotion to Him. May Abraham's piety rebound in our favor!

"The text also reminds us that God spares the boy. Muslims believe that Abraham offered Ishmael up on that mountain in the land of Moriah. In both versions of the story, God spares the child. Can we Jews—or can Muslims—do less? What about sparing each other's kids?

"Israelis and Palestinians are killing each other's children. I'll name only five: the Kahdar brothers, Ashraf and Bilal, aged five and eight, and the three Schijveschuurder kids, Hemda, two, Itzhak, four, and Raya, fourteen. The two Arab boys were killed by shrapnel when the IDF rocketed Hamas headquarters in Nablus on July 31. The Schijveschuurders were among seven children murdered by a suicide bomber in Jerusalem on August 9.

"I have two sons, Joel and Michael. As God would have it, Joel is four—Itzhak Schijveschuurder's age, and Michael is five—like Ashraf Kahdar. Four-year-olds are rebellious.

"Joel says 'I won't!' and 'Try and make me!'

"I imagine Itzhak Schijveschuurder was pretty much the same. Five-year-olds are obedient—particularly to their mommies. Michael falls all over himself to obey his mommy.

"Anne tells him, 'Pick up your underwear from the floor,' and he hops to.

"I imagine Ashraf Khadar was pretty much the same.

"We're not responsible for the sins of the Palestinians. Their suicide bombers—and the Islamist organizations behind them—have made a covenant with death. But I say that even though it was inadvertent, the killing of the Khadar brothers was also a sin. They were innocents. On Rosh Hashana all Jews stand as one before God. He accounts us, scattered throughout the earth, as a single holy assemblage.

"During the Days of Awe, we communally confess our sins and pray together for forgiveness. In memory of the innocent boy Isaac, whom God spared, let's pray for Him to forgive us, His holy people, for killing the Khadar brothers and every other Palestinian child we kill. There have been eight since the last day of July."

Klugman heard grumbling from the crowd.

"I'm having a heart attack."

"Mom!"

"Leslie, call Abe Raskin—his number's in my Filofax. Tell him I'm having a heart attack. I know it. Can't be anything else. My chest—I've never felt such pain. Like a man standing on the middle of my chest. A fat man. He's crushing me. Pain's also down my left arm and up my jaw. On the left side. I'm all clammy. Weak in the knees. And dizzy. I must sit. Oh Leslie, I'm dying!"

"Hang on, mom, I got the number. I'll call."

"Hurry!"

"The line's busy."

"Keep trying."

"Still busy."

"Try again."

"It's busy."

"Keep trying."

"Wait! It's ringing."

Johanna said, "I wanna die. When I die, the pain will stop."

"Leslie Pendleton—that's right. Johanna Rubin's daughter. Johanna Rubin. Doctor Raskin's patient. Tell him she's having a heart attack. I'll wait."

Mom's turned gray. If she dies now, the shock—I could lose the baby. Hell, I'm tougher than that. "Doctor Raskin? This is Leslie Pendleton, Johanna Rubin's daughter. She says she's having a heart attack. Yes, in her chest and down her left arm and up her jaw, on the left side. She feels weak."

Johanna said, "And nauseous."

Leslie said, "And nauseous. We're in our office at 45th between Fifth and Sixth."

"Daddy's probably still in shul. Leave a message on his cell."

"Mom, I can't hear the doctor! No, I was talking to Mom. You want me to put her on? Okay, I'll tell her."

She said to Johanna, "The doctor says don't move. He says I should call an ambulance and get you to Columbia Presbyterian as soon as possible. He'll meet us in the emergency room." She spoke again into the phone. "We'll see you in the emergency room."

Leslie dialed 911, ordered an ambulance, and dialed again.

Johanna said, "Call daddy."

"That's what I'm doing. I got his voice mail."

"Hang up and call again in a little while. Tell him the news in person. No, wait. I may not have time to say good-bye. Let me speak. Artie? Darling, meet me at the Columbia-Presbyterian emergency room. I'm having a heart attack. Oh, Artie, this could be good-bye. Good-bye, darling. I love you."

She handed Leslie the phone and asked, "Who're you calling now?"

"Chris? Listen! Bad news. No, I'm okay. It's Mom. She thinks she's having a heart attack. We're at the office waiting for the ambulance. Meet us in the emergency room at Columbia-Presbyterian."

She said to Johanna, "He wishes you luck."

Leslie hung up.

Johanna said, "Give us a kiss."

"There! And one for good measure." She wiped away a drop of sweat from Johanna's chin with her fingertips.

Johanna said, "I've peed in my pants."

The words and melody of a spiritual went through her head: "Death, ain't you got no shame."

Johanna in the ambulance: Please don't let me die! That was a prayer. A prayer! From me! I'm crazy with fear. All hooked up to oxygen, an IV drip, an EKG. Just like on TV. What's the EKG say?

The Korean paramedic said, "Don't lift your head, lady. Lie back and relax. You'll be okay."

He took her pulse. Warm fingertips pressed the inside of her left wrist beneath her thumb. The touch of a human hand. For the last time. She watched Leslie dial her cell phone from a padded bench. She's green around the gills. Why, oh why, did she have to witness this? Four months pregnant. Her pregnancy and my death; they'll be linked forever in her mind. It can't be helped. She's got through to Artie. The siren. Can't hear what she's saying.

Leslie: "Dad will meet us in the emergency room."

I won't make it. Poor Artie! I'll bet that right this minute, he's taking a stiff drink. Or two. Or three. He'll drink plenty from now on. He missed a spot shaving this morning—above his right upper lip, in the corner. His whiskers are white. His hairy right ear—Esau. I won't trim Esau again. And Artie and I won't fuck at the Monaco in Venice on the night of February twenty-second. No fortieth anniversary for us. Why don't they give me something for the pain?

The paramedic took her blood pressure. How high is it? I can't tell from his inscrutable face. He's cross-eyed. The last face I'll ever see—a cross-eyed Chinaman.

Artie will remarry. A younger woman. He'll get her to trim Esau. And balance the checkbook and manage his investments. He has a deep need to be taken care of by the woman he loves. I gave in to him, though his helplessness infuriated me. His mother spoiled him. He's a mama's boy. With a child's imagination. He'll dedicate his new book to my memory. He knows I want to be cremated. Mom's ashes in that cardboard box were greasy and filled with bits of singed bone. Dad and I scattered them among the rhododendron along the backyard fence in New Rochelle. At least five pounds of them!

Artie in the cab heading uptown: three stiff drinks and I'm cold sober. If Johanna dies, I'll kill myself. But how? I'll find out from the Hemlock Society.

Sept. 19, 2001. Wed. 11:30 p.m. *Just before noon, while I was in shul, Johanna suffered an acute coronary occlusion in her left main coronary artery. Arterial plaque—a clot—has blocked the flow of blood to a segment of her heart, killing some of its muscle.*

She's in the coronary intensive care unit at Columbia-Presbyterian, under the care of John Starkie, a distinguished cardiologist—the head of the cardiology service at the hospital—who was brought into the case by Abe Raskin. Starkie supervised an angiogram, then sat me down in the waiting room with Leslie and Chris. I took notes on what he said.

"Your wife has a life-threatening mural thrombus—a large clot on the wall of the ventricle. Because of extensive damage to her heart muscle, an operation isn't feasible. We're treating

her with anticoagulants to prevent the clot from propagating and embolizing. We're also giving her morphine and Celexa for her pain and anxiety."

"What're her chances, doctor? Tell me the truth."

"Half such patients die within 8 to 12 hours."

Starkie allowed me a minute or two with Johanna when the morphine took hold.

She yawned & said, "I want to say good-bye, but you look so sad, I haven't got the heart. So to speak. I don't feel anxious. Or pain. I don't feel anything. Except drowsy."

I left Leslie and Chris in the waiting room about six, when I went home to walk and feed Muggs. I brought a pizza & Cokes back to the hospital, where we stayed till midnight.

Then the nice head nurse in the coronary ICU said Johanna has passed the first crisis, and sent us home to get some sleep.

Well, what do you know! I lived through the night. Any pain? No pain. Must still be on morphine. Everything's at a remove: discs stuck across my chest, wires, tubes from my nose, the catheter in the vein in my left arm, the puncture from the angiogram in my left groin, the yellow blips on the screen. My heartbeat. Blip! Blip! Tick-tock!

Chris will help Leslie through my death. He's thoughtful and kind. Ruddy cheeks. And what lovely, thick hair. Ah, youth! He'll never go bald. A young good-looking blond and blue-eyed Aryan. Leslie never dated a Jew. Not one! I suppose it's Oedipal. She needed a man completely different from Artie. Chris is so physical! He plays tennis, squash, golf. He sails. Bet he's a great lay.

Artie was good but unimaginative, which is odd for such an imaginative artist. He didn't like me on top. It put him off his rhythm. I loved it. Skewered, astride him. His dick seemed to reach from my clitoris to the roof of my mouth. Still, doing it his way, we always came together.

Because of Chris, Sam won't be circumcised. Leslie told me that Artie told her sorrowfully that he's the last Jew in his family. No loss.

Chris will be a loving father. And Leslie will be a loving mother. I was a loving mother. I mothered Mom during her depressions. One breakdown after another all through my childhood and adolescence. She was allergic to those early antidepressants. What're they called again? They stopped her from peeing. Once, at fourteen, when Daddy was in LA on business, I rushed her to the New Rochelle Hospital emergency room at three in the morning to be catheterized.

Mom said to the resident, "This is a new low for me. In addition to being suicidally depressed, I can't pee. My bladder's full, and I can't empty it. Help me! I'm about to burst!"

Mom's life was sad. Mine was happy. Death, ain't you got no shame?

Artie caught a couple of hours sleep, then went back up to the hospital at six thirty, where he spoke in the waiting room with Starkie.

Starkie said, "Your wife's doing okay. But she's not out of the woods yet. Not by a long shot. Her enzyme count is high—very high, which means severe damage to her heart muscle. She has two continuing serious symptoms. An extra ventricular beat, which is in essence an extra heart beat. And ventricular tachycardia. Her heart's beating too fast. This can develop into ventricular fibrillation, which means that instead of pumping, the heart quivers. We're hoping the anticoagulants will work. We'll just have to wait and see."

"Can I visit her?"

"Not yet. I know you want to stay here and hang around the waiting room all day, but do yourself a favor and go home. Waiting all day in the waiting room doing nothing makes you crazy. I'll call if there's any change in her condition.

"By the way, I like your book on Southwestern American Indian mythology very much. Particularly the section on Navaho myths. The Five Worlds, First Man, First Woman, the Flood. I grew up on a Navaho Reservation called Fort Defiance in Arizona. My father was a Presbyterian missionary."

Artie thought of First Man standing on the eastern side of the First World. He was the Dawn, the Life Giver. First Woman stood in the west. She was Darkness and Death.

Ella came in at noon. When Artie told her about Johanna, she prayed, Master, spare that good woman. She be a Jew. If she die now, she burns in hell. Sweet Jesus, let her live. Give her this last chance to accept You as her Savior.

Sept. 20, 2001. Thurs. 3:15 p.m. *In spite of everything, an idea just came to me for an illustration. A* photo—*i.e., a digital image—of Odin in the Land of the Dead taken at the moment he learns he must die.*

Subj. Johanna
Date: 9/20/2001 3:30:30 PM Eastern Daylight Time.
From: Artjo
To: Danik

Yesterday Johanna had a very serious heart attack. It's touch & go. Can you recommend a digital artist I can hire to help me with an illustration?

Love to Alice,
Artie

"Artie?"

"Dani?"

"What're you doing for dinner? Let's eat together. I can be in the city in less than two hours."

"That's sweet of you. You're a good friend. But I'm eating at Leslie's."

"You'll want to be with your family, of course. Never mind. We'll have dinner some other time. I've the name of a digital artist for you."

"Let me get a pencil and paper. Okay. Shoot."

"Tal Raz. He's Israeli. An old army buddy. And a fellow student at Bezalel. He does image retouching for Razorfish—a big interactive agency in New York. I'll tell him to expect your call. His cell phone number is (646) 112-6474."

"Thanks. I'll ring him first thing tomorrow. I must work or I'll go nuts. I'm very touched by your offer to shlep into the city to be with me. Thanks again."

Dani said, "*B'vakashah*," in Hebrew: "You're welcome." Then he said, "I hope Johanna gets better soon." Then he said, "Go ahead and cry. Cry your eyes away."

Artie sniffled and said, "Out."

"What's that you say?"

"The expression in English is cry your eyes out."

"So cry them out. It'll do you good."

Citigroup 36.30, Intel 20.50, Cisco 12.88, Microsoft 50.67, Johnson & Johnson 52.35. Leslie emailed Johanna's ninety-five clients.

Dear ——,

Mother has had a bad heart attack. There's no telling when she can return to the office. I am familiar with all your portfolios so until she recovers I will serve you and guide your investments. In these turbulent market times, you will have many questions to put to me about my guardianship of your funds. Please contact me as often as you wish and I will advise you to the best of my ability about your investments.

Sincerely yours,

Artie put off telling Shirley till 7 p.m., just before he left for Leslie's. He didn't want to get into a long discussion on the phone about Johanna's condition. Talking about it made him feel cold and strange. He gave Shirley the bare facts and promised he'd keep in touch.

She said, "How are you, Artie?"

"I'm fine. It's Johanna I'm worried about."

"Is there anything I can do for you?"

"No, I'm fine."

He's in a fog. He doesn't know what he's in for.

Artie, on the living room sofa, said to Muggs, "Johanna may die. What's to become of us?"

Muggs cocked his head left and right.

"I tell you one thing. Walking you three times a day

for the rest of your life will be a pain in the ass."

Artie had a buzz on from two vodkas and a glass of California pinot noir. He said to Leslie, "I wish it were me instead of Mom."

She looked down from the teak deck at the two pear trees in the garden. And so do I.

Artie said, "And so do you."

"Not true! I love you both the same."

"And we love you. You're all we got. You and the baby. The truth is—we have to face it—Mom might not live to see him. The next few days will tell. Our own Days of Awe."

He said to Chris, "These ten days between Rosh Hashana and Yom Kippur are called the Days of Awe. Religious Jews believe God decides during this time who'll live and who'll die in the coming year. They confess and repent their sins in hopes of being spared. Johanna and I live in a world from which there's no appeal."

Leslie appropriated Artie's phrase. From then on, to amplify the unbelief she shared with Chris, she said, "We live in a world from which there's no appeal."

Johanna said to the tall rabbi in a black silk kaftan standing at the foot of her bed, "Congratulate me, Rabbi! I made it through another night."

The rabbi said, "Seen any good movies lately?"

"You're not allowed to smoke in here."

The rabbi sucked furiously on his cigar—a Havana, Johanna recognized the smell—and the smoke drifted in the fluorescent light that gave his face and hands a waxen sheen. The lustrous, reddish beard that covered his chest reminded Johanna of a fox's tail.

The rabbi said to his wife, "It's a bad business. Very bad! Disgusting! It's no way to behave. Disgusting!"

His beard and payess trembled from anger. His wife was wearing a long, black, silk dress and a strand of pearls around her scrawny neck. A black velvet bonnet covered her shaved head. She said to the rabbi, "Chill out! With me, the truth comes first. And the truth takes thinking."

"Spare me the small talk."

Johanna said, "Rabbi, your cigar stinks." She didn't have the strength to speak the rest of her thought: and a lit cigar is dangerous in here because of all the oxygen,

The nurse said to her, "Take it easy, Mrs. Rubin. There's no rabbi here. You're hallucinating from the morphine."

The rabbi said to Johanna, "Don't fuck with me! I'm armed to the teeth."

Johanna thought, A hallucination! How about that? I've got a pushy bushy rabbi on the brain! She smiled. It serves me right!

The rabbi raised his voice, "I'm dreaming. Don't wake me."

Artie left Tal Raz a message on his machine: "I'm

Artie Rubin. Dani's friend," etc. etc. "Please get in touch with me as soon as you can."

Leslie's phone rang all morning. The fifth call she got from one of Johanna's clients interrupted her conversation with Artie, who was waiting to hear from John Starkie. Rita Painter was on the line. Leslie flipped through the Rolodex in her head and came up with art dealer, fifty-five, way too thin. Bony arms.

Rita said, "I'm sorry to hear about Mom, but this gives me a chance to ask you about something that's been on my mind. I've been worried that my portfolio might contain too many stocks from older companies that are no longer market leaders. And since you're from a younger generation, I'd like you to review my entire portfolio and call me back with recommendations.

"I hope your mom gets well soon. Send my love. We go back a long time. I'm grateful to her. She made me a bundle in the eighties and nineties. But this market scares me. I need her advice. But right now—sadly—she can't give it. I must rely on you. I know that Mom has great faith in your financial acumen. That's good enough for me. I put my money in your capable hands."

Leslie said, "Thanks for your confidence, Rita. I'll get on this right away."

John Starkie on the phone to Artie: "I'm cutting back on the morphine drip. She was hallucinating. Says she can't wait to describe what she saw to you. You can visit her this afternoon for five minutes."

"What time?"

"Let's talk first. Meet me in the waiting room of the coronary intensive care unit at one thirty."

"I'd appreciate that. I have lots of questions to ask you."

"Mr. Rubin, I'll tell you right now. I don't have all the answers."

"Call me Artie."

"Then call me John. I'll see you at one thirty. We'll be speaking together a good deal in the near future. Artie, I know you're going through a bad time. So long as Johanna's my patient, consider yourself in my care, as well. A good cardiologist treats a coronary patient's family as well as his patient."

Artie said, "You're very kind. I'm grateful."

He was astonished by the tears that welled up in his eyes.

Subj: Medical expenses
Date: 9/21/01 11:07:49 AM Eastern Daylight Time.
From: Adamlaw
To: Artjo

I hope Johanna makes a rapid recovery.

In the meantime, a few tips from your lawyer. Buy a cardboard box with hanging files. Keep all medical bills, hospital records, copies of prescriptions, correspondence. Photocopy all letters about $, date everything, including year. Copy everything you submit to insurance companies for reimbursement. Don't forget ambulance bill!

Call or email me with any questions.

Best. Adam

Subj: Re: Medical Expenses
Date: 9/21/01 12:15:12 AM Eastern Daylight Time.
From: Artjo
To: Adamlaw

Dear Adam,
Thanks for the tips. Just bought box with hanging files & will follow your advice.

Almost 40 years ago, by mutual agreement, Johanna completely took over the management of our finances. I was relieved, but felt ashamed. My masculinity was impugned. I never shucked my shame until this morning, when I bought box & files in Staples for $15.95. I confess this only to you, old friend: because of Johanna's heart attack, I suddenly feel more of a man.

Love to Shirley,
Artie

PS. The ambulance cost $500 plus mileage. However, it's covered by Blue Cross.

Leslie got back to Rita Painter at one fifteen. "I've reviewed your portfolio and agree with you. You probably are a little too heavily weighted in companies that are no longer market leaders. Here's what I'd do. I'd lighten you up on Coca-Cola, General Motors, GE, and Proctor & Gamble. You hold five hundred each of Coke and GM, and four hundred each of P&G and GE. I suggest selling two hundred shares of each of them. Then I'd buy two hundred shares of Amgen, and five hundred each of Cisco and Intel. They're all down right now, but I think they have very good prospects for the future. If we do this, you end up with just over twenty thousand in cash. Sitting on some cash in this unstable market is a good idea. You may want to talk with your accountant about your capital gains exposure on those stocks we sell. On the GE and P&G particularly, your cost basis is quite low. You may need the cash next April."

Rita said, "Sounds good to me. Go ahead. I really appreciate this, Leslie. I'm with you all the way. I'll sit on the cash; it's a comfy seat these days. Send love to Mom."

John and Artie talked in the Coronary ICU waiting room; a middle-aged black woman, seated in the opposite corner by the windows, stared into space.

John said, "You can visit Johanna for five minutes every day. Her heartbeat is still irregular, but I think it'll regularize. At least I hope so. And once it does, she should be able to resume a pretty normal life. Yes—including sex! It's hard to say how long her recovery will take. Do you have any questions? How are you holding up?"

Artie noticed the tic in the black woman's right eye. "I'm good."

"What're you writing?"

"A book of Norse myths."

"Well, you did well by the Navaho."

"Thanks. What was it like growing up on a reservation?"

"Lonely. I was different from the others kids—never close to them. I was not only white, but the son of the missionary. That defined me. I was first and foremost the missionary's son." John was still irked by memories of his annual Christmas presents: worn clothes from the missionary barrel, donated by the Presbyterian Missionary Society. He never forgot a red plaid flannel shirt, with frayed cuffs, and faded brown corduroy pants, with a threadbare seat. He said, "I wore hand-me-down pants that were always too short."

Artie kissed Johanna's forehead. She smiled beneath the nasal tubes.

He said, "John Starkie says you're gonna make it. It'll take time, but you'll be okay. We'll fuck again! What did you hallucinate under the morphine?"

"I saw a tall bushy rabbi, all in black, smoking a Havana cigar."

"Serves you right!"

"That's what I said!"

They laughed together and had the nearly identical thought: this my first laugh since (my) (Johanna's) heart attack.

"Leslie and Chris send their love. She says not to worry. Everything at the office is under control. The people there, especially Steve Tobin, wish you well. Leslie's handling your clients. They all send their best. I have regards from the Pendletons, the Jacobsons, Sandra Grossman. Everybody. Ella says she's praying for you. The Pendletons, too.

"Richard said, 'Tell Johanna we remember her in our prayers.' I'm touched, in spite of myself.

"Muggs checks your side of the bed in the morning, then wakes me. He puts his front paws on my back and licks my left ear. Always the left. But he won't hug me. He only hugs you. Come home quick! I'm tired of walking him three times a day. He waits for you by the front door. He just lies there with his back against it.

"I haven't done any work since you got sick. I got an idea for an illustration though. Something new for me. A digital image. I've contacted an Israeli digital artist. He called me just before I came here. We're going to meet this evening.

"Leslie had me to dinner last night. Tonight I'll order

in Chinese. You hooked me on croissants with honey. I have one every morning for breakfast. Soon I'll be buying them again for you.

"Are you in pain? Don't talk. Just nod or shake your head. No? Thank God for that. I blame Abe for not seeing this coming. He didn't take your hypertension and high cholesterol seriously enough. And we're both at fault for ignoring your symptoms last weekend.

"You look good. You're all eyes. I was struck again last night by how much Leslie looks like you. She sure has your eyes."

Johanna pulled herself together and said, "They're giving me anticoagulants. Made me bleed. Yesterday afternoon, my wound from the angiogram opened and bled. The blood soaked the sheets. Betty Hartog, my nurse, pressed the artery in my groin for two hours till it stopped bleeding. Her hand, in this ghastly florescent light, was like a white lily. Yuck! It looked dead."

Rabbi Klugman recited Psalm 21, Psalm 23, and—for himself—Psalm 51 over his mother's grave in Beth Sholom cemetery off the Interboro Parkway in Queens. His father, Iz, whose Hebrew was rusty, picked out buildings on the Manhattan skyline in the west. There's Citicorp, between Lex and Third, and the black Trump apartment house across from the UN. But, Jesus! No Twin Towers.

He asked his son, "Do you believe in the World to Come?"

"I believe we live on after death as thoughts of God until we're resurrected at the End of Days."

"Resurrected! You don't say! That's good to hear. Mama alive again! In the flesh! And me and Nora! I know you've never approved of my remarrying. But I fell in love. And Nora loves me. I'm a lucky man. I've loved two women in my life, who've loved me in return. I only hope they hit it off in the World to Come."

"I hope so, too, Papa."

"But suppose not! What do I do then? It boggles the mind!"

Tal Raz had a dimple in his left cheek. A well-built guy in his mid-thirties. Dani's army buddy and fellow art student. Tal, who spoke with a slightly guttural accent, told Artie he had studied computer graphic design at Bezalel in Jerusalem. His wife, Michal, had danced with the Batsheva dance company. Their seven-year-old daughter was named Anat.

Artie said, "Anat was a Canaanite war goddess—the queen of heaven, mistress of the gods."

"The queen of heaven! Mistress of the gods! My little Anati! You don't say so! I had no idea. Anat's a popular Israeli name for girls. My sister-in-law is also named Anat."

Tal and Michal came to the States nine years ago, so Tal could continue to study digital art at the School of

Visual Arts. "Then I got good job at Razorfish, where I've been ever since."

"Are you and Michal American citizens?"

"Since four years."

Artie was sorry to hear it. He thought young Israelis who became American citizens were leaving their country in the lurch.

The two got down to business. Artie explained he wanted a digital image that looked like a photo of the god Odin in the Land of the Dead for an illustration in his book on Norse mythology. "I want my reader to see a photograph of a god on the page. Not a drawing or a painting, but a photograph. Taken from life at the moment he learns he must die.

"This is the text in which that moment appears. Please read it and share with me any ideas you have for the illustration. I want to work closely with you on this. Digital art is new to me. I need all the help I can get. Are you interested?"

"Very. I've never done anything like it. It's a real challenge. I'll do it."

"What will it cost me?"

"Fifteen hundred dollars, more or less, depending on the prices—and numbers—of the images we license to reproduce."

"Fifteen hundred, more or less. Agreed. When can we start working?"

"Tomorrow evening is okay by me."

"Good. I'll see you here tomorrow at eight."

"We have to work on my computer. Come to my house. Five West 86th Street, apartment 2C. No good. I forgot tomorrow's Saturday. We're eating out with friends at eight thirty. Can you make it at six? We can put in a hour's work."

Artie said, "Six it is."

"A photo of a god! That's cool."

Saturday, a little after 2 p.m. "This morning, I cleaned up the apartment after Ella. Washed the soap dishes and wiped the faucets. Picked up those little strings from the mop she leaves on the bathroom floor. Then I scoured the backs of the shelves in the fridge—they were sticky from spilled milk—and dusted the crossbars under the dining room table and behind the lamps in the living room. I also polished the mirrors and changed the sheets. Everything's spic and span, waiting for you to come home.

"I met with that Israeli digital artist I told you about. We're going to work together. Handsome. Has a dimple. The young are lovely to look at. He speaks English almost flawlessly. He and his wife are American citizens. Israelis in voluntary exile. The consummate irony of Jewish history.

"Yom Kippur begins Wednesday evening. I'm going for Kol Nidre. I love the melody. Tolstoy said Kol Nidre was the most beautiful melody he ever heard. I read somewhere it's Babylonian in origin. What melody's going through your head?"

Johanna said, "What else? The rondo from the Waldstein."

She was trying to replace the theme with another tune, but none came to mind. She was at this moment listening to the trill. The rondo's power to make her vanish into its music scared her. It's so easy to drop out of things. I must hang on to myself with all I've got.

Artie wanted a drink. When his five minutes with Johanna were up, he grabbed a cab home and walked Muggs around the block. Two hours to kill before working with Tal. He unscrewed the top from a chilled bottle of Absolut, then thought, make yourself useful. He returned the bottle to the freezer, went downstairs and took a cab to Pier 54.

He was back in the familiar territory of the bereaved: one aisle for victim's families, one for uniformed personnel, six or eight semi-enclosed booths, piles of manila folders on the carpeted floor by the card tables, a play area for kids. Judy was Artie's first client.

The ID pinned to his shirt gave her a hunch. "Are you *the* Arthur Rubin, the writer—Leslie Pendleton's dad?"

"I am."

"I went out with Sut Pendleton and knew your daughter. She was nice to me. How's she doing?"

"She's four months pregnant."

"Congratulate her and Chris for me. Running into

you like this is so New York! I left Sut for Guy Steward, who jumped from the 102 floor of the North Tower. We were engaged to be married on June second. It was either jump or burn. I told him over the phone to jump. Since then I can't swallow solid food. I've a permanent lump in my throat. I live on milk, baby food, and canned beef and chicken broth. I've lost eight pounds in ten days. I need psychiatric help. Can I get that here?"

"I'll arrange it."

"I teach kindergarten at Trinity. I can't afford expensive therapy."

"It's free."

"Sut and I are going tomorrow to Guy's funeral in Philadelphia. The Falls of Schuylkill Baptist Church. His seventeenth. He's been to seventeen funerals in a row. I don't know how he does it. How will I get through tomorrow?"

Artie thought, she's worse off than me. They're all worse off than me. That's really why I'm here. To be around people worse off than me.

Sept. 22, 2001. Sat. 11 p.m. *John Starkie called earlier. Johanna's heartbeat still irregular.*

Back at work. Began digital image of Odin this evening with Tal Raz, digital artist, who told me the following making the rounds among his fellow Israeli expatriates: One

Arab says to another, As you know, my son Ali, 15, was a martyr. Now my son, Ahmed,13, is a martyr too. The other Arab says, Our kids blow up so fast.

Raz says his sister-in-law, who lives with her family in Jerusalem, has thoughts of having a second child in case her son Ron,10, is killed on a bus by a suicide bomber.

Raz asked what emotions I want my digital image of Odin to convey.

I said, "Horror, anguish, anger at the revelation of his mortality. He's after all a god, who thought himself immortal but now realizes he must die. I want that realization embodied in the structure of his face. I want to see the skull beneath the skin of his bearded face."

Raz went online to Getty Images, an image bank with access to thousands of digital images in various categories. We spent the rest of the hour searching hundreds of faces under the category "God" & picked the image of the bald old man because we were both struck by the tonality, texture, & different colors of his skin—the pallid forehead & nose, the touch of greenish yellow on the rt. side of its bridge, the blotches of red around his eyes & on his cheeks. His skin tone combines photographic & unexpected painterly qualities.

Price to download: $240, charged to my Visa card.

Guy's funeral at the Falls of Schuylkill Baptist Church in Germantown was scheduled for 1 p.m. Sut and Judy caught the 10:05 at Penn Station. When the train came out of the tunnel, they looked through the window to their left, towards lower Manhattan, at the space beyond the oaks along the ridge from which the Twin Towers had been expunged.

Sut said, "I've gone from bad to worse since 9/11. At first, for five days or so, I cried every morning in the shower. Then I lost the idea of heaven. I can't conceive of it anymore. It no longer exists for me. It's a fantasy, a myth made up to sucker people into behaving themselves on earth. Only earth and what happens here is real. My getting drunk and oversleeping, Guy jumping from the North Tower, the man I saw falling, with his red tie standing straight up next to his neck. And that burned head on the roof of the car.

"Heaven's a dream. I can't imagine feeling joy at being there. As a matter of fact, joy, happiness, love—all bullshit; they're just words to me. I can't feel them. I don't believe they exist. That's worst of all. I can't conceive that love or joy or perfection exists."

He looked out the window. "There. The abandoned redbrick factory, with the broken windows. That's what heaven's like to me now."

Judy stared at the broken windows, a rusty bridge, two power lines, two chimneys, a box car in a siding, a car park, another rusty bridge, and then said, "You ought to see a therapist. I've a date to see one next Friday."

"What's wrong with you?"

"I can't swallow solid food. I've lost eight pounds."

"I thought you looked thin."

Judy said, "I lost weight and you lost heaven. All because of 9/11."

"Sounds like the words to a song."

Leslie visited Johanna at two, while Chris kept Artie company in his apartment. Artie offered him a glass of red wine, which he took to be polite. It was too early in the day to drink. They hadn't been alone together since their talk last month at the 79th Street boat basin. Chris was astonished how much Artie had aged in such a short time. The furrows that ran from either side of his nose to the corners of his mouth were deeper; his skin was gray. He asked after Chris's business.

Chris said, "We're negotiating to buy a complex of twelve rental units in White Plains. How's your new book going?"

"It's coming along."

Chris had a premonition that Johanna was going to die. His hairs bristled on his arms and at the nape of his neck. Are her cholesterol and high blood pressure hereditary? Leslie might be in danger. I could also be left alone in my old age. He had never before thought of himself as being old—with deep lines running down his gray face. At least I'll never go bald.

Artie said, "Johanna's heartbeat is still irregular." He took a sip and said, "But where there's life, there's hope."

The cliché, parroted with conviction, touched Chris. Poor Artie, drinking alone in his apartment with a smelly dog that needs a bath.

He found himself saying, "Would it make you happy if we had Sam circumcised? I'm talking a Jewish circumcision. With all the trimmings."

Artie smiled. "All the trimmings. That's very witty. Was the pun intentional?" Then he said, "A bris? You'd do that for me?"

"Wouldn't that make you happy? I want to make you happy about something."

Chris was sorry as soon as the words were out of his mouth. What possessed me to sacrifice Sammy's foreskin to this old Jew's god?

Artie put down his glass of wine, stood up from the sofa, crossed to the ottoman, bent over and kissed Chris's right cheek—the first time Artie's lips had touched Chris.

Artie said, "I appreciate your offer—I can't tell you how much I appreciate it—but you'd be sorry for the rest of your life. And you'd come to resent me. I couldn't bear it. Not now, that you're like a son to me."

"Diana? This is Sutton Pendleton."

"Leslie told me all about your experience on 9/11. How you survived because you overslept. I can't imagine its effect on you. It must be profound."

"It is. I'm a changed man."

"How so?"

"Find out for yourself. Have lunch me with me next Sunday. At the Union Square Café at one."

"I don't know. Our first meeting was a bust."

"It was my fault. Forgive me. My girlfriend had just left me. I behaved badly."

"You certainly did. You paid no attention to me."

"I noticed your pearl earrings. They glowed in the candlelight. Like your face."

"You win. I'll see you a week from Sunday at the Union Square Café at one. I have an idea! Meet me outside Grace Church at a quarter to eleven. We can go to services together."

"I don't go to church anymore. Except for funerals. I told you. I'm a changed man."

Sept. 23, 2001. Sun. 11 p.m. *John Starkie calls me every eve. at 7. Johanna's heartbeat still irregular.*

Tonight, Tal said, "I'm against the Occupation. I've been against the Occupation since May 1992. Beginning August '91, Dani and I were members of a special 12-man commando recon team fighting in Lebanon against Hezbollah. Hearts thumping—you say 'thumping'?—dry mouths, faces painted black, night ambushes in wadis—that sort of thing. We were sometimes called to the Territories on special missions. Usually, there was intelligence from the Shin Bet that a well-

known terrorist was hiding in a certain house for the night and we'd go in and kill him. These were guys with 'blood on their hands,' as we say in Hebrew."

"In English too."

"Yeah, well, those missions were easy to justify. I remember feeling lucky not having to deal with the civilian population. Then, at the beginning of May '92, we were posted for four days to a house in the middle of Jibaliya, Gaza. This refugee camp is one of the most densely populated spots in the world. Sandy, dusty, unlit streets, running with sewage, piles of rotting garbage. And the stink! Shit, piss, rot, smoke. There was always something burning. The stink stuck to your uniform, your hair. It got in your ears and under your nails.

"We enforced a strict curfew; anyone out after dark was shot.

"Day three. A lieutenant, who's a representative of the IDF Civil Authority arrives at our compound. Round glasses, very thin. He's what we call a jobnik—a pencil-pushing bureaucrat who's never been in a fire fight in his life. He says a certain somebody in the camp is late with the payment of his water fees. He owes 67 shekels—about twenty bucks. Our job is to collect it.

"Nu, we bust in the guy's door with our rifle butts at two thirty in the morning, according to regulations, yelling Gesh! Gesh!*—'army' in Arabic. Black faces, SLS night-goggles,*

lasers at the tips of our shortened M16's, Maglights taped to the barrels. The Maglights are on. Dani leads me and two other soldiers into the bedroom. We train our barrels and the maglights on the bed. The guy is fucking his wife. They're about the same age as my parents—in their mid-fifties. The guy sits up between his wife's legs, naked, with a shiny, wet hard-on. She covers her head and breasts with a torn sheet. Not a sound from either of them. The guy's hard-on droops. Is that the word? Droop? I see it in the beam of my Maglight. Down it goes!

"I can't look the guy in the eyes. I look at the concrete floor. In comes the jobnik, shuffling his papers."

Tal & I picked a digital image of a skull ($139.95) which I asked him to fuse with the God image—the old man's face. Tal aligned & overlaid both images to the same scale by pressing a combination of a few keys at the same time, or the up and down arrows & the shift key.

I said, "That's it! Now hide the skull's left cheekbone. What do you think? You're right. Get rid of the skull's jaw, too. That's good. Yes, and the nasal cavity. Expose the right cheekbone. No, cover it with skin. But accentuate the skull's left eye socket and the teeth."

He hit keys, overlaying a series of images, masking some of their components, and the skull's left eye socket & bared teeth showed through the old man's mottled flesh.

Artie said to Johanna, "Chris became like a son to me yesterday. He offered to give Sam a bris—with all the trimmings, he said. The man has wit! I had to smile. I told him he'd come to resent me for doing it, and turned him down. He looked relieved.

"The digital image is developing, but not in the way I expected. My original conception, as you know, was a replication of Odin's photograph—not a painting or drawing. But the image is turning out to have a painterly quality as well. Its color balance, hues and contrasts—they make the skin look like it's been painted in oils. No, it's not what I expected. But I'm going with it. I like the effect."

Johanna said, "Make sure Ella throws out anything that's gone bad in the fridge. And ask her about cleaning supplies. Buy what she needs. Check the toilet paper in the back closet. We may be out. And Kleenex; also paper towels. You're on your own about English muffins, milk, sugar, and fruit."

"I don't eat English muffins for breakfast anymore. I told you. I'm hooked on croissants."

"It was wonderful seeing Leslie yesterday. If I die, scatter my ashes, mixed with fertilizer, in her garden, where our grandson will play. Toss them around the tree trunks, among the roses. Ashes are particularly good for roses; fertilize all the flowers in the flower beds with me. Speaking of flowers. Water the azaleas in the dining room every five days. I did it Tuesday. It's overdue. Do it today. The same goes for the orchids in the living room."

When Artie got home, he watered the azaleas and the orchids, then walked Muggs to 84th and Riverside Drive and back. The sky was cloudy; it looked like rain. Good. It was already raining inside him. Lawrence, the handsome black doorman, asked with a look of pity about Mrs. Rubin's health.

Artie answered, "She's holding her own," and thought with surprise, I've become one of those people that others pity.

He decided against going to Pier 54. I have nothing left to give anybody else. The storm inside him leaked two tears; he wiped them away. He settled on the living room sofa with a vodka on the rocks. He remembered making ham and cheese sandwiches in the kitchen with Johanna and thinking, as he brushed her elbow, this is happiness. Will I ever be happy again?

Sept. 24, 2001. Mon. *7* ***p.m.*** *John Starkie phoned to say Johanna's heart beat has stabilized at 86!! The irregular beats have stopped!!!*

11 p.m. Tonight, Tal overlaid the digital image of the portrait of a mature man with long white hair & beard (royalty free) on Odin's emerging face. We kept the upper-left cheekbone, the nose, hairline, beard, & mustache. Tal then adjusted the image's color balance, its hues & contrasts. The different layers, reacting to each other; make the skin translucent.

At seven fifteen in the morning West End was deserted, except for the night doorman outside 400 across the street, smoking a cigarette. Artie walked Muggs to 85th along the curb, under the pear trees, the oaks, honey locusts, and beeches. A few shriveling leaves had fallen underfoot. Artie was his old self: he admired the symmetry of a dried oak leaf on the sidewalk.

He said to Muggs, "We're not gonna lose her."

Johanna said, "My relief is physical. I feel physically lighter. Like I put down a heavy load. And just think. I'll hold my grandson in my arms."

Artie said, "You know, before this crisis, I feared dying like Dad at seventy-three. I couldn't shake it. Well, now it's gone. Poof! A dose of reality cured me."

"I worried so about worrying you and Leslie. That's over, too. Do me a favor. Bring me my comb, hairbrush, and lipstick tomorrow. And the makeup mirror in the bathroom. I must look a mess."

"You look good to me."

"You look tired."

Artie said, "I am. I'm not working with Tal tonight. I'm going to Sandra Grossman's for dinner. Myra and Ira Birnstein will be there. Not Fuchs. He's deteriorating. Myra's hired a full-time home attendant. Oh yes, Judith Benai, an Israeli. Fuchs's Hebrew translator—she's coming too."

"You think Ira's gay? In my opinion, he's sexless. With that leonine hair of his! Sandra once told me he lives on a trust fund with two Siamese cats in a one-room rent-controlled apartment in Chelsea. Why do I remember that? He learned Yiddish as a kid from a beloved grandfather. My head is stuffed with miscellaneous information. I was terrified that it was about to be emptied of everything."

Artie had a yen for Central Park. On his way there, he dropped five of his shirts off at the cleaners on 83rd between Broadway and Amsterdam. He continued walking east. I'm always astonished. This neighborhood, a few blocks from West End—another New York. De la Cruz Barber Shop, All Modern Styles, Garcia Custom Tailor, El Quiosko Mini Grocery, St. Michael Botanica, The Best Palm Reading. What do I know about the life of the little brown man sitting on the freshly painted brown stoop? Not a fucking thing. Nor do I give a shit.

Myra Fuchs said, "Last night, Jacob had a completely lucid moment when his memory returned and he knew exactly what's happening to him. He begged me to help him kill himself with sleeping pills. I quoted him his poem, 'Der Onzug'—'The Message.' Translate, Ira!"

Ira: "The message for the living from the dead: 'Rejoice!'"

"He says, 'You call this living?'

"I said, 'Auschwitz was living? You composed the poem in Auschwitz.'

"He said—I can't forget a word he said—'You needn't remind me. I remember! I remember! I see the spring sky. Pale blue. The white frosty haze is gone. I made it through another winter. The poem wrote itself. Knowing my mind is dying is worse than being in the Lager. The SS couldn't take the sky from me. Whenever I could, I lost myself for a minute or two watching clouds change or the sun set or the moon rise. Now, in a minute or two, I'll forget the sky exists. I want to die.'

"Jacob used to say, 'I can't believe I still must die. I came so close in the Warsaw Ghetto and Auschwitz.' You know the line from his poem, 'I was death's slave, at his beck and call for five years. My bones rattled like chains.' He survived the October 1944 selection in Auschwitz. And the death march as the Russians approached the camp. He was liberated in Bergen-Belsen while recovering from typhoid fever.

"He used to say, 'After all that—I can't believe it—I still owe death a debt.'"

Ira said, "'The Message' is the shortest poem in Yiddish. Seven words. There's a rumor going around town that the Mossad's behind 9/11. I heard a black guy in my supermarket say that the Israeli secret service hit the Twin Towers after tipping off the Jews who worked there to stay home that day."

Judith Benai said, "'The Message' is even more condensed in Hebrew. Six words."

Artie said, "We four will be remembered because of Jacob Fuchs. He's one of the enduring writers who witnessed and wrote beautifully about the Holocaust. Jacob Fuchs, Emmanuel Ringelblum, Primo Levi, the single, glorious goy Tadeusz Borowski, Jacob Presser, my favorite Etty Hillesum, who wrote from Westerbork, the Dutch transit camp for Auschwitz, 'I want to be the thinking heart of the barracks.' She was gassed at twenty-eight.

"Then there's Paul Celan, Abraham Sutzkever—and so on and so on...Anne Frank. Don't forget the prose of Anne Frank. Her visualized details! Her description of the yellow cat piss seeping through cracks in the attic floor. Dripping into the potato barrel. What an eye for details!"

Judith Benai said, "Beautiful writing. An eye for details. Cat piss. You aestheticise the Shoah. You turn it into mere literature."

Artie said, "I don't know how else to deal with it. It gets me down. The collapse of European civilization, Christianity, the Enlightenment. Europe's embrace of barbarism—the frenzied murder of the Jews. It's incomprehensible. The older I get, the more incomprehensible it becomes."

Myra: "I watched the moon rise over the East Side while I was out shopping around three thirty. It's half full."

Sept. 25, 2001. Tues. 11 p.m. *Ever the Jew, I always expect bad news. My heart skipped a beat this afternoon when*

I recognized John Starkie from the back at the foot of Johanna's bed. He turned around & smiled.

"The clot has in all probability dissolved. If everything keeps going the way it is, Johanna can go home in two or three days. Then another six weeks—as the son of a missionary, I prefer the biblical sounding forty days and forty nights—of gradually building up her strength—increasing her normal activity at a pace that seems comfortable to her—and she'll be good as new."

Johanna (wearing lipstick) asked John, "When can I get my hair cut?"

"Wait a week or two."

"A week or two! I can wait a week or two! Or three. Isn't that right? Even four. A whole month. More. I have time. A miracle! Time's been restored to me. I'm so scared of dropping out of time."

Tonight downloaded digital image of Hysterical Woman with Hair Standing on End ($249). Her hair now belongs to Odin.

Red, green, & blue make up the range of colors in the image. Tal reduced the red & blue values & increased the red saturation levels until Odin's hair, beard, & mustache turned brownish-red. Then he masked out some strands of Odin's beard & unsaturated the color till it turned grey.

First thing next morning, Fred Levy called Rabbi Klugman at his office and said, "I got Dad's death certificate. The funeral service is at ten on Sunday at Riverside. I hope you can officiate. It's what he would have wanted. I'm only doing it for him. I'm sorry to say, Rabbi, your psalm doesn't work for me. No text works for me anymore. I can't pray. I'm not coming to Yom Kippur services."

"I don't blame you, Fred. I wish you'd join us, but I don't blame you. Of course, I'll officiate at your Dad's funeral. Let's talk again Saturday night."

Dearest God! This evening I'll lead a congregation of Your holy people in prayer at the beginning of the Holiest Day of the year. You've entrusted some fifteen hundred precious Jewish souls to my care. We're a portion of Your Divine Presence on earth. Tonight and tomorrow we confess our sins. Help us repent and turn to You. I lost Fred Levy. Help me make up for it. Give me another chance, with the fervor of my prayers, to turn somebody in his place to You.

"All this morning, the Mills Brothers sang 'Daddy's Little Girl' in my head. Know what I have now? Eddie Fisher singing 'O, Mein Papa.' I hear the orchestra—

violins. So you're going to shul this evening to hear Kol Nidre. I can't remember how it goes. Are you going to fast on Yom Kippur?"

"No."

"It wouldn't do you any harm to lose a pound or two. Are you going to shul tomorrow too?"

"Tomorrow morning they chant Vidui—the Confession. Dad used to tell the story of the rabbi who prayed, 'If the children of Israel didn't sin, who would chant a confession so beautifully to You, O God.'

"But I'll be here at two."

"Stay in shul. Enjoy the music. Tell Leslie to visit me. What're you doing for dinner?"

"Shirley invited me. We eat at five. We're having lasagna. She makes it too spicy for me. Adam's feeling well enough to go to services with us. He's always stoned."

Artie said, "Dad used to rush home from work in the late afternoon, wolf down a big supper to prepare for his fast, smoke two cigarettes in a row. He suffered horribly not being able to smoke on Yom Kippur. Then he hurried off to shul with me while it was still light to hear the first notes of Kol Nidre. I owe him my introduction to the melody."

Adam took a drag on his joint and said, "Kol Nidre is a Jewish love song to God."

He blew Shirley a kiss.

Shirley said, "When I was a teenager, I prayed for my

period on Yom Kippur so I wouldn't have to fast. Mama would let me off if I had my period."

Rabbi Klugman said, "Today, as I was leaving the house for shul, Michael, my five-year-old, asked me the question I've been dreading every Yom Kippur since he learned to talk. He pointed to my kitel and asked, 'Daddy, what's that you're wearing?'

"Now kitel means 'gown' in Yiddish. This white silk gown will be my shroud. Thus, in my burial clothes, I face my Maker for judgment on Yom Kippur. I said to Michael, 'I wear this white gown to especially honor God on Yom Kippur.' I decided, standing there in the open doorway, to spare him the gory details till he's seven. That's time enough to learn about death.

"Death is on our mind tonight. We think of those who were here with us last year and are now gone. I think of Jonathan Levy, may he rest in peace. He was killed by the direct hit of the plane that crashed into the South Tower. His son, Fred, who witnessed this, needs our prayers and attentiveness. Jonathan's funeral will be at Riverside at ten on Sunday. I urge you all to attend!

"Mindful of death, we think tonight of how many of us in the last year got cancer, had heart attacks, strokes. Who's next? Am I? That's the fear which must fuel the passion of our prayers on Yom Kippur."

My heart's fluttering. I've got butterflies in my chest.

Johanna's EKG showed she was in ventricular fibrillation: her heart had lost coordination in its beat. It quivered. The bells went off in the nursing station. Betty Hartog, the head nurse, was weepy because that morning, she'd had to put down her thirteen-year-old arthritic Welsh terrier, Beau. She called the arrest team, then dashed with two other nurses to Johanna's bed, thinking, She's got about three minutes worth of oxygen left in her brain.

The nurses tried to keep Johanna's blood flowing until the defibrillator arrived. Johanna felt them roll her onto her left side on her left arm. I can't move my left arm out from under me. Can I wiggle my toes? I can't tell. I've lost control of my extremities.

Hartog slid the plastic arrest board under Johanna and rolled her on her back.

Klugman said, "Chant—sing—the beloved opening melody of Kol Nidre with me. Share in its beauty! It's chanted in the setting of a formal rabbinical court. Pam Bernstein and George Friedman, on either side of me, holding Torah scrolls, constitute with me a *beth din*—a court of three, required by rabbinical law for legally granting dispensation from vows. Kol Nidre means 'all vows.' Before the sun sets, we pray that all the vows and oaths we took in the last year shall be nullified. Some scholars say this prayer with its holy melody arose amongst us to solace Jews forced to convert to Christianity by the Visigoths in seventh-century Spain, and again during the persecutions by the Inquisition.

"Whatever the truth, the theme of Kol Nidre's words is nullification—a reminder on the Day of Atonement that all things end."

Betty Hartog's pounding my chest. She's giving me CPR. Not a good sign. Like those fluttering butterflies. (Thump!) Two yellow butterflies chasing one another around the lawn in New Rochelle. (Thump!) A hummingbird. A pink trumpet honeysuckle. Where was that? (Thump!) I can't remember. My mind's emptying out. No, wait a sec. It was at the Jacobson's. Labor Day weekend. My memory's still intact. I can pick my last memory. (Thump!) That's easy. Giving birth to Leslie. I broke water on the kitchen floor. (Thump!) Artie mopped up. The first contractions. Artie forgetting my suitcase and rushing back upstairs. (Thump!)

He says, "Don't worry. I'll do the laundry."

And I say, "When have you ever done the laundry?"

(Thump!) The white electric clock, with black hands, on the delivery room wall. Click. 9:16. Tick-tock. The room was freezing. Why do they keep hospital rooms so cold and dark? I feel so cold and sleepy. I no longer feel the thumps. It's not dark. I'm blind.

Quick! Where was I? The epidural. My epidural let me be fully awake. It took effect only on the left side. The contractions on my right side were excruciating, and I couldn't push. But I can't recall the pain. Even from the episiotomy scissors. I remember thinking at the time, I'm being cut in half. One stitch got infected. That pain went on for days. I can't recall it. But the contractions let up the instant Leslie was born. She looked like she was covered with slimy cheese. And when they put her howling on my left breast, and she mouthed my nipple and was still. Ecstasy! That I won't forget. Ah, but I will. I will.

Johanna's heart stopped. Her EKG went flatline. Betty Hartog thought, She's dead, and smeared more lubricating conduction jelly on Johanna's chest. Betty smeared jelly on the two defibrillator paddles in the hands of Harold Harlow, the senior resident in charge of the arrest team. He clapped the paddles on either side of Johanna's chest, yelled "Clear!" pressed the button and zapped Johanna's heart with 200 joules.

She gave a rigid jerk, opened her eyes, and said, "What're you doing to me?"

Betty Hartog went back to mourning Beau. She saw herself on 72nd Street carrying him in her arms to the vet that morning. Lucky dog didn't know he was a goner. Did Mrs. Rubin know? What went on in her mind?

Johanna said, "I died, didn't I?"

Dr. Harlow said, "Yes."

"You mean I have to go through it all again?"

"All vows and oaths we take, all promises and obligations, we make to God between this Yom Kippur and the next we hereby publicly retract in the event that we should forget them, and hereby declare our intention to be absolved of them."

Gobbledegook, Artie said to himself. The words are gobbledegook. They survived because they got attached to a rapturous melody. Klugman has a nice baritone. It's unusual for a rabbi to have a good singing voice and double as a cantor. He's a talented guy. Adam looks better. As usual, Shirley's lasagna was too spicy.

Klugman chanted Kol Nidre the requisite three times. The second time, Artie joined in singing its famous opening motif with every adult in the shul: my Jews. I'm a voice in your deathless chorus.

September 26, 2001. Wed. 9:30 p.m. *John Starkie informed me over the phone that Johanna went into ventricular fibrillation late this afternoon—around the time I was at Kol Nidre. Her heart stopped beating & quivered—like "a bag of worms." That's what some doctor says on the Web: "During ventricular fibrillation, the heart quivers like a bag of worms."*

Then Johanna died & was resuscitated by a defibrillator. Dead about two minutes. No brain damage.

Starkie said, "Because the heart repairs itself, the myocardium—the main heart muscle—becomes inflamed.

Inflammation is part of the healing process. But it irritates the heart, which sometimes triggers the quivering."

"So it can happen again."

"Yes. That's why we're giving her an ICD—an implantable cardioverter defibrillator that includes a pacemaker. The pacemaker speeds up a heartbeat if it's too slow. The ICD should reconvert—restore—her normal heart beat if she has another attack of ventricular fibrillation. I said, 'should.' I used the word advisedly.

"The truth is, Johanna could die at any time.

"Meantime, she's recovering nicely. Her heart's back in good shape. A regular beat. If all goes well, she'll be home in three or four days."

Artie drank three vodkas, called Leslie and told her the news. "The healing process itself causes the heart to conk out. They're giving Mom what's called an ICD that should prevent another attack. The doctor said 'should' advisedly. It might not do the trick. Mom could die at any time."

Sept. 27, 2001. Thurs. Yom Kippur. 4:30 p.m. *Prayed in shul this morning for Johanna's recovery. I stood up, called out her name, then—adding my own words—prayed (in*

English) with the congregation praying in Hebrew: "May He who blessed our ancestors, etc. etc., bless and heal Johanna, May the Holy One in mercy strengthen Johanna and heal Johanna soon, without irritating her myocardium, together with others who suffer illness. And let us say: Amen."

Fessed up in the hospital to Johanna, who said she prayed in the ambulance. "I was crazy with fear."

"The same here."

"Let's forget it."

"Done!"

She's having an automatic implantable cardioverter defibrillator (AICD) put in Monday morning. Ventricular fibrillation. The words now make me think of a squirming bag of worms.

Muggs farted from the floor on Johanna's side of the bed. Artie looked up from his pillow. Would that it were you.

The next afternoon, Artie asked Johanna, "What's dying like?"

"I went blind. But I didn't care. I wasn't scared. My mind was clear. I got to pick my last memory. I relived giving birth to Leslie. In a way, I gave birth to my death. I'm now curious. What will my next experience be? Curiosity isn't an emotion I previously associated with dying.

"John explained ventricular fibrillation to me. That healing kills—what an irony! A paradigm for the whole shebang. He, John, said the AICD prevents another attack of ventricular fibrillation. But he also told me, and I appreciate his honesty, that I could also have another coronary occlusion. I'm on Coumadin, an anticoagulant. No matter how you cut it, I'm in deep shit.

"If all's well, I'll be coming home Tuesday morning. How's Muggs? I can't wait to see him. I'm embarrassed by how much I love that dog. His black ears and big black nose. The patch of white fur on his grey rump. I look forward to his hug. Hugs from Muggs! He looks me in the eye. He's the only dog we've had who looks me in the eye. He catches my eye in bed every morning. Though, to be honest, his eyes are devoid of intelligence. They're glassy—like brown marbles.

"Oh, to sleep in my own bed again, past five thirty. They wake you up around here at five thirty. I look forward to reading in bed by the soft light on my night table. Damn this deathly fluorescent glare. It makes everybody look dead. You too. I sometimes feel I'm surrounded in here by walking corpses. I'm the only one alive. I'm alive! Can you believe it? I came back from the dead! I'm hungry all the time. I look forward to Chinese food—particularly spare ribs. Two spare ribs can't do me any harm."

"I associate spare ribs with Leslie telling us she's pregnant."

"Right! We were having dinner at Shun Lee. I remember. I so look forward to being a grandma. Do I dare look forward to anything? Should I? Or should I try living in the moment? Why ask you? What do you know about facing death, all alone, at sixty-four? Sixty-four! This can't be happening!"

Klugman to Artie, over the phone: "Mr. Rubin, I noticed on Yom Kippur morning before the prayer for the sick that you called out the name Johanna Rubin, who I presume is your wife. I hope she's doing okay."

"As a matter of fact, she's still in great danger."

"I'm so sorry. What's the trouble?"

"Late Wednesday afternoon, at Columbia-Presbyterian, she died from ventricular fibrillation and was resuscitated with a defibrillator. She could possibly die again at any time."

"God forbid! Did I hear right? She died and was resuscitated?"

"With a defibrillator."

Klugman spoke in Hebrew.

"I didn't catch what you said."

"I gave the appropriate blessing on hearing that your wife died and was resuscitated."

"Is there really a blessing for that?"

"Oh, yes." Klugman slowly repeated a short Hebrew phrase.

Artie made out one word: *Baruch* "Blessed..." Blessed something something. He couldn't translate the rest.

Klugman said, "Blessed be He who revives the dead."

"That was a doctor named...I must get his name. I've been meaning to thank him."

"That's appropriate too."

Sept. 28, 2001. Fri. 11 p.m. *This evening, at dinner, I was too ashamed to tell Leslie & Chris that I'd prayed for Johanna's recovery in shul on Yom Kippur.*

We sat out on the deck wearing sweaters. Moon almost full. The pear trees in the garden reminded me of Johanna's request to have her ashes scattered around them. Dread of her sudden death; palpitations, sweaty palms, shortness of breath. One of Chris's Klonopins plus two vodkas calmed me down.

Leslie asked Chris, "Are you asleep?"

"Not anymore."

"I caught a whiff of Dad before he freaked out about Mom. He smells old. Like my grandmother in New Rochelle when I was a kid. A mixture of sweet and something I can't put my finger on. Slightly acrid."

Johanna to Artie, "Last night I dreamed a doctor

sawed the hump off a humpback. All that blood! I woke in a sweat. Then I felt happy to be alive to have had a nightmare. What's been going on in the market?"

"Haven't the vaguest."

"Tell Leslie to come tomorrow and fill me in."

"Let's plan our fortieth. Venice in February is cold and damp. Maybe we ought to go south. Or to Hawaii."

"I hate the beach. You know I hate the beach. We'll do Venice! Like on our twenty-fifth."

Their thoughts met again among red and green traffic lights reflected at night in dark canals, the top of the Campanile hidden by mist, the black gondolas crammed with Japanese tourists. Artie remembered a funeral procession of black motorboats crossing the lagoon. The glassed-in coffin near the floating hearse's stern was heaped with white roses.

Sept. 29, 2001. Sat. 11 p.m. *Late this afternoon, Tal & I finished digital image of Odin. The last—most difficult, most important—element was his blue rt. eye, for which Tal licensed a close-up of a young woman's eye ($210). He & I worked 2 hrs., separating out her cornea, pupil, eyeball, eyelid, etc. with their color layers, to get the eye to reflect light & focus on the viewer. Fitted together more than a dozen segments.*

Finally Tal said, "Nu, here's the image of your god. But not to worry. We're allowed. It's not a statue or a mask."

"A statue or a mask?"

"The second commandment. 'Commandment' you say? In Hebrew we don't say commandment. We say dibrah. *I don't know the English for it. The second whatever you call it goes, 'You shall not make a statue or a mask.'"*

"Ah! We say, 'graven image.'"

"Whatever. The Hebrew is 'statue' and 'mask.'"

Artie had trouble falling asleep. He thought about the service on Yom Kippur morning—the communal Confession: we jeer, we kill, we lie. I let Mom die alone. Forgive me.

Diana checked the Sunday *Times* weather report: today, cloudy, windy, and cool, high sixty-two. She put on her pink sundress with little red and green flowers and threw her black cardigan sweater over her shoulders; both church and restaurant would be air-conditioned. At the last minute, she put on her pearl earrings and gathered up her hair so Sut would notice them. Relax. It's not a real date. It's just for lunch.

She fixed her mind on church—on her hope of meeting Christ that morning between the stone walls, before the altar, among the jumble of her thoughts and prayers.

Sut got to the Union Square Café at twelve forty-five and had a Gibson at the bar. Bars are my milieu. He felt at home facing a row of polished martini glasses on the shelf to his left and three rows of liquor bottles stacked on the shelves reflected in the mirror against the wall.

Diana was prettier than he remembered; he was flattered that she wore her pearl earrings. Diana noticed that he noticed them. She blushed. She saw he also noticed that. They were seated at the table to the right of the foot of the stairs. Sut ordered another Gibson, Diana had a Diet Coke.

The second Gibson loosened Sut's tongue. He said, "I like your hair up. It's very becoming. And those earrings! I take your wearing them as a compliment. Thanks. But I must tell you. I brought you here under false pretenses. During our disastrous dinner, you mentioned you're a psychologist. I need your advice."

Shit! It's not a date. Still, he feels comfortable reaching out to me. That's something. He must feel we have a connection to each other.

Diana said, "Tell me what's going on," and he told her almost everything that had happened to him since the night before 9/11. He spared her the burned head.

When he was done, she said, "Thank you for confiding in me. It must have been very difficult for you."

"Pray for me."

"I will."

"I never realized how much my faith meant to me until I lost it."

"There's one thing I must know. Do you have suicidal thoughts?"

"All the time. I keep thinking I'd be better off dead."

"Do you have active plans to kill yourself?"

"No, just thoughts. I no longer think suicide's a sin—I've lost my belief in sin—but I couldn't do it. I could never kill myself. I love my parents and my brother too much to do that to them."

"I thought you said you've lost the capacity to love."

"It was nearly extinguished, till this moment, when you showed your concern for me. You blew on my ember."

"No, you did. It was your breath."

"You mean, there's hope for me?"

"You bet there is. With help. Let's talk while we eat."

Diana ordered the tuna salad sandwich, without bacon, on white bread, with arugula and garlic potato chips, and Sut had the shell steak sandwich, medium rare, and a glass of Merlot.

He munched a potato chip and said, "Would you help me?"

"I can't see you professionally. We have, however tenuous, a personal relationship, and it would be unethical for me to treat you as a client. I can, however, recommend another cognitive therapist for you to see."

"Is he a Christian?"

"She's Jewish."

"Then how can she help restore my faith?"

"Your loss of faith is a symptom—like your inability to feel emotions. She'll do her best to restore both."

"What's cognitive therapy like?"

"You're suffering upsetting thoughts that are affecting your emotions and behavior. This therapist will help you understand where they're coming from. But most important, she'll help you modify them and restore your feelings."

Sut ordered another Merlot. "It sounds good to me."

He looked at her—and she saw it—with affection, but then the second Merlot sloshed over his glowing ember; he felt it fizzle out.

Leslie thought she was coming down with a cold, so she didn't visit Johanna. Artie went instead. Johanna gave him Dr. Harlow's office number, which she had gotten that morning from John Starkie.

Artie said, "We'll call him from home tomorrow."

Blessed be Dr. Harlow who revives the dead.

Subj: (no subject)
Date: 9/30/2001 11:38:48 AM Eastern Daylight Time.
From: Raz
To: Artjo

Dear Artie,

It was a good working with you. Let me know when you

want to make image of another god. I looked up *dibrah* in my Hebrew-Eng. dictionary. It's statement, pronouncement in Eng. Commandment in Heb. is *mitzvah*. Plural, *mitzvot.*

Later this week I'll drop off with your doorman the digital image of Odin that I burned into a CD-ROM so your publisher can transfer the image to the printed page.

I hope Mrs. Rubin gets well real soon.

Best,
Tal

To celebrate Johanna's homecoming, Artie dropped off Muggs to be bathed and groomed at A Cut Above, at 83rd and Columbus. It would take from ten till about four and cost ninety bucks, plus a ten-dollar tip for the groomer.

"They implanted my ICD this morning. With a mild anesthetic. Took an hour and a half. I couldn't tell if I was awake or sleeping. It's under my skin, here. Imagine! My heart's wired. I have two electric wires in my heart. Shocking! No wonder I'm all wired! I'm a nervous wreck! I must hold my cell phone on the opposite side of my body from the ICD. And keep my distance from running engines. It seems running engines generate magnetic fields. The ICD won't prevent a heart attack. I have to have the bandage changed next Friday.

"Abe Raskin stopped by afterward. His phony smile gives me the creeps. He said my blood pressure's 150/95 and my cholesterol is down to 250. He told me exercise. Exercise! I'm scared to go pee. I mean it. I'm terrified some movement—a slight exertion—will kill me. I have this fantasy that if I lie in bed, without moving, I'll live."

The next morning, a Doctor Finkle gave Johanna's ICD an electrophysiological test to make sure it was triggering properly. Artie picked her up at eleven fifteen. Starkie discharged her in his office on the sixth floor.

She asked him, "Can I have a couple of spare ribs for dinner tonight?"

"Absolutely. Don't live in fear. Live normally. Nothing you do will increase the chances of your death."

Johanna read the hand-printed parchment under glass on the wall behind his desk:

Beauty Way: A Navaho Ceremonial

I walk in front of me beautiful
I walk behind me beautiful
Under me beautiful
On top of me beautiful
Around me beautiful
Everything is beautiful.

Oct. 2, 2001. Tues. 5:30 p.m. *Johanna's stretched out on the sofa listening to the Waldstein. 15 min. ago we thanked Dr. Harlow by phone for resuscitating her. Stuck since then with the dread that unless I recite blessing "Blessed be he who revives the dead" in Hebrew (!), she'll die. Don't know the Hebrew.*

Sweaty palms, palpitations, shortness of breath. Like in the garden Fri. night.

6:15 p.m. Mellowed out by 2 vodkas & a Klonopin, from a prescription Starkie gave Johanna.

She can't keep her hands off Muggs's clean fluffy fur. "You feel so soft. And smell so sweet. Give me a big hug!"

Shirley called at seven. "Welcome home! So you were in the Valley of the Shadow. What was that like? No, don't tell me. I don't want to think about it. That's the way I deal with death: I don't think about it.

"Next Monday, Adam starts giving himself injections of Interferon three times a week for two years. Half of what he takes now. He's afraid to get off pot because of his nausea. It decked him. He could only drink cold fluids and eat odorless meals. Then Jerry and Hal turned him on. The nausea vanished. And he's not so depressed. He was stoned in shul on Yom Kippur. The pot made him ravenous; he left in the middle of the afternoon service, went home, and broke his fast with a bagel and cream cheese.

"Of course, we don't have sex. We haven't had sex in over two months. But I suppose you can't have sex either. That's none of my business. Forgive me.

"We have good news. Jerry and Hal's adoption agency hooked them up with a pregnant woman in Minnesota. She's due in April—like Leslie. We'll be grandmas together!"

"Oh, Shirley, I'm so happy for you!"

"Jerry will be the primary caregiver, the stay-at-home mommy. He was always maternal. He loved playing with dolls when he was a little kid. He'll be on maternity leave from his job for three months.

"Artie, you know, prayed for you in shul."

Johanna said, "He told me."

"You could have knocked me over with a feather. I prayed for Adam on Rosh Hashana. At first I felt, this is absurd. Then I figured, what harm can it do? And it was good praying in a big room packed with my fellow Jews who also were praying for Adam."

Artie later told Johanna, "I felt the same. Good. Like Shirley said, it was good praying for you with my fellow Jews. I prayed aloud in English. The Hebrew being chanted all around me charged my words—I can't explain it. I truly felt like a Jew, one of the Eternal People."

Johanna ordered in from Ollie's: a large order of spare ribs, eight steamed little juicy buns, sautéed mixed vegetables, beef with scallions, and Moo Shu pork. Leslie, who turned out not to have a cold, set the dining room table for four with chopsticks. Artie opened a bottle of Sancerre. Chris put out three wine glasses. Leslie was sipping a Diet Pepsi.

Artie tipped the Chinese delivery man eight bucks and got an effusive thank you.

Artie said, "Do me a favor and ride your bicycle in the street. Not on the sidewalk."

He said to Leslie, "I'm scared that one of these days I'm going to be run down on the sidewalk by one of those guys on a bike."

Leslie said, "I'm scared of taking the subways. Since 9/11 I'm scared a suicide bomber's going to blow himself up in a subway during rush hour."

Chris said, "I have to admit: it's crossed my mind. I can't get my mind around America being vulnerable to attack."

Sucking one end of a spare rib, Artie dreaded that Johanna would die if he didn't recite "Blessed be the One who gives life to the dead," in Hebrew. What's the matter with me? Am I going nuts? He drank another vodka, excused himself, took two Klonopin in the john, and sat back down at the head of the dining room table. The booze and pills worked fast. I'm high as a kike—uh—kite.

Chris, feeling guilty that he'd thought of Artie as "this old Jew," raised his glass of wine and said, "*L'chaim* —to life. The toast Artie taught me—the best toast I know."

Artie said, "*L'chaim.*"

They clinked glasses. Johanna noticed their big knuckles. She looked at Leslie's slender fingers, picking up a steamed bun with chopsticks. Johanna watched Muggs, seated near Leslie's left foot, intently watching her swallow the bun. Leslie sneezed twice. Muggs barked. Leslie sneezed again.

Johanna said, "Bless you." Maybe she has a cold, after all. Or an allergy. Then Johanna looked again from left to right, at Artie, Chris, and pregnant Leslie, blowing her nose in a Kleenex. She's all flushed, and shining. She's radiant. The men looked at her tenderly. Around me beautiful.

She said to Leslie, "Starkie wants me to stay home six weeks, but I can do some work. I thought I'd call all my clients and let them know I'm back in business."

"Why don't you email them?"

"No, I thought I'd speak to each. It's more personal. I know you did a good job, but you've your own clients to worry about. I want to reassure mine that I'll be looking after their portfolios again full time. Particularly when the market's so lousy."

"Don't overdo it."

Johanna said, "I won't. Starkie says I have to take it easy for the biblical forty days and nights. What happened in the Bible for forty days and nights?"

Artie said, "Well, let's see. It rained forty days and nights, and Moses stayed forty days and nights on

Mount Sinai where he got the ten commandments."

Not to worry. We're allowed. It's not a statue or a mask.

Johanna said to Artie, "I'll walk Muggs. You go get us fresh croissants."

"You sure?"

"Get the croissants."

They left the house together. Artie went to Broadway, and Johanna walked Muggs down 80th Street toward Riverside.

Exhausted. Should've stayed in bed. The street was strewn with gingko leaves shaped like miniature fans. I once read that gingkos are among the world's oldest trees. Survivors. Like me.

Muggs crapped on Riverside. My God, I'm scared to bend over and pick it up. No matter what John Starkie said, I'm terrified that just bending down will bring on a heart attack. Well, I won't live that way.

She scooped the crap up in a page from yesterday's *Times* and dropped it in the garbage pail on the corner. That was one of the bravest things I've ever done!

Oct. 3, 2001. Wed. 11:30 a.m. *Johanna's in the dining room on the phone with her clients. My joy at having her home. My anxiety about having another attack of dread.*

Artie went into the dining room for the pleasure of hearing Johanna's voice around the house again.

"I feel fine. Yes. Six weeks. In the meantime, I'll be reviewing your portfolio. I know you're worried because the market has been negative recently. Leslie kept her eye out, as you know. Thank you. I'll tell her. I'll be monitoring the market from here, where you can call me at any time. You have my number."

Johanna went back to bed and closed her eyes for half an hour.

Ella came in at one and said, "Mrs. Rubin! God be praised! Welcome home!

"Thank you, Ella."

They hugged, then Ella said, "Mr. Rubin, he tell me you died and come back to life. Is that true?"

"Yes. I was dead for two minutes."

"Did you see Jesus?"

"No."

"An angel?"

"No."

"A bright light at the end of a tunnel?"

"No."

"What then?"

"Nothing. I can't remember a thing."

"Aha! You can't remember! That explains it!"

"Ella, you've let things slide. The house needs a good going over. The tile walls in the bathroom and the shelves in the medicine cabinets are dirty. Mr. Rubin's studio needs dusting. Also the top shelves—behind the books. And please change the sheets."

Oct.4, 2001. Thurs. 8:30 p.m. *Another attack of dread. 1 vodka, 2 Klonopin eased my palpitations, sweats, shortness of breath. But all I think about is that Johanna will die unless I recite "Blessed be he who revives the dead" in Hebrew. Can't expunge the thought.*

Subj. Hebrew blessing
Date: 10/4/2001 9:01:50 PM Eastern Daylight Time
From: Artjo
To: Raz

Dear Tal,
A favor. Spell out the Hebrew words of "Blessed be he who revives the dead" in English.

Best,
Artie

Johanna was asleep. Artie waited for the Ambien to kick in. The full moon shone through the window to his left on the wrinkled nape of her neck.

Johanna let Artie walk Muggs the next morning. She snoozed on and off till ten—the first time she'd slept past seven in years. When her eyes were fully opened, she looked around the sunny room and thought: Willa Cather says happiness is being dissolved in something great and complete. Wrong! Happiness lies in feeling part of ordinary things—my dresser and night table, recumbent bike, TV, our green wicker laundry hamper, Artie's sheepskin slippers with their flattened backs, left on the carpet by the radiator.

In the shower, she cupped her hand beneath her left collarbone to keep the bandage on the pacemaker dry. Add a warm shower to the list.

And work. Work makes me happy. Johanna spent the next forty-five minutes consulting on the phone with three clients. She extended her list. I'm happy their accounts are doing reasonably well—considering the market. I'm happy Sue Lathrop and Linda Salzman referred their friends to me because they're pleased with the way I've handled their accounts. I'm happy that Alan Berger asked my advice about his youngest son's portfolio—the kid who lives in LA. I'm happy that beside that fracas with Steve Tobin about Intel my firm's on the up and up. I'm extravagantly happy.

Oct.5, 2001. Fri. Noon. *Another attack. This time, 3 vodkas & 2 Klonopin.*

Johanna smelled the vodka on Artie's breath.

He said, "Remember Leslie's riding lessons at Claremont? How old was she? Eleven? She was in love with a big gray gelding named Samurai. Remember Samurai? A spooky nag. She bolted at the drop of a hat. Leslie wasn't scared of him though. She had a good seat. Riding was her only sport. Ever. She doesn't use the golf clubs Chris gave her for Christmas. Even before she got pregnant. I remember you in your eighth month, with your pear-shaped tummy, rolling over on your right side in order to sit up in bed. I could use another drink."

"I notice you're also at my Klonopin. You've taken six in less than a week."

"You don't miss much."

"What's going on? You're running off at the mouth. Your eyes are bleary. You're stoned at two o'clock in the afternoon. Why?"

"I'm too embarrassed to say."

"Embarrassed? What're you so embarrassed about? Why are you stoned on pills and booze in the middle of the afternoon? What's eating you? "

"I'm too embarrassed to say."

Artie went into his studio and shut the door. Johanna made an appointment with Eddie Piero to get a haircut next Monday at two. Why is Artie so embarrassed? Did he fuck another woman when I was in the hospital? Did he discover he's gay? Is that possible? Why not? Eddie came out at sixty-one after two marriages.

Subj. Re: Hebrew blessing
Date: 10/5/2001 4:04:18 PM Eastern Daylight Time
From: Raz
To: Artjo

Baruch mekhayei hameitim

Sub. Re: Hebrew blessing
Date: 10/5/2001 5:12:26 Eastern Daylight Time
From: Artjo
To: Raz

Thanks. I recognized *baruch*—blessing, life—*chay*—the root, I gather, of the verb revive. They're among the few Hebrew words I know. *Meitim,* I presume, means the dead. I'd like to be conversant in modern Hebrew. The revival of liturgical Hebrew as a living language is a unique achievement of our people. Life from death.

Best,
Artie

Artie printed out Tal's email and slipped it between the pages of the paperback *The Prose Edda* by Snorri Sturluson that he kept on his studio desk.

A little after two in the morning, Artie got out of bed, went into his studio, took the email out from between the pages of *The Prose Edda*, and read aloud:

"*Baruch mekhayei hameitim.*"

Oct.6, 2001. Sat. 3:20 a.m. *The blessing works like a charm. It is a charm. Pronounced it once in a solemn voice & my dread vanished instantly. Have memorized it.*

Johanna unobtrusively sniffed Artie's breath the whole next day. He hasn't taken a drink nor any more Klonopin. What was that all about? "I'm too embarrassed to say." Embarrassed by what? Another woman? Is he gay? I have a right to know after almost forty years of marriage.

Artie thought of the blessing as the brocha—a Yiddish word from the Hebrew meaning "benediction." He made the brocha twice that Friday: once before noon and once at four fifteen. And each time, his dread that Johanna would die dissipated instantly.

The next day he was fine. And the day after that, till late in the afternoon, when Tal dropped off the CD-ROM of Odin.

Oct. 7, 2001. Sun. 6 p.m. *I now dread that my digital image of Odin, despite what Tal says, is idolatrous—that it violates some rabbinical injunction against making any religious images—& offends god with fatal consequences for Johanna. He's jealous, this god of mine.*

Have a call in to Rabbi Klugman.

After dinner, Johanna made reservations online for five nights at the Hotel Monaco in Venice, beginning February 20, at two hundred and sixty a night. She also booked a dinner reservation for two on the twenty-second at Da Fiore and two round-trip airline tickets on Delta.

October 7, 2001
Darling Artie,

I'm writing this in case I die. I'll leave it in my top dresser drawer, on top of a pile of family photos I never got a chance to put in the album. There's one of you kissing Leslie on the left cheek I took during our weekend with her and Chris at the Cape at the beginning of July. I kissed your faces in the photo and wept. I grieve that I won't have the chance to see you both change over the coming years. The worst thing about dying is that I'll miss out on the future. I won't see you grow old, Leslie become a matron, Sammy a teenager. It makes me so angry. I'm desperately trying to reconcile myself to my fate.

You and Leslie will keep me in your thoughts, but I shall eventually fade some in your minds, just as my parents have faded some from mine. Don't feel guilty about it.

Ever since I was 15 or 16, I've been fascinated by the mystery of dropping for a while from eternity into time. I'm grateful to have spent so much of my allotted time in time with you and Leslie.

Love,
Johanna

Monday morning, coming back from shopping at Fairway, she ran into Noah Levin in the lobby. He and his kitchen designer had just measured the kitchen in 2D. Levin's black suit and broad-brimmed black hat reminded Johanna of the bushy rabbi in her morphine hallucination, and she broke into a smile that Levin took for a warm greeting. He smiled back; it became a grin as he recalled her loud fart at the Admissions Committee meeting. Johanna found she was grateful to see him. I'm grateful to see anybody nowadays.

They made polite conversation, while she thought, My gratitude at being alive is wearing thin. Likewise my extravagant happiness. Maybe Willa Cather's right: happiness is dissolving into something complete and great. Ordinary things—the doorman's console, the double glass doors—they lose their savor. How can I recapture the joy they gave me the afternoon I stepped into the lobby out of the cab from the hospital?

Jerry and Hal had Leslie and Chris to Monday night supper at their apartment on Charles Street. Hal made a mushroom polenta pie, topped with tomato wine sauce. Jerry and Leslie had known each other all their lives. They went to West Side Montessori kindergarten together. Though they weren't close, they shared memories of Thanksgiving dinners and Seders that their folks had celebrated over the years. Leslie, who was eight months younger, had the right to ask the Four

Questions, but she always alternated them with Jerry.

Leslie remembered getting poison ivy one summer at the Jacobson place in Columbia County. The rash spread between the fingers of both hands, swelling the flesh so that her fingers looked webbed.

She said, "I'm turning into a frog."

Jerry said, "I'm the princess."

Leslie loved his humor, and the way he furrowed his forehead as they sat thinking, side by side, on the grass between the vegetable garden and the pines.

Now each had a sick parent and a baby on the way.

"Ours is a boy, too," Jerry said. "We just found out. Haven't yet picked a name."

Leslie said, "I see lots of play dates in our future."

"Anytime you say."

Leslie said, "You know, it's conceivable that our kids could practically live forever. I mean, in their lifetimes, old age and death might be indefinitely postponed."

Hal said, "Let's drink to it."

Chris said, "Let's. Long live our kids! Down with their old age and death!" Christ, I just hope Sammy's straight.

Oct. 9, 2001. Tues. Noon. *Klugman returned my call about 10.*

Asked him if my digital image of Odin violates the rabbinical injunction against making a pagan god's image. He explained that, though according to the strictest interpretation of the Second Commandment, it's impermissible to make a visual image of anything, most contemporary rabbis would allow a Jew to create an artistic representation of such a god, so long as it's not worshiped.

The dull dread I suffered on & off all weekend is gone.

Klugman was gratified by Artie's sudden concern about committing idolatry. He was no longer surprised when a nonobservant member of his congregation came to him with a question about observing *Halacha*—Jewish law. More and more Jews are returning to the Faith of our Fathers. It's a good time to be a rabbi.

Walking Muggs up Broadway for a change, Artie saw Molly, in her wheelchair, coming out of McDonald's on 84th Street. She was talking with a black guy with a jutting jaw who begged around the neighborhood. Next time I see her I'll buy her a meal.

Johanna came home from the hairdresser at three fifteen.

Artie said, "You got a good haircut. I like the shape."

"It's got a good shape now. But I always keep my fingers crossed on how it'll grow out. I read somewhere that your hair grows after you're dead. Not mine. See to it that mine goes up in flames."

"Why say such things?"

"I apologize. It was cruel of me. I'm frightened and angry."

Citigroup 42.02, Intel 21.27, Cisco 14.35, Microsoft 56.74, Johnson & Johnson 55.05

Leslie felt the baby kick. My darling Sammy! What I said Monday could very well come true. Yours could be the first generation that won't age and die. I once thought Mom and Dad would stay young forever. They're getting old. Maybe Sammy won't age.

Oct. 10, 2001. Wed. Noon. *Thought of Dad teaching me to put on tefillin for my bar mitzvah. Can't remember how. But I fear for Johanna's life, unless I do it right, with the appropriate prayers, every morn. It's suddenly clear to me. Despite myself, I'm being driven, step by step, to become an observant Jew. 2 vodkas & a Klonopin.*

Johanna said, "What's eating you? Tell me the truth. Have you had an affair? Have you discovered that you're gay?"

"I've got religion."

"What're you talking about?"

"I've developed this dread. If I don't become an observant Jew, and perform the required rituals, you'll die."

"What kind of rituals?"

"I now have a compulsion to put on tefillin in the mornings. Phylacteries to you."

"I know perfectly well what tefillin are."

"Well, I suddenly have this need to learn to put them on and pray."

"But that's crazy."

"You're telling me."

"Next you'll want me to keep kosher."

"Don't give me any ideas."

"Go see a psychiatrist."

"I've been thinking about it."

"Leslie knows this clinical psychologist. Maybe she can help you."

"Maybe she can. The thing is, I also think, maybe I'm having a genuine religious experience. Maybe my dread that you'll die unless I become observant is God's way of bringing me to Him."

"I can't believe my ears."

"Maybe what they say is true. 'The fear of the Lord is the beginning of wisdom.'"

Johanna went cold. She said, "Listen to yourself. That's not you talking."

"Maybe it is. The real me, who all along was waiting to emerge. Maybe my lifelong love of mythology conceals my desire for the one true God. The God of Abraham, Isaac, and Jacob. He was, after all, Pascal's God as well. Yes! The God of Abraham, Isaac, and Jacob. Pascal loved Him. Geniuses have worshiped Him throughout the ages. I'm just sharing my thoughts with you.

"Maybe the stories—the myths, if you will—in the

Torah are distorted memories of literal encounters between Jews and the Creator of the universe who exclusively revealed Himself to them to the degree that their unanalytical, mythopoeic minds could grasp. Maybe the whole of Israel, including the West Bank, really is the Holy Land that God promised them and their descendants. Maybe Jewish history has cosmic significance. Maybe, at the End of Days, a Jew will redeem the world. I say 'maybe.'"

"You're having a breakdown."

"Maybe so."

"Promise me you'll get some kind of psychological help."

"I promise. Ask Leslie the name of that clinical psychologist."

Artie said, "I'll call her right now. It's not the fear of God, my love, it's the fear of death that's the beginning of wisdom."

Johanna got Diana's office number from Leslie, saying, "Dad's having anxiety attacks." Artie left a message on Diana's machine. She got back to him at five thirty.

He said, "My wife recently died and was resuscitated from a heart attack. I've been suffering ever since from the dread that unless I become an observant Jew and perform the required rituals, she'll die again. For good. Can you cure my dread? After one attack, I live in fear of another. I'm drinking too much and gobbling Klonopin. Can you help me?"

"I'd be glad to consult with you, but because Leslie and I are friends, I can't treat you. That would be unethical. After we talk, I'll recommend somebody you can trust."

"When can we meet?"

"How about next Friday, the nineteenth, at one?"

"I'll see you then."

Diana thought of Sut. She had her first glimpse of the symmetry of opposites in life.

Johanna saw John Starkie in his office at two. She said, "Everything is beautiful."

"Really?"

"Once in a while. Sometimes, when I remember I can die at any time. That awareness flits in and out of my mind at odd moments, and my fear is sometimes accompanied—I feel what it says there on your wall: 'everything is beautiful.' Even death."

"Have you any questions you want to ask me?"

"I've lost my sex drive. Is there anything I can do about that?"

"Give it time. It'll eventually come back."

"I have a new relationship to time. It doesn't flow indissolubly like it used to. It's broken up into discrete moments. Like grains of sand in an hourglass. Running down."

Thursday was the eleventh. Sut gave Judy a ring at seven in the evening.

He asked, "How you doing?"

"How about you?"

"I had flashbacks all day. One in particular. People screaming on Church Street. Then I'm covered with black dust and ashes. I can't see and I can't hear. Or breathe. I can't breathe. All I can do is pray."

"I had what I think of as the jumps all day. 'Then jump darling. Jump into my arms, where I'll hold you close for good.'"

Sut said, "I'm seeing a therapist. She says I've got a bad case of survivor guilt."

"That's what mine tells me."

"Then we've got something else in common."

Judy said, "We start out as lovers and wind up friends. Who could have foreseen that?"

"You're the only friend I have."

"Same here. Are you back to praying?"

Sut said, "I beg God to help me in my unbelief."

Oct. 12, 2001. Fri. 2:15 p.m. *Told Rabbi Klugman in his office at Etz Chaim that in gratitude to God for bringing Johanna back to life, I want to put on tefillin every morn. & pray. "But I don't know Hebrew."*

"Then pray in English. Just make sure you don't go through the words, but that the words go through you."

A tallis & yarmulka must be worn with tefillin.

Klugman said, "The Midrash declares that wearing tefillin is like reading the Torah." He taught me how to put them on. It took almost 2 hrs. Complicated ritual. Made extensive notes. It'll take practice to get it exactly right.

There's one tefillin for the head & one for the left arm. Two black boxes made of leather from a kosher animal attached to black kosher leather straps. One box is worn, facing inwards, on the left bicep, the other in the center of the forehead. The boxes contain four parshos*—paragraphs, written on a parchment, 2 from Exodus, 2 from Deut. which includes the* Sh'ma*: "And you shall love the Lord your God with all your heart & with all your soul & with all your might."*

I asked Klugman, "What about fear? I thought we're supposed to fear Him as well."

"I believe God wants us Jews, in so far as we're able, to experience Him in all His aspects. He wants us to feel awe, terror, reverence, and love in His presence as intensely as we can. He wants these feelings to overpower us and—as Ezekiel says—change our hearts from stone to flesh. And when every Jewish heart is changed, death will be swallowed up, and all tears wiped away."

Bought tefillin ($279!), tallis ($50), & yarmulka ($5) along with Tefillin: An Illustrated Guide *($10.50) &* Siddur Sim Shalom: A Prayerbook for Shabbat, Festivals

& Weekdays *($19.95) at West Side Judaica ("A full line of religious articles") on Broadway, between 88th & 89th.*

Is Rubin the answer to my Rosh Hashana prayer?

Artie read in his book about tefillin that it was forbidden to wear them on Shabbes. He looked up sunset in the *Times:* 6:20. He had fifty minutes left; not nearly enough time to learn to put them on correctly. He had to wait until Sunday morning. The dread came to him at night as Johanna flossed her teeth. He dulled it with vodka and Klonopin. It returned at 7 a.m. and lasted three hours. Artie stuck it out without booze or drugs. When it hit him again just before noon, he sneaked a drink.

Leslie joined Johanna for lunch—two shrimp salads from Zabar's. They talked about Johanna's clients. She had worked her way through all ninety-five.

She said to Leslie, "They were all impressed by your performance—except three or four. I'll give you their names and complaints. Think you should call them?"

"Is Max Brooke on the list?"

"He is."

"He's a chronic complainer. Fuck him. What about Susan Glick? I thought so. I'll talk with her. She's going through a transition in her financial planning."

Oct. 14, 2001. Sun. 1:10 a.m. *Holding off dread for*

the last half hr. with an Ambien & 2 Klonopin. Sunrise, when it's permissible to put on tefillin, is 7:06 according to the Web. Set my alarm for 5:30.

Johanna, awakened for a moment from a dream by the alarm, said, "You'll be interested to know there are giraffes on Mars," then slipped back to sleep.

Artie went to his studio, put on his yarmulka and broke out his notes:

1. Wash hands. Recite blessing in Siddur p.3 for ritual hand washing.
2. Meditate (Siddur p. 3) before putting on tallis.
3." " (ibid. p. 5) before putting on tefillin.

He did as he was told, returning in his thoughts to the blessing he'd recited after washing his hands in the kitchen sink, "Praised are You, Lord our God, King of the universe, whose *mitzvot* add holiness to our life..."

So that's what I'm trying to do—sanctify life. I'll buy that.

Oct. 14, 2001. Sun. 11 a.m. *This morn., after an hour's practice, I put on tefillin by myself, reciting the accompanying blessings & verses from the Bible.*

At first, I made the mistake of winding the strap of the arm tefillin toward the inside, rather than the outside, of my left upper arm.

Finally got it right, said the blessing for the arm tefillin, tightened its strap & wound it 7 times around my forearm, and twice around my palm to hold it in place while I put on the head tefillin, while reciting 2 blessings, 1 before & 1 after tightening straps.

Then I finished winding the strap of my hand tefillin, by passing it between the inside of my thumb and forefinger. And after that, I wound the strap around my middle finger three times—the part of the ritual that moves me because it affirms that loving God is a feasible experience.

Each time I wound the strap around my finger, I repeated one verse from Hosea. First winding: "Thus says the Lord: I will betroth you to Me forever." Second winding: "I will betroth you to Me with righteousness, with justice, with love, and with compassion." Third: "I will betroth you to Me with faithfulness, and you shall love the Lord."

Johanna walked in on me at 7:30, took one look at me wearing yarmulka, tallis, & tefillin & said, "I don't know whether to laugh or cry."

Coming out of the Korean greengrocer's on Broadway at three, Artie saw Molly in her wheelchair in front of the steps of the Baptist Church. She was reading a paperback romance novel by Nora Roberts and didn't see him. I want to do a mitzvah. He remembered Dad telling him that according to Maimonides one of the most virtuous ways to give charity is to make sure that the recipient doesn't know who the donor is.

Artie went into Le Bistro, handed the bald Palestinian owner fifty bucks, and said, "I'll give you this every Sunday. I want you to serve Molly—the woman in the wheelchair—a meal of her choice three times a week from now on. But don't tell her who gave you the money. That's very important. I don't want Molly to feel beholden to me."

"I will do as you say, sir. You're a compassionate man. God favors the compassionate." Even a Jew.

Artie told Johanna what he'd done. She kissed him on the mouth.

Molly collared Khalid, the Palestinian owner, that evening when he offered her a free dinner. "Fess up!" she said. "Who's my benefactor?"

"I'm sworn to secrecy."

"Is it a man?"

"I can't say."

"It must be a man. Men are more generous to me than women. But don't he realize that I have my pride? I want to thank him. But I can't. His kind of charity is humiliating.

"Well, beggars can't be choosers. I ain't had but a carton of orange juice all day. I'm starved. Give me your hanger steak, medium rare, with mashed potatoes and carrots. And a double espresso. Please."

"Dessert?"

"Why not? Chocolate ice cream. I ain't had ice cream in a dog's age."

Oct. 16, 2001. Tues. 10 a.m. *This morn., as I wrapped the first strap around my middle finger, I remembered that I'd forgotten to recite the blessing after tightening the head tefillin. Took tefillin off & put them on again. This time, correctly. (Tefillin must be removed in the reverse order they're put on.)*

Rabbi Klugman rang up Artie in the afternoon and asked how things were going with the tefillin.

"Good. I put them on first thing every morning and pray. I like the betrothal prayers best."

"They're my favorites as well."

"Tell me honestly. Do you ever experience loving God?"

"Occasionally, while praying, I experience You! You! You! Everywhere, You!"

"I envy you. How I envy you!"

"Then learn to pray. But I warn you. It's heart-breaking work. One should strive to be a prayer oneself."

Oct. 17, 2001. Wed. 1:15 p.m. *Putting on tefillin wards off my dread. No attack since Sun. Johanna says she's counting the days till I see the psychologist. (Friday @ 1 p.m.)*

Blocked. Why does Odin become a poet?

Subj. Myra & Jacob Fuchs
Date: 10/17/2001 5:59:39 PM Eastern Daylight Time
From: sgrossman@verizon.net
To: artjo@aol.com, akahn@aol.com, rachelklein@verizon.net, petergold@hotmail.com, jginzberg@earthlink.net, banai@hotmail.com

The following letter, addressed "To Our Dear Friends" was found by Jacob's caregiver this morning near Myra's corpse.

October 17

Dear Friends,

For months, in moments of rationality, Jacob has been begging me to kill him. I can't live without him so I'm committing suicide after I kill him. I read how in a book from the Hemlock Society. Over a period of two months, I got a prescription for 60 Seconals from Dr. Glass. I told him I needed something very strong for my terrible insomnia.

We'll eat a light meal—tea & toast, like the book says—then take 20 pills with a glass of schnapps apiece (I hate schnapps) & (I hope) quickly fall asleep.

I want to thank you, each and every one, for your friendship over the years. The love you have given Jacob and me made us feel part of a loving family that neither of us have on our own.

Goodbye.
Love, Myra

PS. We have a plot in Mt. Harmon Cemetery in Westchester. I found out from the manager their policy on burying suicides. They have a rabbi who declares we suicides are out of our minds and therefore not responsible for our actions. Bury Jacob on my left, where he slept for 52 years. No funeral, please. And don't say kaddish for us. If you want, hold a memorial service for us later. No more than 10 speakers, 5 minutes apiece. Let Ira choose & read 20 poems by Jacob in Yiddish & English.

PPS. For Ira. As our executor, please buy us a simple tombstone & have it inscribed with our names, dates, & in Yiddish & English,

"The message for the living from the dead: Rejoice!"

According to the paramedics & the medical examiner, Myra immediately passed out & died within 45 minutes. She forgot to add Dramamine to their cocktails. Apparently Jacob became nauseated after a few minutes &—not uncommon

in these cases—vomited up the phenobarbs & survived. He lay in his puke all night.
He's now at Roosevelt Hospital. He keeps asking for Myra. Ira hopes to get him into the Hebrew Home for the Aged in Riverdale.

Sandra Grossman

Johanna said to Artie, "Don't put on your tefillin tomorrow. Don't pray, for one day at least, in Myra's memory. And for Jacob's sake. For one day, at least, don't worship a god who allowed such a thing to happen to our friends. It's degrading.

"And if you can abstain tomorrow, maybe you'll be able to hold off the next day, too. Take it one day at a time. Free yourself from this mishegas that's taken possession of you. Come back to me and my world. Don't put on tefillin tomorrow. Promise me!"

"I can't."

Diana asked, "What did you do?"

Artie said, "I held off. Around two, I got an attack. The dread is always very specific—focused on a specific mental picture—a brief scene. I saw myself here, in your office, which I pictured with a desk something like yours actually is. My cell phone rings. It's a call from Leslie telling me Johanna is dead."

"Did you take any Klonopin?"

"Two. They reduce my physical symptoms—the palpitations, the shortness of breath—but the scene plays over and over in my head. It's playing now. Horrible! It's horrible!"

Diana: "You're suffering from a form of obsessive-compulsive disorder—magic think—a traumatic response to the knowledge that your wife may die at any time. Underneath, you feel powerless to help her. Your religious rituals empower you and temporarily reduce your anxiety. But the anxiety builds again, necessitating an anxiety-reducing ritual. When you give in to one, you feel better for a while, but then a new demand appears."

"Do you believe in God?"

"I do. I'm an Episcopalian."

"How can I be sure that my need for these rituals doesn't come from Him?"

"Put Him to a test. Don't perform the ritual. Endure the anxiety. It'll eventually diminish, and your need for a ritual will be weakened. If you repeat this process enough, your need for religious rituals will fade away."

Diana said, "But look who's talking! I regularly take communion. I fast on Ash Wednesday and Good Friday. I believe in baptism, the forgiveness of sins and salvation. And I suppose that underneath it all is a dread of suffering eternal death if I don't affirm that Christ is my Savior. But I'm not conscious of it. What I do is out of love. I believe that God is love. But I don't kid myself. His love is harsh and dangerous."

Artie said, "I don't know what God is. Is it He I feel inside me? I must find out. I want to separate my observance of religious ritual from my dread of my wife's death. I want to seek God of my own free will."

"I can recommend a cognitive therapist who'll help you."

Artie told Johanna, "I made a date for next Thursday at one with a cognitive therapist who teaches at Rutgers. He'll teach me techniques to overcome my obsessive thought that if I don't perform certain rituals you'll die. You're a smart cookie! The technique is similar to the one you suggested. It involves my abstaining from putting on tefillin, one day at a time."

"What about tomorrow?"

"I'll see. This dread wears me down. I'm having an attack right now. I'm scared you'll drop dead if I don't put on the tefillin tomorrow."

"Don't do it! We're drifting apart—after almost forty years. Don't let it happen. Don't let God come between us."

"I can't help it. I want to love Him."

"Whatever for?"

Artie said, "I want that joy. I want to love the source of life and death."

"Since I've been sick, I sometimes do."

"Then let me experience it, too."

"Whatever it is, the source of life and death isn't a personal God. You can't have a reciprocal relationship with it."

"Part of me knows you're right."

Artie was up before the sun.

Bargaining with You for Johanna's life is a cheap ploy. I'm a better Jew than that. Let me love You without hope of reward. For Your sake alone. Change my heart from stone to flesh.

Johanna was still asleep. Muggs would soon breathe in her face. Artie went into his studio and put on his tefillin at sunrise.

"I will betroth you to Me with faithfulness, and you shall love the Lord."

I'm trying.

The fat man's standing on my chest again. Where's Artie? Can't speak. I hear the rondo—the trill—and smell lilies. Yuck!

Rabbi Klugman made a condolence call that night. Artie said, "I've been reading my Siddur. The mourner's kaddish isn't translated. I can't remember how it goes in English."

Klugman said, "It goes—let's see—'Glorified and sanctified be God's great name throughout the world which He has created according to His will.' Uh. Give me a minute." He stroked his beard, then said, "May He..."

Artie interrupted. "That's enough. Thanks."

Oct . 27, 2001. Sat. 8 p.m. *Today I was alone for the first time in a wk.*

Bought copy in Barnes & Noble of Final Exit: The Practicalities of Self-Deliverance and Assisted Suicide for the Dying, *by Derek Humphry. Read some. The surest way to kill myself is with a plastic bag over my head tied tightly around my neck. I'll use up oxygen within the bag, replacing it with* CO_2 *& leaving behind nitrogen that'll let me breathe while I pass out. It doesn't say how long it takes to die. Recommends using a ribbon to tie off bag. Where will I get a ribbon? Will use scotch tape.*

"You can commit suicide just with a plastic bag but it gets a little uncomfortable because you breathe out carbon dioxide and, as the carbon dioxide increases, then the body adjusts to this and you find yourself breathing more deeply & that can be mildly distressing, though not the same as having your respiration blocked."

Need to take sufficient sleeping pills to ensure 2 hrs. sleep. Have two Ambien & Zabar's plastic bag. Gave bag a try for a minute or so. My breath got warm, the plastic crinkled in & out every time I inhaled & exhaled. Heart beat faster. Glasses fogged up.

8:30 p.m. Leslie called, said, "I'll see you in the morning about ten."

Wept together. It hit me she'll find my corpse. Why hadn't I thought of this before? She'll find my corpse—& the mess poor Muggs, who won't have been walked, will leave. Dog shit, piss, & my corpse.

I can't kill myself because of the effect my suicide will have on Leslie. Used the Zabar's bag to take out the garbage.

Nov. 21, 2001. Wed. 11:15 p.m. *This eve. I scattered your ashes, mixed with a 5 lb. bag of 5-10-5 fertilizer, among the pear trees, the oak, the evergreen, the rosebush, impatiens, marigolds, & petunias in Leslie's garden. I long to join you.*

I'll never forgive myself for praying while you died alone.

The god in me is dead. I refused to say kaddish & praise him at your death. I've resumed living in your world, from which there's no appeal.

Leslie tells me that what Sut now calls his Day of Awe (9/11) left him groping for Christ.

I donated my tefillin to Etz Chaim. Klugman accepted them graciously, but I could tell he was disappointed that I didn't ask him to conduct your funeral. 250 people came to the memorial service at the Atheneum. Leslie & I & Chris & Shirley & Adam & Sandra & Jerry & Steve Tobin spoke.

Tobin called you the most honest broker he ever knew. "Johanna's honesty restored my faith in human nature."

Leslie gave me a copy of her eulogy. Among the things she said: "I not only lost my mother, but my oldest friend and business partner. Mom made me an equal partner in our business on August 28—the same day I first felt my baby quicken in my womb. Now he'll grow up without his grandma's love or the benefit of her wisdom. I shall raise him as she raised me: encouraged to express anger toward her without fear of retribution. And when I lose my temper, I'll apologize to him, as she apologized to me.

She said to me on August 28 that she wanted me as an adult to feel her equal in all things. I want that for my son and when I tell him so, I'll think how Mom looked across her desk at me on a summer day long ago, and relive my surge of love for her that left me speechless."

I knew from your pallor that you were dead. Yet I gave you mouth to mouth. Your deflating lungs expelled one of my breaths, and it moaned passing up through your larynx. I thought for an instant that you were still alive. The moment after that—when I realized I was wrong—was my worst ever. My best? The moment I fell in love with you on our first date. I was behind you, holding your chair, as you sat down in that little Italian restaurant—what was it called?—on East 54th. I noticed the two soft auburn curls, loosed from your upswept hair, on the nape of your neck & wanted to bend over & kiss them.

Nov. 25, 2001. Sun. 3:15 p.m. *Today I earned one of your kisses on my mouth for anonymously giving another $50 to feed Molly.*

Ira got Jacob into the Hebrew Home for the Aged. He's a celebrity there but doesn't know it.

Cancelled our plane tickets, hotel, and dinner reservations in Venice.

I read your letter of Oct. 7 over & over. I too am grateful for spending so much of the time allotted me in time with you.

Leslie & Chris will give our grandson a middle name—Jo—after you. Leslie worries about my drinking. So do I. I never expected to outlive you. I was counting on me dying before you.

How will I bear the coming years alone? The arthritis in my big toes is excruciating. I hobble on the street like an old man. I wish I were. I wish my memory were gone, like Jacob's, so I'd forget you were dead.

Muggs rested his head on your side of the bed at 7 sharp this morning. Where are you?

Nov. 28, 2001. Wed. (Odin's day) Noon. *You'd be glad to know I'm back at work.*

This morn. I stole a word from Jacob & tacked it onto my rewrite of a short Norse poem, translated by your beloved Auden (& Paul Taylor, an Icelandic scholar). The poem is from a collection, ascribed to Odin, called The Words of the High One, *that was written down in the 13th C.*

"Odin was filled with secrets he had learned in the Land of the Dead. He decided to teach them to us. Odin knew that it's easiest to memorize verse. He became a poet by drinking three draughts of the mead of poetry, made of fermented honey and the blood of a wise man by the name of Kvasir, who had been renowned for his way with words. Then Odin changed himself into a tall, one-eyed, fifty-five-year-old warrior, and went among men.

"Late one winter day, he wrapped himself up in his long, blue woolen cloak, and trudged through the drifted snow, against the north wind. The snow crunched under his boots. He held on to his broad-brimmed hat with his left hand; in his right, he carried his spear, Gungnir, on which he leaned like a staff. The end of its shaft pierced the snow's icy crust and left a trail of deep holes in the drifts.

"He crossed the frozen Vindel River, then trudged through a long, narrow pine forest, and a snowy meadow, west of the trees, that belonged to three farms. He knocked on the door of the first house, on his left, and asked for hospitality. He was welcomed inside by a rich old farmer named Egil, who sat Odin

by the fire and served him a drinking horn filled with ale. Egil was skin and bones; his legs were stiff.

"Egil's sixty-six-year-old wife was named Gudrid. She refilled Odin's drinking horn, and said, 'Join us for supper, stranger. We're having salt pork.'

"'I'd be delighted,' said Odin.

"Egil said, 'Sir, I see by your spear and one eye that you're a warrior. The chances are you'll die in battle and go to Valhalla, where you'll feast and fight to your heart's content. What about me and Gudrid? We'll soon die of sickness or old age, and rot in the Land of the Dead. What solace is there in life for us?'

"Odin spoke a verse:

'Rejoice in these things at nightfall:
Another day lived,
Your beloved's love,
A burning torch,
Ice crossed,
Dry boots,
Ale drunk.'"

Hugh Nissenson is the author of eight books, including the recent illustrated novel, *The Song of the Earth*, which received a number of superb reviews in *The New Yorker*, the *Washington Post*, and the *Los Angeles Times* among others. His previous novel *The Tree of Life* was a finalist for the National Book Award and the Pen-Faulkner Award in 1985. He lives in New York City.

Sources for passages from the Jewish liturgy that appear in *The Days of Awe* include *Siddur Sim Shalom*, edited with translations by Rabbi Jules Harlow, published by The Rabbinical Assembly, The United Synagogue of Conservative Judaism, New York; *Mahzor for Rosh Hashanah and Yom Kippur*, published by the Rabinical Assembly, New York; and *Etz Hayim, Torah and Commentary*, published by The Rabbinical Assembly, The United Synagogue of Conservative Judaism, produced by The Jewish Publication Society.

A Conversation with Hugh Nissenson

Q: You made your early reputation as a writer concerned with Jewish themes. Then you wrote a novel whose characters are all Christians, and another which is concerned with Christianity and the formation of a new religion in the future. What led you to return to Jewish issues in *The Days of Awe*?

A. I felt that, in my later years, I wanted to confront once more the mystery of my relationship with Judaism and the Jewish people. It's been a persistent fascination throughout my whole life, although not always the theme I've chosen to write about. I wanted to write about a contemporary American Jew, an illustrator and a writer, who's secular and liberal in orientation, an archetypical Upper West Sider—a man somewhat like myself, and yet, of course, not myself—who has a profound religious experience. It is a deeply Jewish book—my mature meditation on what it is to be a Jew at the present time. And what it is to be a secular Jew. Where do we stand, and what defines one's Jewishness? At the beginning, and now toward the end of my career, I address the same questions that have haunted me all my life.

Q. Do you consider yourself a religious writer?

A. My father was a deeply, although eclectically, observant Jew, and my mother was an atheist. Throughout my childhood, my father stimulated my imagination with stories from the Bible. I became obsessed with his obsession with God and his belief that the Jews were the Chosen People. As I matured, I rejected my father's world view intellectually but discovered that it had lodged in my imagination. The conflict between belief and unbelief became the source of inspiration in all of my work. So, yes, as I first said in an interview years ago, I'm an atheist for whom religion is a compelling metaphor.

Q. Do you consider yourself a "Jewish" writer?

A. I'm proud of being a Jew. And my early work—my stories, a memoir about Israel, my first novel, set on the Lower East Side—was all situated within the Jewish milieu. My identity as a Jew plays an important part in my personal and artistic life.

But I'm an American patriot, in love with our country's history. One of the things that has always fascinated me about America is that it continues to be deeply influenced by the Jewish Bible and its messianic message. Americans from the very beginning have seen themselves as the Chosen People. So I would consider myself, first and foremost, an American writer. Passionately devoted to the American language—the American vernacular.

The Days of Awe is a novel that is deeply Jewish. But one can indeed have many identities; I can be a Jew and an American. I see no conflict. And that's what has enabled me to dramatize various aspects of the American tradition—the American experience. My metaphor can be Jewish, it can be Protestant—as in my novel *The Tree of Life*—or pagan—as in *The Song of the Earth*—but my novels all explore the American experience.

Q. How has your love of American history influenced your work?

A. I've written two books set in America's past. *My Own Ground*, which draws to some degree on my father's memories of his boyhood, takes place on the Lower East Side of New York in 1912. *The Tree of Life* takes place on the Ohio frontier during the War of 1812. Both of these novels dramatize, among other things, formative events in the making of our country. *The Song of the Earth*, which is set in Nebraska and New York in the middle of the twenty-first century, is a meditation on the possibilities of America's future.

Q. Critics have called you the last of the Modernists. What does that mean to you and how is it expressed in your work?

A. Ezra Pound, in 1910, enjoined twentieth-century artists to "make it new." I took the belief as gospel and made it my creed. During my twenties and thirties, I learned my craft by writing conventional short stories.

They were all of a piece, haunted by the Holocaust, about Jewish experience in Europe, Israel, and the United States. I desperately wanted to write a novel, but couldn't find a theme, or story, that was commensurate with even the conventional form. Finally, when I hit forty, a plot came to me that I couldn't confine within a short story. It turned into a conventionally constructed novel called *My Own Ground.*

The novel's conventional narrative left me feeling unfulfilled. I was still committed to the aesthetic of Modernism. I was determined to find a way to break up the traditional structure of the novel. I did it in my second novel, *The Tree of Life*, in which I integrated my poetry and illustrations (which I attributed to the book's protagonist) with my prose. The book is written in the form of a ledger/journal, which enabled me to do away with chapters.

Q. In your subsequent works you rely more and more on your poetry and visual images, which again you ascribe to characters, which are integrated into the prose. How do they function?

A. They expand the parameters of the form of the novel. They give the reader a new aesthetic experience. In my last novel, *The Song of the Earth*, I eliminated the authorial voice completely. I tell the story by a series of interviews, emails, visual images, poems, and journal entries, all of which are juxtaposed to each other, without transitions, like a film. In all I made forty-seven illustrations, drawings, paintings, and pieces of sculpture, and wrote a cycle of ten poems, that I ascribed to a poet named Chlorene Welles.

In *The Days of Awe*, there is just one visual image and several poems. I've also included sections from a book about Norse mythology that my protagonist is writing. Once again I've done away with formal chapters and traditional transitions. *The Days of Awe* is narrated by an omniscient narrator who switches point of view, sometimes in the middle of a scene. I've never used this technique before.

Q. What was the genesis of *The Days of Awe*?

A. I began writing the book in the spring of 2001. I had already conceived the outlines of Artie's story. It would be his spiritual history. I knew the action of the book would begin on August 1 of that year and continue through the Jewish High Holidays—the Days of Awe. Then came 9/11. I had to deal with it. I had to integrate it into my plot. What immediately interested me were the religious implications of the tragedy. How did it affect the faith of the various characters—Christians and Jews—in the novel?

Q. Artie is torn between two definitions of what it means to be a Jew—is it a religious or the cultural identity?

A. Artie has long thought of himself as a cultural Jew, for him it's an ethnic identity. As the novel progresses, he becomes increasingly obsessed by Judaism as a religion and the possibility of a personal relationship with God.

Q. You dramatize the impact of the Holocaust and the present state of Israel on Artie and his contemporaries. It seems as if they replace formal religion in the primacy of their impact on his identity. Do you believe that to be the case? Or it is just a literary device?

A. Both of these extraordinary events took place during Artie's lifetime. And mine. They are the most significant occurrences in Jewish history since the fall of the Second Temple in AD 70. I believe that whether or not you interpret these events as having religious implications or as purely historical in nature, their impact on the Jews—on the world—is overwhelming. Of course both of these events mean one thing to Artie and something quite different to his daughter.

Q. Among other things, *The Days of Awe* is an intergenerational novel that concerns familial relationships. It's your most domestic novel. The first book you've written that's set in the present day. Why?

A. I wanted to write a novel that celebrates happy marriages. I've been happily married for over forty years. My wife and I have two daughters—one of whom has gotten married since I wrote the book. I was nearing seventy when I wrote *The Days of Awe*. I've passed into that time of life in which I feel compelled to contemplate the arc of my existence. I look around me at contemporaries who are struggling, as I am, with the existential realities of aging, sickness, and death. *The*

Days of Awe affirms the beauty of the ordinary things in life and the renewal of life's possibilities in successive generations.

Q. You're Jewish. You live on the Upper West Side of New York. How autobiographical is *The Days of Awe*?

A. In one sense, everything I write is autobiographical. My characters, although they assume fully formed identities and are placed in various historical eras, all reflect aspects of my personality or of things that interest me. On the other hand, *The Days of Awe*, which draws more on the details of my daily life than any other book I've written, is no more autobiographical than, say, *The Tree of Life*, which is set among Protestants in nineteenth-century Ohio. My imagination, my capacity to fantasy, provides the inspiration for all of my work.

Reading Group Questions and Topics for Discussion

1. The Days of Awe, in the Jewish religion, refers to the ten days between Rosh Hashana, the New Year, and Yom Kippur, the Day of Atonement, during which time it is believed that God decides who shall live and who shall die in the coming year. Those ten days in the Jewish liturgical calender play an important role in Nissenson's novel. To what other contemporary event does the Days of Awe, when it is decided who shall live and who shall die, refer?

2. *The Days of Awe*, like all of Nissenson's work, is about the religious impulse, the religious experience, and the ultimate question: is there a loving God who concerns Himself with human affairs? Which two characters—one Jewish and the other Christian—who are in a sense doubles, wrestle with their belief in God? As examples of contemporary New Yorkers, they each seek psychological help to assuage their anguish. Why? Does either of them resolve his spiritual struggle? Which character, at the end, is left grappling with God?

3. What characters in the novel have renounced God? Why have they done so?

4. Artie Rubin is the novel's main protagonist. He begins as a secular Jew who is obsessed with pagan mythology. As the novel progresses, who is the deity to whom he turns? Is there an irony inherent in this development?

5. What aspect of Norse mythology is especially attractive to Artie at this time of his life?

6. What Greek myth, mentioned early in the book, prefigures Odin's journey into the Underworld., The Land of the Dead? What is the thematic significance of Odin's mythic journey? What does he learn about his destiny at the battle of Ragnarok?

7. To what contemporary event in the novel is Odin's journey analogous? Why?

8. What other character shares Odin's fate—his death, rebirth, and final extinction? What is Nissenson implying about the relationship of mythology to everyday life?

9. *The Days of Awe* is first and foremost a love story. Artie and Johanna have been happily married for nearly forty years. Her heart attack precipitates a spiritual crisis in Artie. How does Johanna respond to the catastrophe? In what way is her appreciation of ordinary life deepened by her experience of dying and, in a sense, being reborn? How does her fixation on the words of the Navaho Ceremonial dramatize her new vision of life?

10. Artie's final vision of life and death reflects Johanna's. How is it expressed? By what action? By what artistic creation?

11. Chris, Artie's son-in-law, objects to having his son circumcised. Why? How does Artie feel about this? Why? Do you think that child will be raised as a Jew? How will Artie respond?

12. Rabbi Klugman is the truly observant Jew in the novel. How does he express his love for God? And his compassion for his fellow human beings? How do his religious beliefs affect his politics, as expressed in his sermons?

13. How does the Holocaust influence Artie's attitude toward his people? What is the significance of the destiny of Jacob Fuchs? How do his poems reflect his religious beliefs?

14. What role do the current policies of the state of Israel play in the novel? How are the young Israelis living in America portrayed?

15. As his first name indicates, the protagonist is an artist. How does Nissenson dramatize Artie's talent to make words into pictures and a picture from words?

16. What thematic purpose do these examples of Artie's artistic creations serve? Why is he concerned about creating a digital image of Odin? How does this dramatize his growing obsession with Orthodox Judaism?

17. What thematic purpose is served by the poem at the end of the book? How does it dramatize Artie's final vision about life and death?